Book Plate 1928

H. ALLEN SMITH

1906-1976

RETURN OF
THE VIRGINIAN

RETURN

THE

Doubleday & Company, Inc.
Garden City, New York

1974

OF

VIRGINIAN

H. ALLEN SMITH

Library of Congress Cataloging in Publication Data

Smith, Harry Allen, 1907-
  Return of the Virginian.

  I. Title.
PZ3.S64803Re   813'.5'2
ISBN 0-385-03405-9
Library of Congress Catalog Card Number 73–15367

Full measure
this time
for Harold Matson

RETURN OF
THE VIRGINIAN

Mungo Oldbuck was in one of his moods when he made me promise I would never write a book. Not so much as a Pooh-type book, nor even a genealogy of the highborn Hargis-Landrum-Grady clan from the Pennyrile region of Kentucky. The way he made it sound, he was indulging himself in an Oldbuck whim, and something over a hundred and twenty whims boil out of him every day of his life.

He said, "Grady, if I ever catch you putting one sheet of paper in your typewriter with the intention of writing a book, you will perforce become an author, and you will no longer be welcome in this house. And if I catch you writing one single goddamn line about me in your pipsqueak newspaper, I'll raise knots on your head with the butt end of my Dillinger .38."

Mungo is my best friend and I made the promise, standing there beside the big fieldstone fireplace in his Rancho Traseros headquarters. And I made no effort to suppress a grin at his reference to the John Dillinger pistol. Mungo is inclined sometimes to fantasize himself as a dilettante who would never hit anybody except with a collector's item.

So here I sit, at the unchristly hour of 3:40 A.M., in the sable-vested office of the Caliche Weekly *Mud Dobber,* thumping away at the old Royal, breaching a solemn contract, beginning the composition of a book that will be to some extent about Mungo Oldbuck himself.

I consider myself to be an honorable man, too damned honorable for the world I live in, and I suffer from the rare and debilitating disease known as personal integrity. So why am I violating my promise? Possibly because a man in New York once told me that all is fair in love and war and book writin'. A man named Hemingway. Earl Hemingway.

Nobody moves in the downtown side streets at this hour, but I can hear the thunderous procession of trailer trucks on our main drag, Railroad Avenue. This office is two and a half blocks north of Caliche's main street, which is called Highway 90 when it gets out of town. The drumming of the diesels is not disturbing to me. At this distance it blends into a deep soughing sound, as of a wind that rises and falls in the forest; sort of a deep-night murmur.

This is my fourth morning of lunacy, my fourth start on Chapter One, and I think maybe I've got it moving now. I'm minded of the lady novelist back East who said that writing the opening page of a book is like taking the first step on a walk to China. I've finally made it past that first page. It's gonna take a long time.

There's something compulsive about it. I wouldn't be welching on my contract if that solemn Choctaw, Victor Standcabbage, had stayed the hell in Oklahoma with his six pigs. I would be holding fast to my vow if that incredible young fogy Jefferson Cordee had not walked into Kohlick's Cafe at high noon and asked the meanest old man in town why he was eating his pie thataway. I'd be home in bed this minute if that meanest old man, Rustler Smith, had never departed Buffalo, Wyoming.

When I spoke of Victor Standcabbage's pigs I had only one of them in mind. If it would seem strange and improbable that one charming little forty-pound pig named Emily, through sheer porcine witchcraft, could precipitate a shooting war in the cattle-lands of the American West, then let me hasten to explain that this pig Emily was of the Mulefoot breed. There are said to be only a handful of Mulefoot pigs left in the world and those few are in the custody of the Choctaw Indians of eastern Oklahoma. It may be that a scattering of the breed still exists in the islands of Polynesia, where the Mulefoot seems to have originated.

It is generally conceded that the plain barnyard pig is far and away the most intelligent of all our domesticated animals. The Mulefoot is approximately twice as smart as the average cloven-hoofed variety. And from this short distance in time of acquaint-anceship, I can say that Emily is the cream of the Mulefoot crop when it comes to wisdom, talent, and all-round amiability. If there still should be some doubt that such a small and affectionate pig could start a war, let me refer you to the ear of Robert Jenkins, master mariner, which precipitated the war between England and Spain in 1739 and, more to the point, to the fact that the storied Hatfield-McCoy feud on the Kentucky-West Virginia border started out as a quarrel over a razorback hog.

The concatenation of events involving the three men mentioned and the one small pig began concatenating a year and a half ago and the incident in Kohlick's Cafe, which triggered the whole shootin' match, took place on the same day I made that promise to Mungo out at the ranch.

I had spent the weekend at The Pueblo—the name by which Mungo's house was known—as I often did, and we were getting ready for the drive to town. Mungo was bustling around, machine-gunning orders at the hired help, directing Idaho Tunket to get the green Chevvy pickup around to the front door, behaving in that crisp autocratic stiff-backed manner of a born martinet. Always military, Mungo—right down to the square face, the crooked mouth, and the pepper-and-salt Pershing mustache. Any discerning person would take one look at him and say, "Army." Far wide of the mark. Mungo never even made Boy Scout.

He had on a gray business suit with a faint pinstripe, a solid blue shirt with a gray tie, and a dark homburg. No ranchman's boots for Mungo Oldbuck, no sombrero or Laredo hat, never a bolo string-tie with a roadrunner lavaliere on it.

And much the same for me, except that under my arm I had a book Mungo had handed me at the last minute, a book called *Descent into America*. Author: Ian Christchild-Muckeridge.

The breeze coming down from Doble Traseros mountain was gentle and the air was clear and tangy as we shoved across the nine miles of winding gravel road leading out to the Caliche highway, which Mungo called El Camino del Zopilote in honor of the buzzards. Each morning these unpleasant vultures assemble all along the pavement to breakfast on those animals slaughtered during the night by fast-traveling Conestoga wagons. Nine miles to pavement, yet neighboring ranchers sometimes remarked that Mungo was hugging the highway soze he could set at his bedroom winda and keep a check on who's goin' by. Some of those neighbors had their main houses a good twenty miles back in the sand and mesquite.

Mungo was driving and Idaho Tunket had the snakes again. He sat next to the door, with me in the middle. The snakes that ensnared Idaho were not the snakes that whiskey drinkers are said to get, and rarely ever do. Idaho was suffering from the squirms as he always did when he was compelled to ride with his employer, whether in a jeep, a Porsche 911, on horseback, or in a pickup.

His snakes were the snakes that children get in the back seat of an automobile after the first one hundred miles of a long day's cross-country ride—the snakes of impatience, the serpents of rebellion.

Idaho had the look of a man straight out of Marlboro Country. He was near to six feet and a half tall and his face would have had that weather-beaten look if he had just come out of three years in solitary at Huntsville.

And though in his physical aspect he would seem to be the very prototype of the strong and silent cowboy, heroic conqueror of a disorderly West, he was not a member of that romantic calling. He was Mungo's cook. Strong? Yes. Silent? Great God no! Idaho Tunket was a talker from who-laid-the-chunk. Pressed against me in the cab of the green Chevvy, he had hog-tied his tongue and cross-hobbled his lip. This double impediment in his speech was the condition that brought on the snakes. He had been silent for ten long minutes after we hit the blacktop and I could feel the tensions in him. He couldn't hold it in much longer. He had nothing in particular to say but he was much like the generality of women, both liberated and entrapped—he could not forego the ecstasies of talk for an eternity lasting all of ten minutes.

He began trying to talk to himself in a way that Mungo wouldn't hear. He clamped his horsey teeth together and sermonized back of them, but the rude sounds that came out could not have passed muster as a mumble, or even for the borborygmic shifting of gas in his bowels.

"The hell and damn with it!" he suddenly spoke, aloud. Mungo took his eyes off the road for an instant, glancing at his *cocinero*. He started to say something, then changed his mind and returned to his driving.

"Free country!" said Idaho, becoming suddenly heroic, and forthwith gave himself over to the raptures he found in conversation.

"I know you hate her guts, Boss," he addressed himself to Mungo, "but you fool around that woman and you're liable to get a load of buckshot right in your hind end."

"What woman?" Mungo growled.

"The woman whose spread we just come past. Miz Battle."

"What makes you think I'd ever fool around with that woman. You already know I don't fool around with any women. None. Zero. And most particularly the woman you have just mentioned.

I don't want to hear about her this morning. And what's this about
a load of buckshot?"

Idaho was almost too astonished to utter another word. The
Boss had *invited* him to talk. Asked him a question!

"Last week," he said, "she run a man offa her place with a shotgun. Alferd Keller, the water witch."

"The *dishonest* water witch," I corrected him. "That's what
most of the other water witches call him."

Mungo was beginning to realize that he had committed a tactical blunder. With his own hands he had pulled down the concrete
walls and broken the dam, and now the whole State of Texas would
be inundated, buried beneath a flood of Tunket talk. Mungo tried
to stop it.

"Idaho," he said, assuming a parental air, "*you* are the one to
stay clear of that dame. She's as treacherous as Slaughterhouse
Catherine de' Medici. She's too tough for you."

"She's as purty as a new windmill, but the man she run off her
place was about ninety years old and a water witch to boot."

"I'm telling you," Mungo persisted, "you'd better steer clear
of her. For one thing, she's got a prolapsed vagina."

Now I had to wedge my way in, ever eager to acquire new and
useful information.

"A what vagina?" I asked.

"Prolapsed," said Mungo. "The last time I was in the hospital,
Mount Sinai, there was a woman down the hall clacking out nonsense at the top of her voice, all day long and half the night. I
asked my nurse what the woman's trouble was and she said it was
a prolapsed vagina. I asked her what that entailed—pun intended—
and she said it meant the vagina was turned inside out like a sock.
It makes women mean and cantankerous. This nurse said she
hated all women with prolapsed vaginas because they manage to
be unpleasant and nasty twenty-four hours a day. She said she
had a theory that men have prolapsed peters, because they can be
unpleasant and nasty around the clock when they're in the hospital."

"Did she use the word *peter*, Mungo?" I asked. "I mean the
nurse."

"Of course not. You couldn't get a nurse or a doctor to say peter
if they had bushel baskets full of them."

I love medical discussions. "Did she mean that all men who

enter a hospital have prolapsed peters? Men with pneumonia and broken legs and shingles and . . ."

"I think she was speaking figuratively."

"She must have been. It wouldn't seem reasonable that every man who goes into the hospital would have his peter turned inside out like a sock, regardless of what was making him sick."

"Grady," Mungo now barked at me, "will you cut out the talk about . . . it's setting me on edge."

"You brought it up. And before we leave the subject, what makes you say that Asia Battle has a prolapsed vagina?"

"She's consistently hateful and cantankerous, from all I hear, and she comes from a mean and hateful family. That uncle of hers was . . ."

Idaho had been squirming and fretting at my side. He had lost the ball, but now he was determined to get it back.

"What was innaresting," he declaimed, putting large stress on the third word, "was that Miz Battle had heard about Alferd Keller witchin' the T-bone steaks in Bub Gardner's Meat Market. That's the real reason she took the shotgun and run him . . ."

"God help us every one!" murmured Mungo.

"Alferd Keller," Idaho rambled on, "he ain't too popular with the other switchers. They claim he's too commercial. He used to be with State Highway before he retard and took up water witchin'. He goes out scoutin' fer business, and that ain't proper in the witchin' trade. You are sposed to set still and let the business come to you. He charges fifty dollars and sometimes a hunderd, dependin' on what the rancher's worth and what his politics is. Some witches don't charge a red cent because The Parr is somethin' the Lord installs in them and you shouldn't charge money fer a thing like that."

What happened, said Idaho, was that Alferd Keller went to Bub Gardner and told him that he, Keller, had discovered that he was in some kind of spiritual rappaport with cattle, that cows who have passed on often talk to him from The Other Side, and these passed-on cows themselves communicate the word on whether a steak is good er not. Moreover, Idaho continued, he didn't have to use his willer wand at all, but just waved a finger over a T-bone and he'd get the message whether that steak was tender er tough. And damn if he didn't sell Bub Gardner on it.

Idaho said that Bub Gardner agreed that fer ever ten T-bones

Alferd sold by witchin', he would get one T-bone fer himself, free, and Bub he got the word around to the women, and you know women—they'll bleeve that the bumps on their head tell if they are kindly disposed.

He said that the women of the town started flockin' to Bub Gardner's place and linin' up clean out to the sidewalk, and Bub Gardner he had to telephone to San Antone fer an extry truckload uh T-bones, and he took the T-bone play away from all the other stores in Caliche, and then the trouble really started, because . . .

"How did this Keller witch the steaks?" Mungo interrupted.

"He just stood there by the meat case," Idaho replied, "and witched T-bones till his arm might near fell off. He'd stick his middle finger straight out like he was givin' somebody the finger, and he'd wag it around over the steaks and when it got over a tender one, wye, that finger would begin to go up and down like an awl pump, and Alferd would shut his eyes and rare his head back and holler out, 'Moo! Mooooo! Mooooooo!' and all the ladies in line would whoop and cheer, and then he'd pick up the T-bone and hand it to the lady and say pay at the counter."

Mungo now spoke to me.

"Is there a shred of truth in this lunatic's story?"

I said there was more than a shred.

"Did you report it in your newspaper?"

"Not a line."

"Why the hell not?"

"Bub Gardner didn't advertise his T-bone specials."

"He didn't need to," put in Idaho. "Ever'body in town knew about it."

"What about the steaks?" Mungo wanted to know. "What happened when the women got the steaks home and found out they were tough as usual?"

Idaho answered. "The women all said their steaks was tender as a springer, melt in yer mouth, could be cut with the fork."

Mungo already knew about Texas steaks and how they shatter teeth.

"I want to buy half a dozen of those T-bones," he said. "I want to be present when they are witched. I want to test them. I want to be able to make affidavit that such things as this actually go on within the boundaries of the continental United States."

"Yer too late, Boss. The other stores they all ganged up and got the Chamber of Commerce to order Bub Gardner to dezist, and then the women started hollerin' bloody murder, sayin' by God they wanned their witched steaks, and the men in town bein' natchelly against the women, they turned against Bub Gardner and quit speakin' to him and his family on the street and threw him out of the golf club and . . ."

"Idaho," Mungo interposed, "it just occurs to me that we've forgotten about your crooked friend Keller and thé Battle woman."

"Oh," said Idaho. "Wye, Alferd he come out to her ranch all polite like, and told Miz Battle he heard she was runnin' short a water lately, and he'd like to witch her up a couple uh wells, and she says wait a minute, and come back with a Winchester .42 and told him she had heard about him witchin' the steaks and he could haul his swindlin' ass offa her property, and then she called him a dirty word."

"What dirty word?" from Mungo.

"Well, I saw him over to Bullocks-Welcher's Hardware the day after it happened and ast him what the dirty word was, and he said he would never repeat it in public, it was that *dirty,* but he said since I was his friend he would whisper it to me, and so he whispered that Miz Battle called him a morphadyke."

"A *morphadyke!*" Mungo flung back his head and laughed a long substantial laugh. "Idaho, I want to congratulate you. With one word you have advanced the study of sexual aberration by fifty or a hundred years."

"That's what she called him," Idaho insisted, as if his veracity had been challenged. He was mystified that Mungo should find something hilarious in the encounter between Alferd Keller and Miz Battle. Hell's pecker, it wasn't comical. People start takin' Winchesters to one another, it's not a joke. Idaho grumbled a little, staring off at the Chinga tu Madre Mountains, which stretched across the horizon up ahead, and then Mungo turned right and in a few minutes we entered the metropolis of Caliche. Opposite the high school football field Mungo began chuckling again, and saying the dirty word to himself, and then he turned to me. "I think it's possible, all things considered," he said, "that this Alferd Keller really is a morphadyke. He sounds like one."

He drove straight down Railroad Avenue and parked at the bank. He sat for a moment at the wheel and then said, "Grady, you may be witness to a bizarre performance in a few minutes.

You may see a man who considers himself to be perfectly sane, embark on a search for the meanest old man in Blackleg County."

Then he turned to Idaho. "I've got to talk to Peavy," he told the cook. "Take that list over to the Safeway and get loaded up. I forgot to put down the Mexican sausages—*chorizos,* I think they're called. Pick up those things at the drugstore and the stuff at Bullocks-Welcher. Meet me at twelve noon at Kohlick's."

Then he said to me, "Come on in if you've got the time. I'd like for you to be in on this."

I said Yup.

In West Texas the higher a man rises in worldly affairs, the more likely he will be given a lowly and even earthy nickname by his admiring and envious fellow citizens. He will not be offended by this; indeed, he will regard it as an accolade, and even if his sobriquet be Turd Eye, he will have it graven on his letterheads and stamped in gold leaf on his brief case.

The president of the Peavy National Bank in Caliche had been baptized Darwin Peavy, but he was known universally as Chug. He favored that name over Darwin for business reasons ("he calls hisself Chug, don't put on no airs, he's plain as pig tracks").

"Hidy," he said as Mungo Oldbuck and your beloved correspondent walked into his office. He was a big handsome Texan with silvery hair and a flat midsection. He had that air of distinction often found among business leaders and professional men all over the State.

"Have a chair," he said, "and put your feet up and leave us talk about the miserable bastards in Washington."

"Thank you, Mr. Peavy," said Mungo.

"Now just a goddamn minute, Mungo. I've told you once, I've told you X times, in this town we get on a first-name basis the first time we sight one another across a crowded room. Call me Chug."

"Certainly, Chug."

"I won't start off by telling you the latest Aggie story, which I got on the phone from Dallas late yesterday, because I know that you've come in here with a piece of business in mind and I stand ready to accommodate you. Over on a siding near the depot I've got twenty boxcars full of money, but I know that you've already got forty boxcars crammed with fifty-dollar bills and so I don't believe you want to borrow any money."

I hadn't said a word up to this point, but now I addressed Chug Peavy:

"I'll take any extra you've got laying around loose, Chug."

He feigned a scowl and said: "I'm not yet so steeped in folly that I'd risk money on a depraved newspaper bum, especially one who has lived a large part of his life in New York, New York."

It has been said that a banker can achieve wide popularity just as easily as a camel can attain passage through the eye of a needle. I have known Chug Peavy for a good fifteen years and I need to say that his town not only holds him in respect, but entertains a genuine affection for him. Oh, there are a few people around who cuss him blue, but they cuss everybody blue, and they are the ones who didn't get the money. I have heard Chug Peavy refer to himself deprecatingly as a chickenshit banker, but this I know: he will have one hell of a big funeral.

He now said, "State your proposition, Mungo. I'm all ears and a yard wide."

"You've never heard one like this before," Mungo began. "I've come to you because I figure you know the people in this town better than anyone else. Grady here knows them pretty well, but you've been here all your life and you've had dealings with the total population. Now"—Mungo leaned forward slightly—"I want you to tell me the name of the meanest man in this county."

"Are you serious?"

"Serious as a man can be."

There was a long silence in the room, and I finally broke it.

"Listen, Mungo, I don't know what on earth you may have in mind, but I suspect you're on the wrong track. I've often made the remark that this is a town overpopulated with *mean old women*. Walk down any street, stand on the post office steps, shop for groceries, post yourself across the street from any church—everywhere you look, mean old women. And quite an adequate supply of mean *middle-aged* women."

"Every town is overpopulated with mean old women, Grady. I don't want a woman. I want the meanest, most churlish, cantankerous, vexatious, and nasty old man you can find."

Chug Peavy got back into the conversation. "I think it might help if you'd tell us *why* you're looking for this man."

"It won't make a bit of sense to you when I do. I consider myself to be one of the orneryest old men on earth, and I consider my condition to be the ideal condition for living on this planet. Ornery people are mean because they are disgusted with the rest of the race. Ornery, fractious, quarrelsome people are the only people to be trusted. You get no simpering obeisance out of them . . . no fawning, no Uriah Heeping. They mean what they say and they say what they mean. They are dependable."

Chug and I were looking at each other, questioningly, and we were having the same thought: there had to be a catch somewhere. The town banker turned his eyes back to Mungo.

"Tell us *why,* Mungo."

"Not yet. Let me hear first whether you've got the character I'm after. And let me switch the adjective to give you a little more spread. The man I'm searching for has to be *hardheaded*. He has to be ornery, and then on top of his orneriness he has to be hardheaded. You got that?"

"Tell him about Purp Gibson, Grady," suggested Chug.

"Purp Gibson," I said to Mungo, "is our town's enemy of progress. He says he was born in Oregon and . . ."

Chug interrupted. "I don't think he's ever set foot in Oregon. I remember him when he was a kid right here in Caliche. He was an amateur geek. He'd bite the head off a live chicken for thirty-five cents."

"He sounds promising," Mungo offered.

"Anyway," I went on, "he talks about the people of Oregon because they're conducting an all-out war on Progress. They don't want any new people in their state and they don't want any new industry. As you know, Mungo, this is an attitude that is grossly unAmerican and contrary to the laws of God. Purp Gibson stands almost alone in opposing Progress for Texas and Caliche. I say almost because, as Chug knows, I'm somewhat on Purp's wavelength."

"What's ornery about him?" Mungo wanted to know.

"It's the way he goes about his crusade. He spends a lot of time hanging around the little bungalow where the Chamber of Commerce has its office. Tourists driving through often stop at the Chamber to ask about conditions in Caliche. They like the scenery and the clean mountain air and they think maybe this would be a good place to retire. So they run into Purp—he's been quietly laying for them—and he gets them into conversation and in a rambling, unhurried sort of way he begins putting the knock on the town. Sometimes he tells them he's a minister of the gospel and that he's about to move on to greener pastures because he can't stand the way the sinners keep sinning in this town."

"Tell about the drunks, Grady," Chug Peavy urged, "and then tell about the sex maniacs."

"Purp says to these tourists," I went on, "that the town is full of secret drinkers, mostly women, and these women hole up in their houses and drink themselves stiff as nanny goats, and Purp tells these visitors that once he tried to get an AA chapter organized, but all the women drunks sobered up and descended on the first meeting and started yammering that the AA would give their town a bad name, it would make people think Caliche was a town of lushes, and the women said they were not gonna sit still and have their community befouled and besmirched."

"The sex fiends," Chug reminded me.

"Then maybe with another tourist couple, older ones, he'll say that Caliche has more fat-lipped sex maniacs per capita than any other town or city in Texas. He tells them that public exposure is the big thing with the Caliche sex maniacs, especially in the neighborhood of the elementary school. Purp says that sometimes there'll be a pervert on every corner of the school block waving his diddledywhacker at the little girls."

"And," observed Chug, "at the little boys also."

"He's got several other civic sales talks he feeds the tourists," Chug told Mungo. "He sure knows how to attract new settlers. He claims he can spot visitors who have respiratory troubles a mile away, and he always tells them that this is a real good town but that every vacant lot in the community is a solid bed of ragweed, and that the slopes on the edge of town are so loaded with the weed that it looks as if someone was growing it commercially. Then he tells these hay fever people . . . this is the way he talks, Mungo—Purp says, them indiwiduals in this here town that ain't got the azzmy and the hay fever wye they got all kinds of sociable disease like the gone-rhea and the siff that they git from all this here wife-swappin' in this God-besook community."

"Chug," I said, "you ought to go on TV. I'll bet you could do Nixon."

He stood up and bowed, and said, "I was the first in the nation to do Ed Sullivan."

Mungo was in meditation, considering Purp Gibson.

"I think," he finally decided, "that your man is ornery in just one direction. He has something concrete to be mean about. I'm on his side—I think the worst *sociable* disease we've got is the eternal ignorant yelping for Growth and Progress. I'm after a man who is pissed off about *everything,* who gets out of bed mean and grows meaner every hour of the day, and by bedtime is gnashing his teeth at the whole human race."

I was more perplexed than ever, and so was Chug.

"Mungo," he said, "you wouldn't be looking for a hired gun, would you?"

"Not at all. I don't ride with that kind of orneriness. I'm after a man who has the human race added up correctly, the way I have it added up. It is almost essential that he be an old man, because old men are much meaner than young men. I should know. I've turned the corner of seventy and I can out-mean the best of them."

"Hell, Mungo," I interposed, "you know that's not true. You're not really as tough as you think. Underneath all that bluster and cynicism, you're the salt of the earth. I claim that I'm the only true cynic in Blackleg County."

My ranching friend gave me a long salty glare.

"Grady," he said, "you speak hen shit."

Chug Peavy had been gnawing thoughtfully at his cigar, a frown wrinkling his forehead. Then suddenly he came to life.

"Wait . . . a . . . damn . . . minute!" he intoned. "Baker, Charlie, Roger, Over, Under, and OUT! Grady, we forgot Smith. Old Rustler Smith. How the chee-wah-wah did we ever overlook *him?* The milk of human meanness is running out of his ears. He's your man, Mungo."

"Go on. Give me a rundown."

"He came to town two or three years ago," said Chug. "He has a daughter teaches school, purty little thing. Rustler's three years older than Santa Anna's wooden leg, and the girl must be closing in on thirty."

"She looks maybe twenty-two," I put in.

"Ornery?" Mungo said, speaking to Chug.

"The nicest thing I can say about him," said Chug, "is that he is beyond dispute the meanest old man West of the Pecos River. Right this moment I can't give you any specifics. Let me simply say that if Rustler Smith walked into this office right now, and you flashed a warm smile at him, he might bust you one right in the nose for getting familiar. He hits innocent bystanders. He hits women. If a cow should get in his way, that cow gets kicked in the bag. He walks up to . . ."

"Hold it, Chug. You mean he hits women without a bit of provocation?"

"Knocks 'em to the floor, sometimes."

"And he kicks cattle? Where can I find this paragon of human virtue? And why do you call him Rustler?"

"He made his mark in life rustling cattle, somewhere up north. There's not much doing in his line around here any more; we have some cactus rustling, not to mention wife rustling. When he first came to town and people asked him his name, he told them to shut their goddamn heads, or he swung on them. But once or twice he neglected his vile temper and said, 'If I give you permission to do it, you can add-dress me as The Rustler.' I imagine he's the only cattle thief in the history of the Golden West who ever admitted to his profession in public, and even bragged about it."

"God he sounds good. One of nature's noblemen."

"I don't want you to get the idea that he's perfect in every way, Mungo. He does have a few very irritating mannerisms—such as breathing."

Chug glanced down at the seven-hundred-dollar watch on his wrist. The case and the wide band were of burnished gold, a rich tannish glow to match the cinnamon color of his Lincoln Continental. Chug Peavy is not *country*. Now and then at the Peavy house they eat black truffles, fixed between slices of pâté de foie gras and doused with Sauce Périgourdine, which itself is a blend of black truffles and pâté, with a hefty dollop of madeira thrown in. Also at his house you might be offered calf's-foot jelly, a culinary triumph I will not stay in the same room with.

Having established that noon was less than an hour away, Chug said that Rustler Smith eats his dinner and insults people in Kohlick's Cafe almost every day at twelve o'clock.

"And now," he commanded, "you've got to tell us what you intend to do with your ornery man. I can't even attempt an educated guess."

"That won't take long. As you know, Mr. Peavy, I mean Chug, that ranch of mine is worth a good piece of money. You must also be aware of the fact that I have other valuable holdings. I'm one of those people who have so much money that I don't even have to ask my accountants how much I've got. And all you need do

is look at me to realize that I am approaching the end of my life.
I am . . ."

"This time, Mungo," Chug interrupted, *"you* speak hen shit.
You're in the prime, you've got the best years ahead of you. Wye,
hell, you're not as old as me, and I've got plans to stick around
and give people fits till I'm past ninety. You want to locate a mean
old man, look at me. You've got me so inspired that by God I aim
to foreclose on seven consumptive widows before this day is out."

Mungo's smile was one of mere politeness. He was quite aware
of the fact that Chug's Pollyanna-talk was the standard talk used
by most people when some aging person mentions the prospect of
his dying.

"The thing is this, Chug. I don't have any relatives. No wife,
thank God. No children, praise Allah. No brothers or sisters, bless
the Great I Am. Somewhere in middle Massachusetts there's a
cousin, a crackpot named Tolbert. In recent years this cousin has
taken to dressing himself in women's clothes and spending a couple of afternoons a week parading the streets of the town where
he lives, lisping at people. When the cops approach him and suggest that he go on home and knit a shawl, he defies them, and says
he is doing his thing for Women's Lib. The cops are mortally
afraid of those malodorous fishwives who head up Women's Lib
and rather than risk an invasion of the town by the New York
ogres, they let this Tolbert character get away with it."

"He wouldn't get away with it in this town, Mungo," said Chug.
"We'd entice him into a dark alley and relieve him of his nuggets
with a straight razor."

"Very constructive, Chug. I'd go along with that. A man who
would appear in public dressed as a woman ought to be punished,
and it would be a nice touch to restrain him from reproducing his
kind. I'm not a bit tolerant toward the degenerates who are marching and howling alongside the Women's Libbers and whining for
their right to do their buggering thing. The hell with them."

(God eternally damn, I whispered to myself, how I do wish I
had his kind of money so I could give tongue publicly to all my
deep and sensible prejudices, all my hang-ups, all my rage against
the idiot imbalances of this nuthouse world.)

"Obviously," Mungo continued, "this Tolbert moron is out of
the picture so far as my money is concerned. I sent a private dick
up there to look him over and the dick came back to New York

and said to me, 'Mr. Oldbuck, I have cast aside the last shreds of my religious beliefs and I may self-destruct.' His report was negative. So up popped the big question: what am I to do with my money?"

He gave us the old Barrymore pause, and Chug Peavy broke in. "There's always charity," he said.

"Piss on charity," Mungo responded quickly. "I have reference to organized charity. I wouldn't give a dime to the bastards. It has been well established by this time that more than half of every dollar a man gives to organized charity goes into fat salaries for parasitic reptiles who ought to be in prison."

"Now, Mungo," Chug Peavy objected, "maybe a few of them, but I'm sure most of the . . ."

"All of them!" Mungo insisted. "Bloodsuckers, every one of them! They've been exposed thoroughly and completely, a dozen or more times. They get nothing from me. It takes mean people like me, and like your guy Smith, to see through the charity racket. We are the true realists, the straight thinkers unhampered by considerations of good taste and good manners. If Rustler Smith and Mungo Oldbuck had the running of this country in their hands, this might just possibly *become* the best damn country in the world. It's far from that now. You might speak of our intolerance as being diabolical and unAmerican. Nuts. A full-blown English simpleton named Chesterton spoke one good line in his fatuous life; he said that tolerance is the virtue of people who do not believe anything."

Chug and I were giving each other the questioning looks again. Mungo ran his right hand over his face from forehead downward to chin, a mannerism he often affected when he was wrought up about something.

"Are you going to tell us," I asked him, "that you intend to leave your fortune to a complete stranger, someone like Rustler Smith?"

"I didn't say that, Grady, but I must confess something on that order has been running through my mind. I'd like to pick a successor who would follow in my footsteps and wage total war against the hordes of the stupids and the legions of the larcenous and the violators of privacy and all the other ignoble and shameless creatures who surround us."

I felt like arguing. "You're talking crazy, Mungo. You could set up one of those foundations to distribute your money to people and organizations whose views coincide with your own."

"Nothing doing. To the devil with those old farts who try to get right with God by leaving their money to colleges and libraries and disease-chasers. I despise them. They stole the money in the first place and they reason that if they play philanthropist at the end, the gates of heaven will swing wide for them and the archangels will slap their wings in salute. I never stole a dime in my life. My father, who started the publishing house that I ran for thirty-six years, never stole a penny. My old man and I functioned in that forgotten period when the book business was an honorable business, run by honorable men. Look at it today. Look at the . . . Great God, I'm beginning to sound like an upfucked archbishop! Grady, do you want to come along with me and find this man Smith? Or do you have to go piddle with your items? I'll buy you some lunch."

"Folks call it dinner out here," I said.

"I know. I haven't been able to adapt. I was born and brought up on Lower Fifth Avenue."

"I'll come along," I said. "Gene Shallow is over there doing the piddling."

"Who's Gene Shallow?"

"My helper. He bumbles around and screws up the details while I'm away from the office. You'd love him, Mungo. He really believes that this is a *good* world. He's been at the *Mud Dobber* since Cabeza de Vaca came through these parts looking for the Holy Grail."

At the door Mungo turned back to say good-by to Chug Peavy.

"If your pal The Rustler turns out to be adequately nasty, I'll be back, and I may have plans for the future."

"Any time, Mungo. We don't see enough of you around here. You pen yourself up on that ranch like a hermit in his cave. People tell me you've got the handsomest house in the county."

Mungo didn't respond, except with a farewell wave of the hand. He ignored the oblique allusion to the fact that he never invited any of the townspeople down to The Pueblo. I knew that our friendly banker had an irremediable itch to see the house and the ranch and Mungo's gun collection and those daffy horses.

Chug just might make it, I felt, because Mungo liked him and recognized some intelligence in his makeup. Yet up to that time

I was the only man in Caliche who was welcome at Mungo's. I didn't quite know why, unless it was the way we agreed about so many things. And in spite of our commonsense compatibility, my overall view of the human condition is actually not quite as jaundiced as his; I sure as hell can't go all the way with him on his belief that there is no useful function in women. I know at least one.

My acceptance by Mungo didn't enhance my popularity in the town. There were some people who resented my weekends in the shadow of the Doble Traseros so intensely that they quit speaking to me on the street.

For those who seek wisdom and enlightenment in their reading matter, and who have no *español*, Doble Traseros means Double Rumps, after the contour of the peaks that loom on the western border of Rancho Traseros: two sets of buttocks as rounded and as shapely as the one set affixed to the person of Asia Battle. And that single set, I must insist, constitutes one of the scenic splendors of the Golden West. I suspect we shall have more to say about it. Or them.

**Chapter Three encompassing an attempt to
explain and justify the strange and com-
pelling attitudes of Mungo Oldbuck**

3

In my present incarnation there are two conditions under which I
seem to do my best eccentric thinking. The first, when I'm driving
cross-country alone on the highways of West Texas, which are
preposterously long and straight and smooth and desolate of
traffic. The second period in which I fancy myself capable of superior thought lies between the hours of three and six in the morning. This may be the subconscious reason I'm engaged in my
present crazy regimen of pre-dawn composition.

Right now it is a quarter past four here in the office of
The Thunderer of North Leakey Street. This room, housing both
the editorial and business departments of the paper, is gloomy
enough in the daytime; in the little hours before sunrise it is a
dungeon. I catch myself feeling isolated in the backwaters of
space, and somehow my mind seems to function with greater
clarity than it does even on those long lonely highways.

It has just occurred to me, for example, that I have perhaps
done my friend Mungo Oldbuck a disservice. I suspect that a
reader might acquire an unfavorable impression of him from what
I have written thus far. Maybe I've made him sound moody and
sour and forever truculent, a man to be avoided. The truth is, he
is loaded with good humor and possessed of many laudable in-
stincts.

I didn't know him in my New York years, but I knew about
him. It was said of him there that he disliked only three classes
of people, namely: (1) all women, large or small, young or old,
ailing or sound; (2) all authors, regardless of literary endowment
and regardless of sex; and (3) the rest. A harsh judgment and an
unfair one. All three allegations and impeachments are in error.
Right at this moment I propose to challenge the first one.

I asked him once if it were true that he held a grudge against all women. He said, hell no, not all of them—just a few thousand. I said I knew he had been married a long time ago.

"What about your wife?" I asked.

"She was a beast."

"In what way?"

"She had dirt under her toenails and she wrote books. God-awful books, novels of the type the critics call gruesomely Gothic."

Why had the people out here in Blackleg County reached the conclusion that he was a misogynist?

"Possibly because I've had some trouble with the Battle woman."

"Like what?"

"Damn your black unprincipled soul, Grady, can't you ever put aside your piss-ant profession and act like a human being for a while? I'll tell you this much and no more. It started with a run-in I had with her lame-brained uncle about a year after I came out here. As your prying nose may already have informed you, I am a millionaire. I'm not ashamed of it. I was a millionaire the moment the doctor picked me up by the ankles and slapped me across the butt. In all my seventy years I have never been slapped again, and I have never been knocked down . . . but once. I mean hit in the jaw and laid on the sod."

"Asia Battle's uncle flattened you?"

"He did."

"Why?"

"If a son of a bitch is a son of a bitch, I call him a son of a bitch. This one knocked me down. At that moment I was a millionaire, several times over. It was a hard thing to take. One of the disadvantages of being a millionaire is the ingrained conviction that no millionaire should ever be knocked on his solid-gold ass. It's a thing you would never understand because you are a newspaper bum."

"So you really don't hate women?"

"Listen. Fifteen or twenty years ago someone started a rumor around New York that I was anti-Semitic. It wasn't true. I was merely anti- a few Semitts. I said so. It happens that I am always and forever anti-horse's ass, and it also happens that there are Jews who have attained high position in horse's-assery. I say, yes, I know Abe Cohen and that Abe Cohen is a horse's ass, and I am immediately branded as anti-Semitic. I deny that I am anti-

women. I just happen to dislike the type of female we used
to describe as A Knowing Woman. She is still with us, and
proliferating. To the deepest and hottest gullies of hell with her."
I reminded him that local people thought it strange that no
woman visitor has ever been seen at Rancho Traseros. He said
there had been some. One or two. At least one. A guileless
El Paso spinster decided to enlarge her horizons by traveling
across West Texas and selling cosmetics to the wives of ranchers.
She arrived one day at The Pueblo, backed Mungo into a corner,
and began drowning him in a torrent of purple language which
she had memorized off advertising dodgers. He told her to stand
off. He told her to get lost. He told her to hit the Tarmac. She ignored his sales resistance and continued the junk-mail jabber. At
length Mungo simply reached out and seized her head in his
hands, clamping her jaws solidly together, and then he advised her,
in strong language, to cram the lower reaches of her alimentary
canal with soothing cold creams, lanolin derivatives, armpit deo-
dorants, bars of scented soaps, jugs of crystalline bath salts, and
tubes of candied-peach lip gloss. After which, still holding her
jaws clenched together, he jounced her out to her car and pointed
toward El Paso.

"She drove straight into town," Mungo said, "and tried to get
out a warrant charging me with subornation of mayhem, but they
already knew her and gave her the same type of friendly advice
I had offered her. Of course the story got all over town that I had
chased her clear to the highway, cracking a bullwhip at her butt,
and this was disturbing to me . . . because I had neglected to do
just that."

Which brings us, by natural progression, back to the tale of Asia
Battle's using a shotgun to drive Alferd Keller off her property.
A few days after Idaho Tunket regaled us with that Joycean narrative in the green Chevvy pickup, I ran into Jaybird Huddleston,
who was Asia's foreman. I asked him about the Keller episode.
Jaybird said, yes, he had been present, that Alferd Keller simply
asked Asia if he could witch up a couple of wells for her, partial
garranteed, that she said, no, she paid at the office, and Alferd
departed. No shotgun. Nary a morphadyke.

And finally, Mungo's attitude toward authors. As the most book-
minded and best-read person of my acquaintance, he could never
harbor any serious antipathy toward writers as a class; but, once

again, he could hold an aversion toward certain individuals afflicted with the disease. Consider the evidence of Mungo's star boarder —Ian Christchild-Muckeridge. At the time of the heroic events I am describing in this manuscript, Ian had been occupying a guest cottage at Doble Traseros for six or eight months . . . not only a genuine author, but the very worst of the breed: an English novelist.

Several times I've asked Mungo about his reputation as an author-hater and I remember best this comment:

"My feeling about authors is much the same as Clarence Darrow's feeling about the Common Man. Darrow said that he was solidly on the side of the Common Man, and would do everything possible for him . . . except eat with him."

Chapter Four which chronicles the first
meeting between a handsome high-minded
cowboy and an ornery old pie-eater

4

Señor Oldbuck drove me from the bank to Kohlick's Cafe and
then went on up the street to Jack Todd's filling station to leave
his car for servicing. I walked into the restaurant and found Idaho
Tunket was already there, hanging over the front counter and
carrying on two running conversations at the same time.

"It was either the Mescalero Apaches er the Doghead Comanches," he was telling Otis Kohlick. "I know it was one of the tribes
that ranged down into the country whirr I come from and, man,
they loved their mule meat. They were good hunters and they could
of had their pick of any kind of meat on earth—deer, quail,
squirrel, peckry, antelope, duck, must-rat, doves, rabbit—you name
it, and all they'd talk about was how mule meat was better'n va-
nella ice cream with strawberries on it. Wye, Otis, them Indinns
raised . . ."

The proprietor of the establishment had to jangle the cash
register for a tourist who wanted two pralines for the road, and
Idaho switched his subject from Mule Meat to The Ideal Family,
addressing himself now to Fremont Wadley, the photographer,
who was helping out with the loafing around Kohlick's cash
register.

"Three children did you say, Fremont? You couldn't of done
better. Three is exactly right. It works out perfect. One to git
killed in an auto accident. One to turn out sorry. And one to take
care of you in yer old age."

"How many you got, Idaho?" Wadley asked.

"I ain't even married. But I promise you if I *was* married I'd
make it three."

Otis Kohlick had finished with the tourist and was thinking
about ducking into the kitchen, but Idaho was too fast for him.

"Reason I got to thinkin' about mule meat, Otis, and how the
Indinns down around Eagle Pass would trade you three beef crit-

ters fer one mule, was that I got to thinkin' about camel meat. You know what the tastiest part of a roasted camel is, Otis?"

"I don't know any part of a roasted camel," said Otis, showing his irritation.

"The hocks. I met a fella once in Paris, France, that used to cook fer a Sultan out in the Holy Land, and he told me you couldn't beat roasted camel hocks fer good eatin', except he said they were stringy and had little knots uh gristle in them, put him in mind of tough turtle eggs. I've never eat no mule meat that I can remember, and I've never even *seen* camel meat, but . . ."

"I don't care to eat neither one of them," said Otis, now grown quite testy, "and furthermore, I wouldn't allow any of it brought into my place here, and *further* furthermore, I'd ruther not hear any more on the subject."

I can't understand why so many other men seem to get bored with Idaho's monologues; I could listen to them all day.

"I bag yer pardon, Otis," he said. "I just thought that you bein' in the business and all, the subject of . . ."

Mr. Kohlick turned his back and began playing a game of checkers with packages of mints and gum and Idaho shrugged and then noticed me standing by.

"Grady!" he exclaimed, as if he hadn't seen me in a year. "Whirr's the Boss? I was just tellin' Fremont here about an Irishman I met once up . . ."

"What Irishman?" Fremont Wadley asked.

"Name of Boyle . . . I met him up in Kinney County, his pecan grove was tuck by the hick'ry shuckworm and he went inn-sane, but not enough to be put away . . . he just stumbled around and . . . say, Fremont, you wouldn't happen to be Irish, would you?"

"Hell no. I'm Amerr-kin."

"I thought so. What I started to say was, an Irishman he gits a bad run uh luck and he's liable to go bad in the head, that's why you see so many uh them runnin' around loose, and this Boyle he wandered around up there in the Turkey Mountain neighborhood and he got the idea he could listen in on telephone conversations just by pressin' his ear up against the telephone poles, and that fella spent the rest of his life wanderin' around the country and pastin' his ear against the poles and tryin' to hear what people was sayin'. The hick'ry shuckworm done that to him. You ever hear of . . . ?"

"Tunket!" It was Mungo's drillmaster voice. He had come up behind Idaho and caught him in sin. "I told you not to bother Mr. Kohlick or anybody else with your soliloquies," he growled at his cook. "Come on, let's eat and get the hell out of this town." He had forgotten our reason for coming to Kohlick's.

The three of us made our way to a table near the center of the room and gave Lanthy Peeler our orders, Idaho taking the boiled beef, Mungo choosing the Mexican plate, while I went for the breaded catfish. There was little conversation among us while we waited. In Kohlick's it is unwritten law that you spend your first five minutes inspecting the clientele, looking over such freaky tourists as might be present, but devoting most of your attention to the local citizens, waving and smiling at your friends, cutting your enemies cold.

I nudged Mungo on the arm and, concealing my right thumb behind my left palm, jabbed it toward an old man sitting alone at a nearby table.

"Rustler Smith," I whispered. "That's him—in the flesh." I whispered because I didn't want the old bastard to hear me and heave a dinner plate at my head. Mungo gave him a long read. The old boy was wearing a corduroy coat with most of the ribbing worn away, and he was eating with his hat on.

The hat itself was an article the tourists might mention on the postcards they sent home. It was a modified western Laredo-style horror which the old man had likely bought secondhand maybe thirty years ago in outback Montana. I could see, with the naked eye, the grease and sweat-sludge and other precipitates and in my mind I reckoned the hat's gross tonnage at six and a half pounds. It was a hat carrying what might be called a Festus block. Coming upon it lying on the ground, a wild animal would have run from it.

The old man's face beneath the Festus block was seamy, and hawkish. He had a piece of cherry pie in front of him and a fork in his hand. Now and then he would raise his head and his eyes would dart about warily, as if he were expecting a mountain to fall on Otis Kohlick's establishment, or flaming arrows to come flying through the windows. He put me a little in mind of a cornered animal searching for avenues of escape.

Mungo didn't say anything, but his eyes kept returning to Smith. And Idaho Tunket, who had been sitting quietly, suddenly gave us a rare demonstration of his total awareness, his acute sensibility. He had noticed Mungo's inspection of the old man at the nearby table, and he now volunteered a judgment.

"That's old Smith," he said. "Snotty old son of a bitch. He's close related to the smallpox on his mother's side."

"Quiet," ordered Mungo. But Idaho's attention had already been distracted by the appearance of another customer.

A man had just come through the door, a trim young giant more picturesque and downright beautiful than Kodachrome film could ever imbue or delineate. His wide soft gray hat was pushed back on his head; a loose-knotted dull-scarlet handkerchief sagged from his brown throat; and one casual thumb was hooked in the cartridge belt that slanted across his hips. The weather-beaten bloom of his face shone duskily, as the ripe peaches look upon their trees in a dry season. Nothing could have tarnished the splendor that radiated from this man's youth and strength. His sex-glistening dark eyes flicked over the room for a moment, then he moved in with effortless grace, walking with the kinetical flow of the jungle cat, making his way to a table next to the one occupied by Mungo and Idaho and me. He took a chair facing away from us. He removed his hat, revealing blue-black curly hair, and he put the hat on the floor beneath his chair.

Iolanthe Peeler, the redheaded waitress, had spotted him the moment he came through the street door and now she too turned feline and all but pounced in getting to his side. Lanthy was normally a woman as harsh as a sawmill, but now she stood beside the handsome newcomer, her ass akimbo, her lips fixed in the cupid's bow that went out of fashion about the time Helena Rubinstein was born in Cracow. When she spoke, she spoke in what she thought was a soft and sensuous drawl.

"Hoddy," she said. "Stranger in town, right?" She didn't give him a chance to answer. "You sure come to the right place." She didn't say the right place for what. He picked up the menu and she braked herself down a little and said, "The veal cuddelets are motty good today." She was looking at the size of his shoulders as she gubbled the words.

"Oh, thank you," he spoke his first words. He glanced over the menu a moment.

"How's the chicken-fried steak?"

Iolanthe looked back toward the cash register to make sure her employer was not in earshot, and then told him.

"Listen, honey, the chicken-fried steak is mott near the same exact thing as the veal cuddelets. Good. Both of um got a cream sauce poured over. The veal cuddelet is the same piece of beef that's run through the veal cuddelet machine we got out there."

"You mean it ain't actual veal?"

"Well, it comes offa like young cows."

"Maybe I'd better have the chicken-fried steak."

At which point Iolanthe lost all control. I had seen her get the hots before but never quite like this. She simply abandoned all decorum, forswore her proper upbringing, and gasped:

"God, honey, you got the *purtiest* hair! I just gotta run my hands through it!"

And she did. The large young stranger's blooming cheeks blushed redder yet. Lanthy withdrew her hand and shifted her weight from one leg to the other, so the fluid mobility of her behind would become more pronounced. The cowboy responded with a grave demeanor, keeping his eyes averted from her behind. He crinkled his brow, ostensibly debating a choice between the steak and the machine-made veal cutlet.

"Reckon I'll stay with the steak," he finally decided, and with reluctance Iolanthe left his side. Something Vesuvian had taken place deep inside this girl, possibly in the vicinity of her Grappling Iron. Normally she was as hard as the devil's hangnails.

Idaho had devoured the boiled beef lustily, but now the French chef came out in him and he said in a tone of disgust, "The party that cooked up this mess uh slum deserves to be pan-fried in Dutch Boy vornish."

Mungo was toying with his enchiladas and glancing over from time to time at the old man in the Festus hat, or at the wide shoulders of the black-headed cowboy. In the course of one such glance Mungo noticed that the younger man had put down his eating tools and was, himself, doing some staring. His gaze was on the table occupied by Rustler Smith.

Suddenly, as if by impulse, the handsome stranger climbed out of his chair and walked over to the old man in the corduroy coat.

"Sir," he said, "I wonder if you'd mind tellin' me why you are eatin' your pie that way." His voice was gentle, yet firm and unfaltering; he had presence to go with his looks.

The old man raised his head and glared out from beneath the brim-sag of his soggy sombrero.

"Git your onsightly ass away from this table!" he snarled.

"But, Sir," persisted the black-headed man, "I only want to know the reason you eat your pie that way."

Old Smith raised himself slowly from his chair, a malefic look in his eye.

"Listen to me, you he-heifer!" he rasped out. "I been eatin' this pie the way I been eatin' pie all my life. Nobody tells *me* how to eat pie. I said, git away from me, you overgrown pansy son of a bitch."

The cowboy didn't move. "Oh, Sir," he said slowly and almost mournfully, "you shouldn't of called me that!"

Rustler Smith sneered villainously. "I'll call you anything I wanna call you, and I'll eat my pie any way I wanna, and no dideyed-up drugstore cowboy is gonna tell me . . ."

"Sir," the handsome one interrupted, "I'm afraid I'm gonna have to take you out in the street and haul down your britches and give you a . . ."

He got no further. The old man let out a roar of rage, seized the straight-back chair he had been sitting on, and swung it above his head. At the same instant, moving so fast that I couldn't follow his hand, the black-headed man whipped out his six-shooter. With the barrel of the gun pointed straight at his belly button, the old man did not falter. He swung the chair with a surprising show of strength and broke it over his adversary's head, shattering a couple of rungs and one leg in its downward arc and knocking the revolver from the cowboy's hand. He staggered slightly from the blow. He was dazed, but he crouched down and reached for the weapon on the floor.

Another hand got there first. It was the hand of Titus Cottle, Sheriff of Blackleg County.

"All right, cowboy," drawled the lawman. "You're under arrest. Don't say nothing or it'll be used against you."

I couldn't restrain myself. I leaned forward and tapped the sheriff on the arm.

"Titus," I said, "this is the first time in your life that you've been present at the scene of the crime when the crime was being committed . . . except in those cases where you were committing it yourself."

The sheriff whirled on me. He had the cowboy by the arm but he wanted to punch me and he thought of letting go of his prisoner long enough to do it. Instead, he just grumbled, "Grady, I'm warnin' you—I'm gonna break ever bone in your body before I'm finished with you. So help me God."

All over Caliche I make friends like that.

As Titus led his captive to the street, I settled back in my chair and looked at Mungo. He had a flicker of a grin on his lips.

"Tonight, Grady," he declaimed, "the American flag floats from yonder hill or Molly Stark sleeps a widow."

"This government," I replied, "cannot endure permanently half slave and half free."

In moments of high stress, when life takes on an exciting air, Mungo and I sometimes exchange stirring utterances out of the nation's history. It serves as our commentary on the radiant and sempiternal nobility that resides in the souls of men.

Quick rundown on a chauvinist schnook . . .

Forsyte Grady. Age fifty-seven. Writing a book. 4:10 A.M. Office of the Caliche Weekly *Mud Dobber*. Insane purpose: vaguely to make a score, to get enough money whereby it will be possible to escape out of a life long turned wretched and odious.

That's it—The Old Journalism. Who, What, When, Where, and Why. That's the old-style way of saying it in a newspaper and that's still the best way. Balls to this New Journalism I keep hearing about. Bunch of nances back East, flipping their gay tails around . . . please! Don't get me started.

Examine that name of mine. I'm in the same boat as Chug Peavy: nobody ever calls him Darwin, and nobody ever calls me Forsyte. The only nickname I've ever had is Tuck, which stems out of the circumstance that I'm a native of Kentucky, the state that somebody once said has the look of a camel lying down. Most people just say Grady.

I was born on June the fifteenth, 1916, and the day of the month is slightly significant.

The town was Bonaroba in the hill country of eastern Kentucky and my mother, a proud Landrum, put the Forsyte brand on me. While she was carrying me John Galsworthy, over in England, was in the process of finishing up his long family chronicle, *The Forsyte Saga*. My mother had been devoting her sentimental vaporings and most of her passion to this series of novels for years. Relatives have told me that she talked about the Forsytes as if they were her own people. She knew all the quirks and quiddities of each member of the clan from Old Jolyon to Young Jolyon to Philip Bosinney to Jolly and Holly and Val Dartie and Fleur and Little Jon and all the rest. She made me read the *Saga* when I was around ten or twelve, and I hated every word of it. I still do.

In the hospital, after she got her breath back, Mama took note of my birth date.

"Glory to God!" she cried. "June the fifteenth! It's the very date of Miss June's engagement party at Old Jolyon's house in Stanhope Gate! The whole *Saga* begins with that party! I'm going to name him Old Jolyon! Old Jolyon Grady!"

"Good God!" remarked my father, who was in the hospital room and who despised Old Jolyon and all his kin. "Good God!" he repeated. His saying it a second time suggested that he was dispirited over something.

"I know!" she exclaimed, clapping her hands together like a Forsyte. "We'll just call him Forsyte. Forsyte Grady! Beautiful! All the Forsytes were present that day, that June fifteenth. So I'll name him for each and every one of them. Oh, but this is frabjous!"

"Callooh Callay," muttered my father, not quite loud enough to be heard by my mother. He was an unhappy man all the days of his life. Later in that same week, reluctant to settle for a son named Forsyte, he trotted around to the Bonaroba Public Library and did some digging and convinced himself that June the Fifteenth is more important than just being the occasion for a Forsyte tea-slurp in Stanhope Gate. He returned home and, struggling for an air of authority, announced that I should be called Goodyear Grady. He said that June fifteenth was the day in 1844 that Charles Goodyear did it with rubber, hence tires, wherefore automobiles, ergo all these horses being scairt crazy in the streets of Bonaroba and Prestonsburg.

"No," said my mother. That settled it.

My father told me in later years that he really wanted to name me Henry. Himself an inept newspaperman in his twenties, he pretended that he was a relative of Henry Grady, the great Atlanta journalist, and that he had once shaken the hand of Henry Watterson, the celebrated editor of the Louisville *Courier-Journal*. He was lying, but he often lied in an effort to bolster his image as a man. In spite of his lying, I sometimes wish my old man had won that argument and named me for the two Henrys—Grady and Watterson. The fact that such a christening was even suggested was very probably the reason I became a newspaperman.

I did real well in the New York years but now I can only look upon myself as a failure, a washout. Here I sit, publisher in name only and make-believe editor of this sleazy little pipsqueak weekly in this sleazy little pipsqueak town. To augment the tragedy, I have to reflect every hour on the hour that I am tied by law to a sleazy little pipsqueak woman who can outpoint Rustler Smith eighteen to one in calculated meanness. She is altogether responsible for my present sorry condition. I have no trouble deciding which one I despise the most—the town, the newspaper, or That Woman.

For the moment let me say, simply, that I married this wretched newspaper. I married Fern Mobeetie after I met her in the lobby of the Broadhurst Theatre, West Forty-fourth Street in New York City, where Rosalind Russell was opening in *Auntie Mame*. Last day of October 1956, a date that will live in infamy. She dropped her program and I stooped and picked it up. I wish now that in stooping I had broken my back in three places and been rushed off to Polyclinic. As it worked out, she set her Texas bonnet for me and I've always been convinced that she dropped that program to trap me. Three days after the theater lobby she hit the mattress with me and, the mid-fifties being a period of comparative moral stability, I had been jerked across the Rubicon.

So why don't I just pack a couple of bags and hit the trail? For one thing, she refuses to give me a divorce and my only hope of gaining my freedom lies in my staying here and accumulating evidence against her—evidence demonstrating that from the very first months of our marriage she was the town tramp. For another, when a man gets into my age bracket he loses his confidence, feels that the spark has gone from his work, and finds it real easy to set loose. In other words, I am chicken to who-laid-the-chunk. There is only one consoling and compensating thought flowing out of my desolate marriage. Fern has a twin sister named Myrtle Mobeetie. They are much alike. What if the Mormons had won out, and taken over, and today's world was so organized that I found myself married to both Mobeeties?

Not many men are willing to make a public statement to the effect that they hate their wives. Most of them go along with the imbecilic proverb which says, behind every successful man stands a woman. The successful man nods and smiles when he hears it, knowing it to be a lie.

During the years I spent under the same roof with the Mobeetie Monster, I experienced tyranny worse than Robespierre's Reign of Terror, bloodier than Torquemada's, more hideous than Hitler's. How could a man ever, in the first place, marry a woman named Fern Mobeetie? After hearing that name for the first time, any sensible man would take a second look. It is a Texas name. There is a hamlet called Mobeetie in the Texas Panhandle and Fern used to tell me that it came from an Indian word meaning Sweet Water. Untrue. It means water, all right, but water that comes from man. What the Froghop Apaches of the Panhandle used to say, men and women alike, was: "Pardon me, folks, but I've got to go take a mobeetie."

I must speak truth, if only to the wild West Texas wind: I don't expect to ever finish this book and if I should slug through to the end, no man in his right mind would publish it. I'm not built to write books. I have a wandering mind to go with an aberrant nature, and I can't stay on course. Under the rules I should have started right off, in this chapter, with the events that took place that same afternoon our handsome cowboy and Rustler Smith engaged in their cherry pie confrontation at Kohlick's Cafe.

Enter Daphne Whipple, one of our more colorful town characters. Daff is the widow of Coke Whipple, who was county judge for twenty-two years before he fell off a stepladder and killed himself. His well-stacked widow, who was about half his age, took over his job, such being the traditional procedure in these parts. She would fill out Coke's term and then another county judge would be elected. Daff Whipple, however, enjoyed passing judgment on her fellow citizens, especially the sentencing part, and she decided to seek re-election. She had a mysterious hold over a dozen or so of the most influential men in town, and she told them she wanted to stay on the bench, and that they should see to it, and they did.

It was midafternoon when Titus Cottle led the engaging young cowboy into the courtroom and stood him in front of our lady judge. A goodly crowd trailed along after the sheriff and his criminal, including Rustler Smith and Mungo and me. Idaho Tunket had gone to the poolroom, looking for an audience.

I regret the necessity of dwelling on the young man's good looks, but they cannot be lightly dismissed. He was handsome in the way the younger Jack Barrymore was handsome, not in the way these new boy actors are certified as being handsome—coarse, untidy, apefaced plug-uglies with the finely honed histrionic talents of a snubbin post.

County Judge Whipple looked up from a copy of *Cosmopolitan* and inspected the prisoner. As she did so her lips parted slightly and her sensuous mouth fell open as if *Pithecanthropus erectus* had just walked naked into her presence. She had been around, Daff Whipple. Her late husband did real well (over and above his salary) in his years on the bench and Daphne had seen Fujiyama and Bernini's stuff and Mad Ludwig's Castle and she'd et mashed duck at la Tour d'Argent and looked at Stonehenge. But this was something else.

She wrenched her attention away from the cowboy and spoke to the sheriff.

"A gift for me, Titus?"

The sheriff, having no wit in his rude but immortal soul, passed over the question and got down to business.

"Pulled a gun on old man Smith at Kohlick's," he said. "Broad daylight. Mighta killed old Smith if I hadnuh been on my toes and grabbed him." He removed the cowboy's revolver from his pants and laid it on the judge's desk.

"Is it loaded?" she asked.

"Shish-kee-bob!" the sheriff blurted forth his favorite cussword. "Fergot to look."

Daphne clamped her lips together in a thin straight line and gave her top lawman a glance laden with exasperation.

"Day after day," she spoke with feeling. "Don't you ever get tired of playing the butterhead?"

She picked up the gun and gave it a quick inspection.

"Loaded," she observed icily, then turned back to the prisoner. Her manner with the butterhead sheriff had been grating but now her voice softened out and she all but cooed.

"Tell us your name, young man."

"Jefferson Cordee," he said in the same velvety tone he had used when he first spoke to Rustler Smith in the restaurant.

"Stranger in town?"

"Yes, mam."

"Did you pull this gun on that old man?"

"I'm afraid I did, mam."

"Where you from?"

"Lately I've been in Wyomin'. Around Medicine Bow, mostly."

"Medicine Bow," Daff Whipple repeated. "Seems like I've heard of that place."

"It's a real little town, mam, fulla fat people, but it's kinda famous. My granddaddy lived around there when he was a young man and he was kinda famous too. He was . . ."

"Look, handsome. I don't need a definitive biography, at least not at this time. Tell me, why do you carry this gun on your hip? You're not a lawman of some kind, are you?"

"No, mam. I carried it all the time I was in Medicine Bow and nobody seemed to mind."

"Maybe the law is different up there. You must have some reason for carrying it. Are you a movie actor?"

"No, mam. Not likely."

"Well, come on now, tell me why you tote this six-gun around."

"It was my granddaddy's, mam. He always carried it when he was in Wyomin'. When he got to be an old man he give it to my daddy, and my daddy give it to me."

"Well," said Judge Whipple, "I don't see anything here to work up a sweat over, but I'd better go up and check the law. We'll have a ten-minute recess."

During that intermission, while Daff was upstairs, the sheriff stayed within easy reach of Jefferson Cordee, as if he had Billy the Kid in custody. One other thing I noticed. Old Rustler Smith was giving the cowboy some close scrutiny. He kept moving closer in and peering at the prisoner, his eyes squinched up and his face one big question mark. I watched his skittish maneuvering because I suspected that he might commit some fresh assault on the black-headed man. I confess that I had not the slightest suspicion of the thoughts that were going through Old Smith's head. All things considered, I was being dumb about the whole thing.

Daphne Whipple came frisking back into the room with a law-book in her hands, twitching her keester more than seemed necessary as she brushed past Cordee. She took her seat at the desk, cast a winsome smile at the criminal, and opened the book.

"Now," she said, "you had only this gun, right? Did you have on your person any dirk, dagger, slung-shot, blackjack, hand chain, night stick, pipe stick, sword cane, spear, bowie knife, switch blade knife, spring blade knife, throw blade knife? Did you have any of these on your person?"

"Heck no, mam. Not a one."

"Let me see now. Mmmmmm. Mmmmmm. Mmmmmm. Place of business . . . militiaman . . ." Judge Whipple was mumbling to herself as she scanned the statute. "Saddlebags . . . not likely . . ."

The sheriff interrupted her musings.

"Judge," he said, "I got a feeling you're bendin' over backwards tryin' to excuse this gunman outa what he done. I got a feelin' that you're . . ."

Daphne went into a sarcastic imitation of his whiny voice. "You got a feelin'," she said. "You always got a feelin' about sump'm, you dumb bastard. Why didn't you have a feelin' about lookin' to see if this gun was loaded?"

She turned her attention back to Jefferson Cordee.

"Now, young man, you haven't told us *why* you threw down on the old man."

"Judge," the sheriff broke in, still a trifle upset over being called a dumb bastard in open court, "this hardcase here walked right up to Old Smith and started a disrupt and . . ."

"What about, Titus?"

"Well . . . cherry pie."

"I don't read you, Sheriff."

"Excuse me, mam." It was Jefferson Cordee's turn to interrupt. "I only asked him a simple question and I asked it polite. He was eatin' his pie funny."

"It would appear on the surface," Daphne announced, after a brief moment of introspection, "that you people are mixed up."

"He was eatin' it from back to front," said Cordee, trying for clarity. The judge took on a worried look.

"You may not realize it," she said, "but you are making Mr. Smith sound like some kind of a double-jointed contortionist. Please get down to the nitty. How was he eating that cherry pie?"

"He took his fork, mam, and he started from the back end—back where the crust is—and then he worked tords the front, where the point is. The point was the last part he ate. I've traveled around a lot, mam, and I never seen anybody eat a piece of pie like that, and I got curious, and . . ."

A high rasping voice came from behind the defendant. Old Smith couldn't contain himself any longer.

"Judge," he called out, "I don't aim to set here a minute longer and listen to this bantywaist insult me about the way I eat pie. The billa rights says a man can eat pie forrards er backerds er by God sideways if he wants to. My good name is bein' tromped in the mud. This duded-up cowboy gives me any more trouble I'll show him what a gun is for. I'll fill him so fulla holes he'll throw a pokey-dot shadder."

"You sit down, Mr. Smith," ordered Judge Whipple, "or you'll find yourself across the yard in a jail cell, on a diet of tortillas and well water. Not another word." She turned back to the defendant. "The fabled Old West still lives," she said to Cordee. "Two men in a fight over the proper way to eat a piece of pie. Here's your hawg-leg, young man. From now on while you're in Blackleg County keep it in your saddlebags . . . I mean your glove compartment. And stick around. I think you'll like us."

"I can leave now?"

"No. Not just yet. Would you please step closer to the bench, Mr. Cordee?"

The cowboy obliged and she engaged him in a brief whispered conversation. I had my suspicions and they were correct. Daphne Whipple was made of the same stuff as Lanthy Peeler at the cafe. The county judge had the hots. The key question she asked him in that whispered conversation was: did he like chicken-and-dumplings? He nodded enthusiastically. She then said that she was quite famous for her chicken-and-dumplings and that if he'd come over to her house on Fannin Street at five-thirty, she would have a plate of the same ready for his supper. She told him that on account of the inconvenience and embarrassment Titus Cottle had caused him, she wanted to show him that the people of Caliche were good people, salt of the earth, helpful and friendly toward the stranger in their midst.

What Daphne was offering Jefferson Cordee was not, basically, chicken-and-dumplings. It was . . . well, she was making her opening move in . . . the thing that was in her mind was . . . let me ask Webster Third to haul me out of this. The big dictionary says:

> The sum of the morphological, physiological, and behavioral peculiarities of living beings that subserves biparental reproduction with its concomitant genetic segregation and recombination which underlie most evolutionary change, that in its typical dichotomous occurrence is usu. genetically controlled and associated with special sex chromosomes, and that is typically manifested as maleness and femaleness with one or the other

of these being present in most higher animals though both may occur in the same individual in many plants and some invertebrates and though no distinction can be made in many lower forms (as some fungi, protozoans, and possibly bacteria and viruses) either because males and females are replaced by mating types or because the participants in sexual reproduction are indistinguishable.

As near as I can make out, folks, that's poon. Hard porn in good old Webster. Language calculated to set the loins athrob. Thank God the big book still has redeeming social value, the same like the Caliche Weekly *Mud Dobber*.

Chapter Six wherein Asia Battle of the
Two Cross T hires Jefferson Cordee to
cowboy for her

6

Jefferson Cordee had met Iolanthe Peeler and set her Fallopian
tubes to dancing. He had been hauled before Judge Daphne Whipple and Daff's inner core instantly took fire and began to throb
like a great flooding exquisite pain. There was one more confrontation that seemed to be ordained by the planets and the slant of the
cowboy's handwriting. And here it came, just as if it had been
orchestrated by Noel Coward and Neil Simon.

The encounter took place right here—right where I'm sitting—
in the baronial offices of the *Mud Dobber*. In anticipation of its
eventual happening, I had pictured it as a chemical implosion, a
calefaction followed by internal combustion of sufficient force to
leave both principals stretched on the floor, as if from sunstroke.

Here on the one hand was Asia Battle. Didn't I mention Miss
Battle's hinder portions somewhere back yonder? I seem to remember comparing the lady's backside to the Traseros peaks looming over Mungo Oldbuck's ranch. I did not mean to imply that
Asia Battle's buttocks were mountainous. Nor did I intend to suggest that I had had any traffic with them, one or either. Still, I am
firmly in favor of them. In accepting the ancient aphorism which
says a person should try to put his best foot forward, I suggest that
the rules of etiquette and protocol be altered in Asia Battle's be-
half. She should always be permitted to enter a room walking backward. Presenting herself in that fashion, she would stun any
gathering into dead silence.

I don't mean to talk the hind leg offen a mule in this matter of
Asia's bottom. For one thing, it is not good for a man's health to
dwell overlong on such a phenomenon. I'd best cast her posterior
out of my mind and move on to the subject of age. Lanthy Peeler
is maybe twenty-two and we have seen how she was affected by
the mere presence of Jefferson Cordee. Lanthy was so churned up
that she attained a condition almost unknown to her: she lost her

cool. Then Daphne Whipple, at first blush a sophisticated, earthy, discriminating woman in her middle thirties . . . but not quite all of that under her flawless hide. Ordinarily when Daphne set her cap for a man she made an effort to move quietly, to conceal her inner gurglings of passion until her front door clicked shut. Not so with this Wyoming boy. One look at Jeff and she abandoned judicial propriety and forgot about the majesty and the sanctity of the law. I remember reading in a magazine about a straitlaced prudish housewife from Little Rock, Arkansas, who was walking one day with a lady friend in Los Angeles when they came face to face with the actor Paul Newman. The straitlaced lady gasped and stood transfixed as Mr. Newman smiled and then walked on past and, regaining her tongue, she exclaimed: "My God, what I could do with a piece of that!"

Jefferson Cordee turned women on the same way Paul Newman turned on that Arkansas sister. Would he stir Asia Battle? Though she must be close to fifty, she looks thirty-five. My biological curiosity led me to begin scheming some way to have the two meet head on. The scheming wasn't necessary. It was written in the book of Nostradamus.

It was around nine-thirty when Asia Battle came into the office. I find it difficult to scare up the right words needed to describe that special aura that flows out of her, an emanation that almost seems to be a tangible thing. If you saw her walking along the street, sixty or eighty feet from you, you wouldn't pay much attention to her. Those structural qualities might register, even at a distance, but if someone asked you a minute later to describe her in detail, you wouldn't remember. Or if someone introduced you to her at a party, you'd mumble a pleasantry and move on toward the coffee urn . . . you'd have looked fleetingly at just another dame's face. But once you stood before her and listened to the music of that voice, and those classic lineaments began to impress their beauty on your mind, and you looked into those big luminous dark eyes, and at the golden unblemished skin with just a hint of olive, and that wide smiling mouth that could be sensuous beyond all believing . . . AND that glossy hair always drawn tightly back and fastened with some kind of a Mexican silver clip . . . I tell you, friends, that I came up to the front counter and my knees began the crazy trembling that told me I was once again in the presence of a Total Woman. I guess I lived so long with an illiterate common scold that this woman staggered my senses by just standing still.

I didn't know how old she was. She showed no wrinkles and there was no scrawn at her throat, where a woman first begins showing her years. There and in the hands. She had good smooth hands. She had good smooth everything.

She said she wanted to advertise for a ranch hand. She told me something I already knew—that she could get wet Mexicans but she won't hire them. This sets her up locally as a traitor to her class (the ranching class) and a Commie of the Jane Fonda stripe, and a fool. The other ranchers nod and touch their hats and sometimes give her a howdy-mam, but they cast no admiring glances at her as she passes along Railroad Avenue. They say they are not objecting to a woman's doing a job that God laid out for men to do. Such a thing is not without precedent. But dad burn it, she's got these dad burn principles! Runnin' a cattle ranch, or even a sheep ranch, is no place to have *principles*. Hodamighty, Jack, what's this world a-comin' to, anyhow?

I asked her to come back and sit at my desk while I wrote the ad for her. She had on some kind of a tight-fitting light blue pants suit and please don't get me going again on that incredible *derrière*.

The thought came to me as I led her to the back of the room that I knew very little about her. She came in to Caliche every week or so and went briskly about her business, and if anyone tried to get her in conversation she'd talk about little more than how-we-do-need-rain. She seated herself in the chair that has been graced by the bottoms of such world-famous celebrities as Mayor Ford Winkler (dry cleaning) and Darwin Peavy (banking) and Vestal McDermott (Sangre de Cristo Motor Hotel) and just everybody else who is anybody. After she got herself snugged in and had given me another helping of that wide and warming smile, I made an exploratory move.

"I don't know," I said, "whether to call you Miss or Missus or that new thing Muss."

"It's Miss," she said, "but not to you, please. I wish you'd just call me Asia. And I'll call you . . . wye, I don't think I even know your first name. Doesn't it appear somewhere in the paper?"

"Stuck down in a corner, in little bitty type. It's Forsyte, and I don't like it, and I always ask people to call me Tuck or Henry."

"Then it'll be Henry, Henry." She threw back her head and laughed and her fine chest advanced three or four inches in the doing, and in my direction at that, and I felt happy about it. Well, not exactly happy. Jizzled.

"Asia," I said, turning businesslike, "I have a little problem you might help me out with. Suppose the *bandidos* come raiding across the border, the way they did back around 1916, and seize you and carry you off into captivity. I'm going to be in trouble. I'll have to write the news of the cruel abduction, and I won't have any background information about the victim. I won't be able to speak of the good taste displayed by the *bandidos,* because I know almost nothing about you. Could I ask you a few questions and scratch down a few notes?"

She glanced at her watch. "Go ahead," she agreed. "I've got about thirty minutes."

With perfect aplomb she answered all questions. She recounted how she had inherited the Two Cross T from her uncle, Crawford Battle, five years ago. At the time of his death she had been doing well as executive secretary to an important advertising man in her home town, San Francisco. Parents dead. One brother in San Francisco.

"Were you ever married?"

"No."

"That seems hard to believe."

"Why?"

"Two immediate reasons: you are calm, and you are beautiful."

"Henry! I haven't had a man say that to me in centuries! The fellow I worked for in San Francisco," she went on slowly, as if she were choosing her words with care, "wanted to divorce his wife and marry me. He had almost broken me down when Uncle Crawford died and left me this ranch. I had been out here to visit a couple of times and liked West Texas and the mountain air and life on the ranch. I didn't want to go it alone, though, so I agreed to marry my boss if he'd come along with me and help lasso dogies and brand the steers and curry the horses. He said . . ."

I had to interrupt her. "Not for the archives, but just for my personal information—did you love this guy?"

"Ha! That *is* a bit personal, but I don't mind answering it. No. I liked him and enjoyed being with him but, truthfully, I haven't been in love, all-systems-go, since I was in high school. Now.

When I asked him to take the shortcut through the canyon with me, he said no. He hated Texas. A lot of people do hate Texas, you know, a way-down-deep hate, without knowing anything about the State. And he wouldn't consider giving up his stupid advertising business, which I disliked intensely. So there we were, and here I am."

She had enlarged the Two Cross T, buying an adjoining ranch to the west. She had replaced much of the old fencing, keeping the lines straight and using galvanized chain link along the highway for looks; and then she had remodeled the headquarters house, giving it a fine Spanish look with lots of russet red tile underfoot and overhead. At present she was running sixteen hundred head of Herefords and turning a good profit. She was surprisingly frank about everything, where I had expected some evasion and cover-up. There were moments when I half expected her to show me her bankbooks.

Then we got to the important matter of Mungo Oldbuck. She said she had been mystified and perplexed from the beginning.

"A dozen or so of my steers somehow worked their way around a water gap, got across Rinderpest Creek, and invaded Mr. Oldbuck's domain. Nobody knew about it for a day or so, and then his men spotted them. I knew that he didn't run cattle but I didn't know that he hated them. He came out with an elephant gun and shot two of my Herefords and when my boys got there, he fired twice over their heads. I heard the shooting and hopped into a jeep and hurried out there. He was stamping around and swearing and he pointed his gun straight at my head and told me to get my . . . my person off his land or he'd shoot me. I thought he was being rather drastic."

"You knew, of course, that he and your uncle had some trouble."

"I've heard talk about it. The details seem to be lacking. They got into a fistfight out there by the creek, something to do with water rights. There were no witnesses, and Uncle Crawford is dead. No matter what the quarrel was about, I think Mr. Oldbuck needs to mind his manners. He'd better not push me too far."

"I don't think he will."

"I can be a beast when I'm aroused."

"I'll bet."

She gave me a long curious smile.

"There was another incident that you may not have heard about. He had a man working for him, named Tiny, a foreigner of some kind—sleek and oily and swaggering. Sort of a gigolo type. He got into the habit of prowling around my premises in the middle of the night. We have a Mexican girl named Rosa and he was after her. The man was a rapist. I woke up around four o'clock one morning and heard a strange tinkling sound and saw a shadow just outside my French windows. I got on the extension phone and woke up Jaybird Huddleston . . . he's my foreman. He came rushing over and caught this Tiny fellow. Tiny tried to use a gun but Jaybird got it away from him and beat him real handsomely in the face with it. I didn't see the fight—by the time Jaybird arrived I was so frightened I couldn't leave my room. Well, Tiny made it back to the Oldbuck place with a fantastic tale of how he had been tracking down two valuable horses that had disappeared from Mr. Oldbuck's stables. He told Mr. Oldbuck that he had good reason to believe that Jaybird Huddleston stole those horses. Imagine it! He trailed the horses right to my bedroom! Mr. Oldbuck was furious and talked about having me thrown in jail along with Jaybird."

"This happened after he shot the Herefords?"

"Oh no. Before."

"Was this Tiny guy out at the creek at the time of the shooting?"

"I didn't see him. Somebody said he left his job a month or two after Jaybird beat him up. Well, there it is. Mr. Oldbuck must have felt he had three reasons for exploding the way he did when my cattle strayed onto his land. The grudge against my uncle. The old quarrel about water rights. And the thing about the stolen horses."

"Except for his bad temper," I said, "I think you'd like . . ."

The front door opened and Jefferson Cordee came in from the street. Asia turned and glanced in his direction and then, in a low voice, sans tremolo and sans vibrato, she said, "Oh, it's the young man they had in court yesterday."

"Did you meet him?" I whispered.

"No, but I was over there and saw the commotion and stepped into the courtroom for a few minutes. Don't mind me—go see what he wants." No flutters, no feminine giddiness, no vibes, no sweat. I got up and went to the counter.

As I stepped up Jefferson Cordee smiled and took off his big hat, exposing that lustrous black hair. One thing I must say—he was not afflicted with country-boy shyness. He looked me straight in the eye without faltering. He spoke in that slow drawl of his but there was no nervous hesitation in it.

"Mr. Grady," he said, "a man told me that if I came around and talked to you, you might be able to help me get a job, maybe write out an ad for me and put it in your paper. I sorta like this town and figure I might stay around a while and see what . . ."

"You like this town after what happened yesterday?"

"Oh, that was all just a misunderstanding. And the judge, Miz Whipple, was real fair. She even had me out to her house last evenin' and we had chicken-and-dumplin's and she explained how ignorance of the law is no excuse, and boy was it good!"

"Boy was *what* good?"

"The chicken-and-dumplin's."

"I'm sure they were."

"This man told me that if I put an ad . . ."

"Just a minute, young man!" Asia Battle called out from the back of the room. She got out of the chair and came striding forward.

"Did you say you wanted a job?"

"Yes, mam."

"What kind of a job?"

"Oh, anything. Anything at all. I can do odd jobs and I can clerk in a store and pump gas and I'm big enough to handle a shovel and I know how to dig postholes and I can milk. Did you have somethin' in mind, mam?"

"I run a ranch, a big one," she said. "I was just about to put an ad in Mr. Grady's paper for a hand. I mean a cowboy. From the looks of your rig, I'd guess that you are either a cowboy or you would like to be one."

"I've done some cowboyin' . . . up north."

"I'll pay you three-fifty a month and all you can eat."

"How far out is your place?"

"Forty miles south."

"Sounds more than middlin' to me," he said. "When do you want me to start?"

"When you can get there. Do you have a car?"

"Yes, mam." He took his eyes away from her and a slight frown appeared. It was apparent that he wanted to ask a question, but he wasn't sure if he should.

"Excuse me, mam," he finally said. "Out at your ranch do you get TV?"

"Oh, certainly." She gave him a broad smile. "And I can't help wondering what the old-timers like Goodnight and Loving would say if they found out that's the first question a cowboy asks before he agrees to sign on. I'll bet you like 'Gunsmoke.' "

"Some, mam. What I like best is football. And roller derby."

She gave him the directions, sketching a little map on the back of an envelope. I had been watching her closely all along and never once did she give a hint of any emotional stirrings. She might have been talking to a cedar post. But . . . Jefferson Cordee, standing in the presence of a woman who might be twice his age, had clearly begun to feel that glow—that emanation I myself could pick up at a distance of six furlongs from her.

"I'll be there, mam, tomorrow morning. I'll just go straight to the bunkhouse and check in."

She laughed. "Bunkhouse? We have no bunkhouse, cowboy. You'll live in your own cabin, all to yourself."

"Lor-dee!" he exclaimed. "Who ever heard! Look for me before noon tomorrow."

"And," added Asia, "you'll make your own bed and sweep your own floor."

"I can do that too, mam."

She said good-by to me, calling me Henry, and started for the door. Hand on the knob, she turned back to Jefferson, whose eyes had followed her and observed (I assumed) the rapturous contours of her bottom.

"I almost forgot," she said to him. "That gun. Better leave it in town somewhere. I don't like my people having guns."

"But, mam . . ."

"You could leave it with Mr. Grady here."

Jefferson Cordee squared his jaw.

"My granddad," he said, "wore that gun when he lived in Wyomin' and he always said a man should keep a gun handy anywhere in the West. I clean it and polish it almost ever night before I go to bed, the way he did. All that polishin' has wore off all the bluein'. I'd sure hate to go anywhere without it."

"Oh, all right. Bring it along. But keep it out of sight."

Asia Battle departed and Jefferson Cordee, looking now a mite bewildered over the swift pace of life in Caliche, lingered at the front counter. I asked him back to the Seat of the Mighty and he took the chair recently vacated by Asia. I sat down and glanced at the notes I had made on my pad. I had lost a classified ad. A buck sixty down the drain, maybe three-twenty. Possessed of a good head for business, I might easily have manipulated bleachable cottonseed oil futures into the field extrapolated by investors in frozen pork bellies and come up with two want ads instead of none. One of the eight thousand things I don't like about running the *Mud Dobber* is that I have to play businessman and bookkeeper much more than I play newspaperman. I wasn't cut out for commerce, at least not under the rules governing today's marketplace. Meaning no rules. Meaning skin the other son of a bitch even if he happens to be your grandmother.

I crumpled up the notes containing Asia's specifications for a hired hand and threw them in the wastebasket.

"Miz Battle is real nice," said Jefferson. "The more I see of this town the more I like it. I think I like it better than Medicine Bow. I'd have enjoyed livin' in Medicine Bow in the old days. I wonder, Mr. Grady, if you'd be able to find time to show me around, maybe fifteen minutes worth."

I said I'd be happy to. I had to write my weekly column, an essay consisting wholly of emulsified bullshit, innocent of thought, offensive to no one including members of the American Legion. After that I wanted to go back to the cubbyhole known as my private office, the little room where I hold secret consultations with visiting tycoons, the crowned heads of Europe, caliphs of heavy industry, three-tailed bashaws of the Masonic orders . . . the room too where bribes are passed and buggings planned, and where there's a studio couch I keep so that local and state politicians can perform unnatural acts on one another if they feel so inclined. All I wanted was to catch me a siesta, and so I asked my Cavalier of the Unstaked Plains to come back later in the afternoon and I'd give him the guided tour.

I had a feeling that I ought to disabuse this amiable young man's mind of the notion that he had stumbled upon Utopia, but I curbed the impulse and asked him a most casual question: why would he have enjoyed Medicine Bow in the old days?

"It must of been excitin'," he said, "in the days when my granddad was up there. I wish he had lived long enough for me to know him. I'm sure you must have heard about him, Mr. Grady. They called him The Virginian, and he killed a man name of Trampas, and a Mr. Wister in Philadelphia wrote a book about it."

I just sat there and stared a hole through him. I was stunned— not alone by that concluding sentence, but by my obtuse failure to have guessed his identity. There were reasons I should have known or suspected, reasons dating back to my college days, reasons having to do with my own adventitious brush with Mr. Wister's book.

There were questions to be asked, elusive angles and aspects that needed exploration, but they would have to wait. For the moment all I could manage was that stare of incredulity, and the murmured ejaculation that seemed to go with it . . .

"God's eyebrows!"

Chapter Seven posing the question of why
our cowboy is hard on the trail of a man
from Buffalo, Wyoming

7

Jefferson Cordee's revelation of his identity set off a long chain
of thoughts that made me restless and unable to sleep. I ran some
errands around town and then put in twenty minutes of hard news-
writing about a lost puppy answering to the name of Ding-a-ling,
a petition for rezoning a part of Lomax Avenue, and the death in
Arizona of a man named Upshur who got his start in life as a
brushpopper on the old Biggerstaff place. After that I gave it another try and managed a twenty-minute siesta. I'm getting to be
like that old guy Buckminster Fuller, a genius who writes surreal-
istic prose and who achieves twenty hours of work a day by taking
little naps from time to time, the way Thomas A. Edison used to do
it. Buckminster Fuller didn't learn the trick from Edison. He got
it from watching a dog.

Young Cordee arrived shortly after five and I suggested that we
take a walk around the central part of town, so I could point out
the showplaces, such as the Indian teepees maintained by the Jay-
cees as rest rooms for tourists, and the sandstone statue of Pastor
Charles Ochiltree on the courthouse lawn.

He told me before we started out that he couldn't get over the
hospitality of the people he had met thus far, and I thought perhaps he might have had chicken-and-dumplings in mind. I could
have enlightened him about the special friendliness the people
of the town were showing him.

It may be against the law to drag forth a hawg-leg in a public
place, but people here like to imagine that they are of hardy
pioneer stock, made from the stuff of the Mountain Men, the Buffalo Hunters, the Pony Express Riders, and the Indian Fighters.
They like to fancy that there ain't no Rexall Drug, no parking me-
ters, no Safeway, no Osterizer in the kitchen, no Dairy Queens, no
motels with beds that shake for a quarter. And, of course, no Law
West of the Pecos. They admire a man of Jefferson Cordee's stripe

who comes along and plays it the old way, and they dislike a man like Old Smith who responds with a chair instead of a Colt, and they overlook the cold fact that the Mountain Men and the Buffalo Hunters and the Pony Express Riders and the Indian Fighters sallied forth with crotch-crickets snapping at their genitals and smelling somewhat worse than a Kickapoo squaw.

We walked the length of Railroad Avenue and sauntered into some of the side streets and for a long while neither of us mentioned The Virginian or Wyoming or Owen Wister. There were exciting things to point out, such as . . . well, such as restaurants. There are three eating houses on the main drag. Good Mexican food is available at Esperanza's Place on the eastern edge of town. Near the opposite end of the long boulevard is the Tasty Barbecue Pit, an establishment sometimes described by the local gentry with the witticism: "The pit may be tasty but the barbecue sure ain't." The big restaurant, the "downtown" restaurant, is of course Kohlick's Cafe.

Then there is Claude Boggy's filling station. Mr. Boggy, who made his taw as a sheepshearer before becoming a tycoon, keeps a pot of chili going on an electric plate in the office of his gas station, offering it in thick white bowls to transient motorists at two bits a throw, with oyster crackers. Mr. Boggy, an amiable and well-disposed man, believes with all his heart that he serves the best chili on earth, and that tourists who partake of just one bowl will go away and talk about the marvelous town of Caliche for the remainder of their lives. Many of them do. They go away cursing Caliche, its people, its ruling establishment, its domestic animals, and its unborn children unto the next three generations. A most unreasonable attitude, though reasonable.

"Claude Boggy's chili," I observed to Jefferson Cordee, "bad as it is, is not that bad."

"I had a bowl yesterday," said Jefferson. "It wasn't as bad as some I had in Pebblo, Colorado."

When we were standing in front of Boggy's place I made ready to launch on one of the historical lectures I sometimes use to entertain or confuse visitors, especially those of the wise-ass type who come from East of the Hudson River. There's a shambles of a 'dobe shack at the back end of Claude Boggy's lot and in my set speech I describe a meeting that took place within its walls a hundred and ninety years ago come December the Nineteenth—a meeting at which Davy Crockett accepted a million and a half pesos from General Santa Anna with the understanding that he, Crockett, would leave the back door of the Alamo unlatched when the Mexican army arrived.

Two considerations stopped me from undertaking the recital, which is exciting and loaded with sacred traditions that still govern the conduct of public affairs in the State of Texas. I had already concluded that Jefferson Cordee has exactly as much humor in his makeup as you could stuff under a chigger's eyelid. Secondly, I caught sight of Big Jim Deehardt.

Deehardt is sometimes called the Hermit of Leydigs Duct, after the creek that runs past his back door. I have no idea what he looks like in the face. His features are hidden by a thorny gray-flecked beard and his right eye is covered with a black patch. Once when I asked him how he lost that eye he said, "In Parson, Kansas, a drunk plumber threw a soddering nipple at me." That seemed sufficient.

Big Jim stands about six three and I would guess him to be fifty, maybe sixty. It's difficult to gauge a man's years when you can't see his face.

"Grady," he said, "I'm sure you must be well acquainted with the mayor of this town, one Winkler."

"Sure," I said. "Ford Winkler."

"Where do I find the miserable son of a bitch?"

"Wye . . ." I began, stammering a trifle at the gentle designation of our burgomaster, "wye . . . he's probably over at City Hall. Something wrong, Big Jim?"

"Nothing worth mentioning," he said. "You might get an item for your newspaper, though. I'm gonna kill the thieving bastard with my bare hands."

Before I could ask for a few advance details concerning this most newsworthy event, the shaggy hermit moved past me and headed off in the direction of Caffknee Street. Then I felt Jeff Cordee's grip on my arm, and I realized that he had not spoken a word during the brief meeting with Big Jim.

"That's him," he said. "That's the man."

"What man, Jeff?"

"I know it. I can feel it inside my bones."

"So . . . who is he, for Christ's sake?"

"Trampas's son. I should have jumped him while I had him here. Come on, let's go get him."

"Now, hold on, Jeff. That's Big Jim Deehardt. I know him. I know his history. He used to be called the Lightning Rod King of the Middle Border."

"I don't want him to get away. I've been on his trail a long time."

"He won't get away. He may strangle the mayor, but he won't split. Come on back to the office and let's talk about this a little. You've got me all befuddled."

Soon we were settled down again at my desk. We didn't talk during the walk back and I was able to think a bit, and I even approached the conclusion that I was beginning to see some daylight. The picture was still out of focus, and fuzzy, but I was . . .

Jeff now resumed his discourse.

"That's the man from Buffalo," he said. "I've got a kind of sixth sense about it. All those whiskers—that's a disguise. He don't want anybody to recognize him. He don't want anybody to know that he's Trampas's son. But, Mr. Grady, he can't fool me." He stopped talking and stood up. "We'd better get over there. You heard what he said. He intends to kill the mayor, and I'm gonna stop him from doin' it."

I decided to play it tough with this young Hercules. "No you're not!" I snapped at him. "You're gonna get back into that chair and tell me about Trampas's son. I didn't even know Trampas had a son. Or was married, for that matter."

He didn't sit down, yet. He was as taut as a drumhead.

"He comes from a town up in the north of Wyomin'," he said. "Town name of Buffalo. That's the place where his daddy lived. His daddy's name wasn't Trampas at all—it was Henry Smith—and this one's name is Henry Smith too."

"Thar she blows!" The words came out of me in a hoarse whisper, almost unbidden, and Jefferson Cordee didn't even hear them. The Owen Wister stuff was flowing back into my head now, and the picture was coming clear.

"All the time I was in Medicine Bow," he continued, "I was on the lookout for some trace of Trampas's kin. One day I was down in Laramie at the public library and a lady there told me that before he got killed, Trampas had been married to a girl up north in this town of Buffalo. It was this library lady that told me his real name was Smith."

"So," I said, "you went to Buffalo."

"Sure. It took me a while but I finally found an old guy name of Coffin, cleaned septic tanks, said he knew about Trampas. And that's when I found out Trampas had a son, a man named Henry Smith, had a worse reputation than his father. This Mr. Coffin there in Buffalo told me that Henry Smith had got in trouble two or three years back, stealin' a truckload of Swift & Company weenies, and had left town two jumps ahead of the sheriff."

"Alone? Was Henry Smith traveling alone when he lit out?"

"Far as I know. Old Mr. Coffin didn't mention anybody goin' with him. He said there was a rumor around that Smith was gonna hide out somewhere in New Mexico, so I headed south. I followed his trail and it was in a town called Roswell that they told me to have a look here in Caliche."

I was beset and surrounded by perplexities. How could Jeff Cordee have completely overlooked the possibility that Rustler Smith was his man? The question was clearing up a little. He hadn't known that Henry Smith had a daughter, and that the daughter left Buffalo with him. The name Smith hadn't caught his attention —I've heard tell that the country suffers under a glut of people bearing that name. And then I think I hit upon the principal reason for his oversight.

Jeff Cordee simply didn't visualize the son of Trampas as an old man. His mind had been conditioned, through the years, to picturing Trampas himself as a big powerful lusty man in the so-called prime of life. It was natural for him to envisage the son of Trampas as looking the same. The fact that the man himself would now be in his seventies, with creaking bones and withered hide, wouldn't have set right. Big Jim Deehardt came closer to the phantasm.

The big question remained, and I was strangely reluctant to ask it. Why was the grandson of The Virginian prowling the mountains from Montana to the Mexican border, looking for the son of Trampas? It was almost impossible to conceive of this soft-talking young man as a killer. Yet I had been sitting a few feet away when he threw down on Rustler Smith in the cafe. The very fact of his carrying the gun would suggest that he might be planning on using it. But what would be his motive? Trampas didn't bring down The Virginian. Yet, within the hour, I'd heard Jeff say the words: "I should have jumped him while I had him here."

I decided against telling him that Rustler Smith was the man he was after. I simply repeated that Big Jim Deehardt was not. And I changed the subject because the complications were giving me a headache.

"Let's forget about this whole thing for a day or two," I suggested. "I'll come down to Miss Battle's place and we might saddle up a couple of horses and ride across country for a visit with Big Jim. That'll settle your mind about him, and we can have a long talk about things in general."

"But I'll be workin'," he reminded me.

"Maybe I'll come on a Saturday, and I'll ask your new boss if I can take you away from your job for a few hours."

"Sounds great. Let's do it."

"One more thing, Jeff. Don't get sore about this, but I wish you'd tell me what happened between you and Daphne Whipple at her house . . . I mean after you got finished with the chicken-and-dumplings."

He sat in thought for a while, scratching his chin with his thumb.

"A man ain't supposed to talk about such matters," he said. "From the minute I got in her house I knew what she was up to, and I didn't like it. Don't get the wrong idea, Grady. I go for the girls like anybody else, but with Judge Whipple there was just something wrong about it. First place, she was a big important judge. I never dreamed of . . . of doin' it with a *judge*. But the thing that really gave me a bad taste in my mouth was that she called the sheriff a dumb S. O. B. Right in front of ever'body. He's dumb enough, I reckon, but I can't stand to hear anybody called a S. O. B."

"Jeff," I told him, "there's one thing you've got to learn. There are a lot of them out in this part of the country, a whole hell of a lot of them, and sometimes a man has just plain got to call them by their right name. Professor Dobie, who is considered to be about the greatest writer ever produced in Texas, used to know a man who was writing—now, Jeff, you've got to excuse me for using that expression you don't like—a man who was writing a history of the sons of bitches in the State of Texas. He never got the book finished. He said that every time he thought he was through with it, he'd discover another one."

"He could have called them sons of guns," insisted Jeff.

I thought, There may be trying moments with this young man.

Chapter Eight devoted to a definitive
history of Caliche's founding by the
Single-Titter Baptists

8

Caliche is an old town, antedating the Civil War by as many as two years. It once bore the name of Ochiltree, and the story of its founding by a man of that name is an inspiring chapter in Texas history, a moving episode with deep tragic undertones—a tale of courage on the one hand and hateful intolerance on the other—little known even to Texans because it cannot be told without use of the word *tit*.

I have never dared to set down the true account of the town's origin in this newspaper, and I chose not to outline it for Jefferson Cordee during our brief tour of the downtown area. In the course of that stroll amidst the canyons of lower Caliche, he mentioned the Bible at least three times. People who mention the Bible that often would not care to hear about Charles Ochiltree's valiant war with the Four-Tit Baptists, except perhaps in private.

Long decades ago there was a town in Texas named Snow Hill, situated in flat country about twenty miles north of Dallas, in Collin County. It was a small community and could support no more than one church, and that church, to be sure, was Baptist. Among the upstanding citizens of Snow Hill were Coley Brewster and Charles Ochiltree, and both of these good men were deacons in the church.

One day in the late 1850s Brother Coley Brewster, who had a houseful of young'uns, found himself needing a good milk cow. He mentioned this need to Brother Charlie Ochiltree, who had cows to throw away, and Brother Ochiltree said, wye of course, he'd be happy to sell one of his herd to his fellow deacon.

Said Brother Brewster: "You understand, Charlie, that I got to have me a cow that's a prime milker."

Said Brother Ochiltree: "The cow I got in mind, Coley, is a cow that'll dern near drown you in milk. I will garrantee you that she will give you one gallon of milk per tit."

(Please, kind reader, keep in mind that this account of the happenings in Snow Hill is unleavened history, and keep in mind, too, that the events took place in a long-gone era; the temptation is strong upon me to give Brother Ochiltree's milk cow a suitable semi-comic name, but in the interest of historical truth and scholarly integrity, let us be content in the knowledge that no cow name, such as Bossy or Bessie or Fern, has been handed down to us from those ancient days.)

Brother Coley Brewster was pleasured no end that the cow in question was warranted to furnish him with four gallons of milk per day. Jehoshaphat! He'd be able to submerge his kids in milk and have some left over to sell to the neighbors. Judas Priest! A truly Christian blessing!

A price was agreed upon, the money changed hands, and Brother Ochiltree delivered the cow to the Coley Brewster home.

Within thirty seconds Brother Brewster had discovered that a monstrous fraud had been perpetrated. He always had been, in military parlance, a tit man—even unto cows—and thus he was quick to detect that this animal was a sport, a mutant, a dad-burn freak. She possessed an udder of standard size and shape, but depending from that udder was just one single tit. Right in the middle.

There were witnesses to what happened next. Brother Brewster lost his Christian cool. To keep himself from busting Deacon Ochiltree a good one right in the beezer, he began picking up fallen tree limbs, breaking them in pieces, hurling the pieces to the ground, and jumping up and down on them in irreverent rage. All the while he was uttering parts of speech that are normally strange and unpleasant to the ears of churchy people. He charged his fellow deacon with lying and larceny and jactitation of marriage and arson, and Brother Ochiltree responded with the patience of the Savior, as follows:

"Fetch me a milk bucket."

Someone brought the bucket and Brother Ochiltree seized the cow's single spigot and milked her, and true enough she gave a gallon.

"All I said," he declared, "was that she'd give one gallon per tit. That is what she has just give. The Good Lord is my witness."

"I demand my money back!" cried Brother Brewster, but Deacon Ochiltree insisted that there had been no deception on his part, that a deal is a deal and this particular deal would remain a deal.

Brother Brewster took the matter straight to the hierarchy of the Snow Hill Baptist Church. A conference was summoned, patterned after the Diet of Worms, and the purchaser of the one-titted cow told his story. His opponent stood firm. After a while the church leaders said they would take the matter under advisement, but Brother Ochiltree noted that they were casting dark looks in his direction. He smelled real trouble. It seemed clear to him that he was in danger of being unchurched—canned out of the flock. In those days being unchurched was a serious and degrading affair, almost as serious and degrading as being hanged. Nowadays it means you get to be an Episcopalian.

Up to this point we have been dealing with straight history. The story of the quarrel is substantially true. As for subsequent events, it is possible that the legend makers have taken a hand—yet the basic details have to be true. Caliche is a solid fact, and the sandstone statue of Charles Ochiltree is on the courthouse lawn.

Rather than submit to the stigma of being unchurched there in Snow Hill, Brother Ochiltree called together a group of his friends and supporters who had stood beside him throughout his ordeal. He had them all kneel down and pray for guidance. Later that same day he told them that while they were kneeling with heads bowed, a seagull came out of the clouds and perched on his shoulder.

"He spoke to me," Brother Ochiltree told his people.

"What did he say?" they wanted to know.

"He said we should go to *The Place.*"

"Did he mean you should go to The Bad Place?"

"Of course not. I don't know what he meant, but the Lord will surely give me a fill-in."

"You said, Brother Ochiltree, that he was a seagull. What in tarnation was he a-doin' in Collin County? A seagull is supposed to hang around the sea, and the only water we got here is Crippled Toad Creek, and it's dry as a gourd."

"God's seagull don't need no water," said the Leader.

There were, as always, a couple of dissenters.

"What language did this seagull use?" asked wise old Deacon Travis.

"It was halfway between Missouri Ozark and Tex-Mex," said Brother Ochiltree.

"I ain't goin'," said Deacon Travis.

Brother Willie Jim Grimes chipped in his quibble. "Did he say anything, this here seagull, in regards to one-tit cows versus four-tit cows?"

"Seagulls don't bother talkin' cow-talk," Deacon Ochiltree responded.

"I ain't goin'," said Brother Grimes.

"Then get lost," said the Leader. "The Lord go with you and the devil take the hindmost."

"A . . . men!" chorused the great throng of thirty-one loyal Single-Titters.

The following day these faithful ones loaded their belongings into their wagons and pushcarts and departed Snow Hill forever. As their sorry little caravan moved away from the town they were showered with rotten vegetables by the Four-Titter adherents of Coley Brewster, who lost their sense of balance so completely that they began shouting hard-core pornography at the apostates.

There was no welcome for the Single-Titters anywhere along the way. Early in their epochal trek they arrived at the thriving hamlet of Dallas, with a population of 775—Methodists, Cumberland Presbyterians, and Fulminant Pentacostal Christians. Not a Baptist in town. The Dallas folks would have nothing to do with the Ochiltree wagon train, refused to sell them supplies, offered them no jerky (the basic foodstuff of Dallasites then as now), and told them to mosey. For this, on July 8, 1860, a week after the caravan had departed, a mysterious wonder was performed: the whole damn town of Dallas caught fire and burned to the ground.

At Waco to the south, the Single-Titters tried to get some converts, since they had a desperate need of manpower, and they set up a baptismal ceremony at the Brazos River, but nobody showed up except a few rowdy children, who shouted taunts at the visitors, and the Waco Water Commissioner, who said he would pour carbolic acid and paregoric in the river if the pilgrims didn't hitch up and get moving. No provisions. No jerky. Brother Ochiltree appealed to the body politic, but the people told him they were busy trying to get up a college, a Baptist school which they planned calling either Cowper Brann State Normal or Baylor U. They made it clear to Brother Ochiltree that the institution would be non-denominational Baptist, meaning neither one-titted nor quadri-titted. Mosey, said the God-fearing people of Waco, and our

friends from Snow Hill did so. Ever southward. Ever westward.
Ever weary.

On a Sunday morning they straggled into the little German settlement of Fredericksburg. The untidy, limping, hungry train
moved along Main Street and came to the Vereins Kirche, where
services were in progress. Pastor Ochiltree (for now he was so
denominated) spoke to his weary flock, telling them that their
fortunes would change now, that the Lord would smile upon them,
that he had heard tell of this community, that the people here were
kind and generous Teutons, quick to embrace the wayfaring
stranger.

The door of the Kirche opened and people began coming out,
disturbed by the noise the Pilgrims were making and led, no doubt,
by old John Meusebach himself. The Fredericksburghers wanted
to know what all the damn *Radau* was about, and Pastor Ochiltree stepped forward. He spoke of their long and harrowing journey, of the schism in the Snow Hill Baptist Church, of the dire
need his people were suffering. The Fredericksburg leaders asked
for details of the church trouble in Snow Hill and Charlie Ochiltree
stated them, concealing nothing.

The elders of the German community then withdrew into their
tabernacle to gnaw on Bratwurst and say Gott-in-Himmel and de-
bate the thorny question before the house. At length they returned
to the street. We do not know if John Meusebach, the colony's
founder, was present as spokesman but if he was he extended his
right arm, pointed south, and intoned:

*"Du verdammter Kerl, mach dass Du raus Kommst aus unserum
County mit Deiner verruckten Ein-Titten Religion!"*

English translation:

*"Verdammt noch mal! Raus mit you and your crazy Tittenre-
ligion aus unser Gilleppisie Coundy und taken mit you zee dumb-
kopf udder-shtoopid Theorie!"*

Alas! Heads hanging, bellies empty, spirits at their lowest yet,
the Pilgrims moved off toward the Pedernales River, and a gang of
boys followed in their train, howling insults in Low Dutch and
hurling rancid potato dumplings at the tormented wanderers.

At Uvalde the guileless travelers were set upon by Lipan-
Apache Indians who had just captured the settlement. One Single-
Titter was scalped, two were wounded, and four lit into the forest
and are probably still running. At Del Rio the Pilgrims found the

community beset by a plague of rattlesnakes; thousands upon thousands of the venomous vipers were wriggling around in the streets, chasing dogs and cats and iguanas and snapping at citizens, rich and poor alike. The invasion was so serious that the Town Council had imported Mexican bandits to fight the serpents, it being already a well-established fact in Texas that a rattlesnake will run from a Mexican every time.

Pastor Ochiltree surveyed this dreadful scene and felt a sickness in his heart; then he squared his shoulders and spoke to his people.

"It couldn't be any wussen it's been," he said, and forthwith led his disciples out of this snake-town, heading his caravan upriver and into the mountain country. Then one afternoon around four o'clock the wagons reached the crest of a rocky eminence and Charlie Ochiltree looked into a verdant vale, where there was no sign of a rattlesnake, a Neiman or a Marcus, a Lipan-Apache, or a single platter of *Kartoffelkloesse*. The Founder raised himself off his wagon seat, swept his eyes across the glorious prospect, flung his arms Himmelward, and cried out:

"This here is The Place!"

And so they descended with a bang and a clatter into the valley, which was no way near as verdant as it had looked from the cliffs, and they set to work building their church and their town and all hands were as happy as larks.

Thus the story of how Caliche was founded. Most of it, as I have stated, is solid history—Texas history, that is. Some bits and fragments are reckoned by local scholars to be fabricated out of folklore and myth, especially the account of the Hegira itself. No one in present-day Caliche is able to sort out fact from legend. In any case, a dozen years after Patriarch Charlie Ochiltree was gathered to his fathers, the name of the town was changed to Caliche.

A lovely name, Caliche. It means dirt.

Chapter Nine in which Miz Fern casts
some stones and is saluted for her
sexual prowess

9

A full moon hung in the sky over toward the Chinga tu Madres as I walked through the cool and serene streets at three this morning. I didn't notice any rumbling of the trailer-trucks on Railroad Avenue and even the night-roving cats seemed to be sacking out somewhere.

Caliche is at her primordial best in the deep of the night when the population has succumbed to the lures of Ovid's deity Morpheus, or to the slumber induced by lonely bacchanal. The Chicanos over in Chihuahua—that half of the town lying south of the tracks—lay dreaming in their beds and on their pallets, none of them abroad, as many Anglos believed, burglarizing houses and stealing cars and committing acts of vandalism. To borrow from Kentucky's own Irvin S. Cobb, the only night life in Caliche is furnished by aging men whose prostate pressures have brought them off the mattress and into the bathroom.

During my stroll I encountered no sign of human life, though I did run into Slats Peeler, supercop, high school dropout, and brother to Iolanthe. Slats was walking through the shadows of Leakey Street—the first time I'd seen a small-town night patrolman on foot since I was a child.

"Well, pig," I greeted him. "Did your bucket-of-bolts collapse?" It was said in jest, but proved to be true.

"Darn thing give out on me with a sorta sigh, Mr. Grady. Darn flashlight batteries wore out. I cain't find the darn trouble in the dark so I got to go get some batteries."

"Great!" I exclaimed. "Just by-God *great!* I don't suppose you know that Bonnie and Clyde and Pretty Boy Floyd fouled the magneto on you. Right this minute they're in the bank using a meat saw to open the vault."

"I almost woosh it was true. Darn Council so gut-stingy, we needin' a new car for over a year. What's a magneto?"

Save for Slats I had the entire metropolis to myself, with all that gentling moonlight and clean West Texas air, and as I ambled on my way I thought back to the day when Mungo came in from the ranch and asked me to call on the Smiths.

Mungo didn't like our town and often said so. Several times I've heard him say that the trip in from Rancho Traseros gives him jet lag. Another time, when we were climbing into the Porsche to scud up El Camino del Zopilote, he remarked with an air of despair: "The time has come to mount the fairy chariot and return to the nine sources. That, Grady, is what the old Manchu princes used to say when they were getting ready to die. I say it when I'm going up to Caliche." In a more frolicsome mood he once told me: "If you ever run into a perspicacious philosopher who tells you he wants to give Creation a soapsuds enema, take him straight to Caliche as the proper point to begin."

A week had passed since that eventful day Jefferson Cordee introduced himself to Caliche, and it was just after one o'clock on a Thursday afternoon when Mungo walked into the *Mud Dobber* office. He said he wanted me to do him a small favor . . . to find Rustler Smith and his daughter and talk them into attending a meeting that same afternoon in Chug Peavy's office at the bank.

"You really thinking about giving your ranch to that old billy goat?" I asked him.

"It's a little more complicated than that."

I flashed him a clownish grin. "Listen, Mungo," I said, "I let a big one slip by me. You want yourself somebody real mean, just check me out for nastiness. If I put my mind to it I can be more malevolent than Rasputin and Lucrezia Borgia working as a team. Why the hell that smelly old thief?"

"Grady," he said, "you have a rough and barbarous exterior which you acquired working for that godless atheist newspaper in New York, but under the skin you're almost as civilized as me."

"Nuts. I was born tough and I grew up tough. Why have you picked *me* to go out and tackle Old Smith?"

"He'd recognize you for what you are—a sweet man with a kind heart. If I went to see him he might attack me with a skillet. You'll know how to soft-soap him."

"I'll do it," I said, "but I do wish you'd level with me about this proposition. I'll keep your secret."

"There's no secret. I tried to explain it that day in the bank.

For a long time I've had this whimsical notion that mean, rebellious, and cantankerous people are the best people we've got. They're loaded with qualities that most people can't see. The villains of the world could be the greatest leaders of the world if they could be given a nudge in the right direction. And I've had a strong feeling that I could take a man of classical orneriness and leatherheadedness, and turn his talent into new channels. Transmute his villainous genius into a constructive force. It sounds crazy but . . . well, what else have I got to do?"

"Sounds to me as if you were trying to play God."

"To the contrary. I'm practicing psychiatry. I'm convinced that I could take your Rasputin in hand and make a benevolent Czar out of him. Or Machiavelli, Iago, Solomon Pross, Fagin, Maugham, John Dillinger—even that smelly old toadfrog Roy Bean . . ."

"Watch it, Oldbuck. Judge Bean sprang from the same part of Kentucky that produced the Gradys."

"My apologies. I hasten to correct the image. He only looked like an old toadfrog, and you couldn't smell him much if you were standing upwind from him."

"And did you say Maugham? Willie Somerset?"

"The same. Meanest goddamn author in the whole history of literature. Hateful, right down to his heels."

I heard the street door open and glanced up. It was the charming Miz Fern Grady, nee Mobeetie. My estranged wife seldom came near the paper, even though it had been the source of her family's livelihood since three nights before the *Titanic* went down. Whenever she did turn up at the *Mud Dobber's* palatial quarters, it was reasonable to expect trouble.

"Forsyte, you son of a bitch!" she sang out from the front counter, unperturbed by the presence of Mungo Oldbuck at my side. I suspected that she was unsettled about something.

"Forsyte!" she repeated in her stridulant Texas voice. I sat steady, just staring at her. "You listen to me, you smartass bastard . . ." I made a rough guess that she was angry—this grossly immoral bitch rarely indulges in vulgar language. I reckoned, too, that she was sozzled. And when she bent down, disappearing for an instant behind the counter, I suspected what was coming. Rocks.

She came up with a dornick in her hand, a rock about the size of a Presidio cantaloupe, and let fly. It thudded against the door to my private office, just behind me.

"Man the lifeboats!" cried Mungo, dropping to the floor. Another rock came zinging down the line and would have scalped me if I hadn't ducked below the level of my desk. Two more wild pitches followed and then she went stomping out, carrying the tin bucket which she used to transport her ammo.

Mungo came slowly off the floor.

"Your good wife, I believe," he said, a little sheepishly.

"It wasn't Somerset Maugham."

"How in the name of sweet leaping Christ did you ever get mixed up with a matron of that caliber?"

"Don't let it upset you," I urged. "Fern's just being her everyday normal self—the All-American Girl-Next-Door. This is the second time she's been here with her rock bucket. The first time they weren't very big—about the size of Idaho potatoes. I relish the thought of her next visit—she'll come at me with cannon balls."

"What the hell's eating her?"

"I hear she's lost another boyfriend. Virge Decker."

"Who's Virge Decker?"

"You've probably seen him around—a big powerful redheaded guy, used to play football at Gateway Christian, mumbles a lot to himself. Got canned out of college for overscrewing co-eds. That's a practice that is frowned upon at Gateway Christian."

"How do you overscrew a co-ed?"

"In platoons. Never one at a time. Never even Indian file. So they bounced him out and now he's home and driving an oil truck. His principal occupation, though, is servicing the hungry wives of the community. Lately he and Fern have been playing motel. I'm not complaining—I simply don't give a damn. As Harry Golden might put it, she's entitled. The boys over at the poolroom tell me that Virge has a jock like a plumber's snake. I'm mystified that he'd have anything to do with Fern, except for maybe a one-night wham-bam-thank-you-mam."

"My, you're educated," said Mungo wryly. "I can't imagine any man getting within a country mile of her. She's a monster. She loses a plumber's snake and takes it out on you. Why doesn't she just throw you into the street instead of pelting you with rocks? She owns this paper, doesn't she?"

"She's drunk, Mungo. And she wants to harass me out of this office and out of this town. But like I told you, I'm tough and mean. And there's such a thing as a community property law."

"Don't take it for granted. If her old man bequeathed the paper to her and to her alone, then you have no community rights in it and she could fire you. I'm pretty sure about this, but you'd better talk to a lawyer."

"I wish to God someone would fire me out of this rathole. I'd go out and prance a mazurka right down the middle of Railroad Avenue."

"I hope you'll forego that pleasure for a while, and do that little errand for me—go get Old Smith and his girl. I'll set up a meeting for around four."

"Okay. But you've seen how muleheaded he can be."

"That's the way I like him. You can tell him that there might be some money in this for him."

"Right."

And so Mungo departed. I went around and picked up the rocks and surveyed the damage, which didn't amount to much, and my thoughts drifted back to the days in Manhattan just before my departure for the new life in Caliche, Texas. There were conflicts in my thinking at that time. I knew from past experience that I was heading into a contrary kind of existence, a world of stultifying dullness and provincial complacency. I tried to give these cancer-blights a better assessment by picturing the serenity of small-town life as well suited to a man of advancing years. I was a tottering forty at the time, and I should have known better. I should have known that village life is a microcosm of universal life, and is steadily more eventful and exciting than residence in the middle of Manhattan.

I carried the four dornicks out to the trash can in the alley. Then I sat for a while at my desk, reflecting on the evil streak that dominates that muttonheaded wife of mine. She has scarcely a handful of friends in Caliche. Her poisonous tongue, which she inherited from her mother, helped her toward that condition, as did also her stinginess, which she acquired from her father . . . the consecrated boob who spent his life studiously doing everything the wrong way.

Still, there were half a dozen women in town who put up with Fern's perverse eccentricities and drank coffee or booze in her company. Foremost among these was Daphne Whipple, that self-same county judge who lured Jeff Cordee into her chicken-and-dumplings web. Daphne and Fern spent a lot of time together. A telephone conversation between these two could stagger the mind of a tapeworm. I know. I have heard them. There is no single wretched program on television as protracted and as gut-wearying.

Among the menfolks of Caliche Fern has no friend, though she has always had lovers among the able-bodied and a few of the crippled. At which juncture I must, in all fairness, speak of her one glowing attribute. Granted she is an intellectual nerd. She has to be faulted in housekeeping, the social graces, personal hygiene, the culinary arts, and temperance. She draws D-minus for her indifference to books and her obsession with any and all moronic manifestations of the occult. These latter characteristics—her insensibility to books and her preoccupation with signs of the zodiac, transmigration of souls, crystal-ball video, faith healing, a blind acceptance of any and all preaching-worms as functioning under Divine Guidance—all these moonrakings were the principal cause of trouble between us.

And her one attribute? The very best. In the domain of the Biological Urge she stands supreme. Minks and rabbits are frigid creatures, sluggish in their love life, alongside Fern. She was always cyclonic on a mattress, in the shower, out in the woods, on the kitchen floor, in the back seat, on a Ferris wheel, dogging it, roaring down Track Sixty-nine, and anywhere else except in or near her church. She was never tired, never had a headache. This is a fairly good commodity to have around the house . . . for a while. Eventually it tires a man out, whips him down, takes weight off of him, destroys his appetite, and gives him an ailment vaguely related to Parkinson's disease. In the beginning years of my marriage to Fern, a meal at our house consisted of poon for the soup course, an entree served at table, and nookie for dessert.

As for her lack of interest in literature, she never cracked a book unless it had something to do with those fatuous superstitions that have 88 per cent of the American people in thrall. Strangely, she wouldn't even read the New American Novel with its flamboyant treatment of constipation and degeneracy, the romance of same.

It came to pass that her nymphomania became a tribulation to me, and I would catch myself shuddering whenever she'd begin firkytooting around, and I arrived at the abnormal state of mind where I didn't give a damn how many other men she was giving the Mobeetie bear-hug. And I must make it clear that for all her wild and tempestuous dexterity in bed, her sensuality could not compensate for her ugliness.

That ugliness extended even to her table manners. She slurped and slobbered and snorted when she ate and sometimes when she had finished wolfing down a huge meal she'd push her chair back from the table and holler, "Calf rope!"

She never hollered calf rope in bed.

In short, a real dog.

Rustler Smith and his daughter Holly Ann lived in a small rent house constructed of a material known to Caliche folks as sment blocks, painted a ghastly yellow. The old man came quickly to the door as soon as I punched the buzzer. He stood and glared silently through the screen, and then spoke.

"You're that newspaper churnhead," he snarled. "I got no use fer newspaper churnheads."

"Daddy!" His daughter had come up behind him.

"I wanted to talk to you for a few minutes, Mr. Smith," I said. "It's not newspaper business. It's something else."

Old Rustler didn't respond but Holly Ann quickly asked me to come in and she jostled her father out of the doorway to clear a path for me. This was as close as I had ever been to her. She was real pretty in a wholesome 4-H Club sort of way . . . an impression that was a little out of reckoning, considering her ancestry. Everything inside was plain and old-timey but neat. Rustler groaned himself into a chair and I did likewise and Holly Ann suggested coffee. I begged off and asked her to listen to what I had to say. I sensed that strong support might come from her and I was sure I'd need some support.

Out of some subconscious promptings I chose to approach the old reprobate as one approaches a child afflicted with chronic distemper. Gentle persuasiveness and simple declarative sentences made up of small words. I think it worked pretty well; he didn't once try to coldcock me with an overstuffed chair.

I spoke rather glowingly of Mr. Peavy, the friendly banker, and of Mr. Oldbuck, the congenial rancher, and then said that these two men had become interested in Mr. Smith in the joint belief that he, Mr. Smith, was not too happy with life in Caliche.

"They would like to have you come down to the bank," I said, "for a little talk, because they think they may have something in mind that would make life a little more pleasant for you."

My clever employment of artifice, my gentle guile, are almost always effective, especially with older people.

"Tell them both," said Rustler Smith, "to go fart up a chimbly."

"Daddy!" Holly Ann was genuinely distressed.

"But, Mr. Smith," I pushed on, "they are both your friends, or want to be your friends."

"I don't want no friends. Friends are a pain in the . . ." He cut his eyes toward Holly Ann and decided to expunge the word. "Friends are always tryin' to borry things from you, includin' hard cash and horses and whiskey, and they are always goin' on the make fer your wife and daughter, and you get 'em in court and they'll testify again you ever time. Anyway, you ain't foolin' me. You're tryin' to lore me into a trap. You Texas churnheads are as ontrustworthy as the Nez Puss Indinns. You cain't . . ."

"Daddy!" his daughter broke in again. "You behave yourself now."

"Mr. Smith," I said, taking a new tack, "I think there might be a piece of money in this for you. Legitimate money."

"Fer doin' what? Somebody want me to kill that slick-headed bird from Medsen Bow? Hell, I'll do that fer free. Sorta plannin' on it anyway."

He paused for a moment, staring at the yellow wallpaper.

"What's that slick-headed dude got to do with this, anyway?" he demanded truculently. "I know he's out to get me."

"If you mean Jeff Cordee, he's left town—gone to work on a ranch forty miles back in the boulders."

"Then why'd you say he's out to get me? You're talkin' through your John B., churnhead."

"Now, Mr. Smith, please. Cordee's not a killer."

"The hell he ain't. He's another Tom Horn and another Slade and he's got more notches in that gun than you and me put together got toes on our feet. I know his breed. Wuss nor Billy the Kid.   When-you-say-money-how-much-money-you-got-in-mind?" Those final words came out of him fast, like machine-gun fire.

"I have no idea, Mr. Smith, but I do know you'll be dealing with men who are well acquainted with lots of money."

"I don't like the looks of it," he spoke slowly and reflectively.

"But tell you what. If I go down there with you, my time is worth exackly one dollar per minute. You got a stopwatch?"

"Daddy!"

Holly Ann sure had to use that word a lot.

"I'm certain they'll accept that figure," I promised, happily spending other people's money.

"One dollar per minute and I'll stay twenny-five minutes. No more. That'll add up to twenny-five bucks. Right?"

"Right."

"You want Holly Ann to come along?"

"Certainly."

"That'll be an extry ten dollars."

"It'll be no such thing!" his daughter protested. "Get your hat, Daddy, and we'll go. Right now."

"You listen to me, Miss Feisty. Don't go orderin' me around er I'll take a lenth of britchin' strap to you."

She gave me a big wink.

Mungo and Chug Peavy were waiting for us in Peavy's office. I introduced the Smiths, a ceremony which evoked nothing more than angry little grunts from The Rustler. He was alive with small herky-jerk movements, testifying to his suspicions and his nervousness. He was like a small dog in an encounter with a snake, tensed and ready to spring away at the slightest sign of danger.

When we were all settled down, with the Smiths seated together on a red leather couch, Mungo opened the proceedings.

"Mr. Smith," he said, "I like the way you eat pie."

"I don't eat pie to suit you," said The Rustler.

Mungo was not deterred. "One of the most brilliant men I ever knew, an engineer back in Connecticut, eats asparagus the same way you eat pie. He begins at the butt end of the stalk and works his way up to the tip. He argues that . . ."

"I don't eat 'sparagus a-tall," growled Smith.

"Let's get straight to the point," Mungo suggested, not at all dismayed over being rebuffed. "For several months I have been scouting around for someone to live in the guest house at my ranch and help me run the place. I've been looking for someone with special qualities I think are needed in the job. I was present in the restaurant that day, Mr. Smith, when you faced up to a man with a gun in his hand and clobbered him with a chair. The thought crossed my mind that you might be the person I was looking for."

"You made a mistake," said Smith. "I spent most of my life rustlin' cattle. I'm plannin' on takin' it up again soon as I get to feelin' better. Sciatica been botherin' me lately. I got a hankerin' fer these Charlie Ray white cattle I see around these parts. In my time I've rustled ever kind of a goddern cow you ever saw, except a Charlie Ray. I aim to rustle a few."

"If you aim to do it," Mungo assured him, "then I'm certain you will do it. I judge you to be a dependable man, Mr. Smith. I don't think I need mention the sorry condition the world is in today simply because there are no more standards. It is impossible to have faith in anyone. The only real friend I have in this town is Grady here, and I can't be altogether sure about him. I don't know for certain how he'd shape up in a crisis. I'm beginning to take a liking to Banker Peavy, but as of this moment I wouldn't trust him forty feet up the alley. There was . . ."

"Bankers," put in The Rustler, "are usely no good."

"Thank you, Mr. Smith," said Chug Peavy. "I'm in full agreement with you. I much prefer the company of rustlers and road agents."

"There was a time well within my memory," Mungo picked up the thread of his lecture, "when it seemed that most men were reliable and worthy of trust. That time . . ."

Rustler Smith broke in again. "There wasn't ever no such of a time in *my* mem'ry. Everbody I ever met was ontrustworthy."

Mungo gave him a long approving look. "You're a good man, Smith. I like you. I like the way you eat pie. Now, as I was saying, I walked away from a thriving business because I couldn't find a single soul in that entire city of New York that I would want to have lunch with. Not a one."

Holly Ann now threw in a question. "What is it, Mr. Oldbuck, that you would expect us to do at your ranch?"

"You would live in that guest house," said Mungo. "It's a six-room residence, built two years ago, quite a handsome house. Two bedrooms, two baths, refrigerated air conditioning, television, fully furnished, a quarter of a mile from any other house."

"It sounds great," said Holly Ann, "but what would you want us to do?"

"That's right," snapped her father. "What's the ketch? How 'bout puttin' yer cards on the table?"

"I need someone," said Mungo, and I thought I detected a little nervousness in his voice, "I need someone with a hardheaded attitude toward the human race. Mr. Smith would be . . . well, let us say he'd be my foreman. He could take a lot of bothersome detail off my hands. But . . . wait a minute. I haven't even asked you, Mr. Smith, if you know anything about ranching. After all, rustling is now . . . uh . . . it's not what you might call scientific ranch management."

Old Smith was wounded by this oblique slur at his profession. He leaped to its defense. "Rustlin'," he said firmly, "is one of our best sciences. After a man learns all there is to know about ranch management, then he's ready for rustlin'. You got to know more to be a good rustler than you got to know to be a Yew-nited States Senator." He seemed pleased with his own panegyric, saluting the vicissitudinous trade to which he had devoted so many of his years. He felt like continuing in a philosophical mood, and he did. "Trouble is, like you said, this is a sorry world and nobody cares a bit any more about doin' a good job. Whirr's the new talent comin' from? The kids of today ain't interested. Turn their backs on rustlin'. Goin' into electrommics, servicin' these computers, playin' games on the TV. Gettin' so nobody wants to rustle cattle any more. Kids of today goin' around . . . Tell me somethin', Mr. Oldcock. You happen to know that young dude that pulled a gun on me? Somebody said he was workin' on a ranch somewheres. Wouldn't be your place, would it?"

"No." Mungo didn't seem at all upset over being addressed as "Oldcock." I would have bristled.

Smith lowered his head and stared at his square-toed shoes, deep in reflection. He mumbled something to himself and because I had my attention focused on him, I heard it. He said, "Son of a whipper-snapper-bitch ain't satisfied with one killin', wants to clean out a whole fam'ly." Then he looked up and said he wanted to hold a private confab with his daughter, and they went across the hall and into another office. They were back in five minutes.

"I decided we'll resk it," said Smith, "but I don't want anybody thinkin' I can be swayed by money. I got no money worries." He glanced sternly at both Chug and Mungo. "Fact is, I could buy and sell both of you."

Holly Ann smiled. "What he means," she said, "is that he's on Social Security."

"And also Medicare," added her father. "A hundred seventy-four dollars and some odd cents ever month of the year, and also Medicare."

Holly Ann now turned to Mungo. "Don't you think we ought to have some kind of an agreement? I mean a paper? And we'd want to come down and have a look before we sign anything."

"Understood," Mungo told her. "We'll draw up a proper contract. Make it, say, for two years. If we should get to warring on one another, the paper will say you can pack up and leave and I'll pay off the contract a hundred per cent."

"That's real generous," she said. "I'll be happy to quit my job at the school. I teach English but the kids don't seem interested in learning anything about it."

"That's good," observed Chug Peavy. "You teach 'em English and what comes after that? They learn to read contracts, and then we're all in trouble."

And so I said good-by to everyone and headed for my office, wondering along the way just how in the hell a Wyoming cattle rustler gets himself on Social Security.

Chapter Eleven incorporating a veracious
account of the great B. M. Bower em-
broilment

11

Rustler Smith and his daughter loaded their personal possessions
into a U-Haul and drove down to Rancho Traseros on a smiling
Monday morning when the Spanish dagger was in bloom and desert wildflowers were splashing their myriad colors across the stony
landscape.

A few days later, it needs to be noted, a young Mulefoot pig
trotted briskly up the long entry road and stood in pensive con-
templation before the headquarters house of the adjoining rancho,
Asia Battle's Two Cross T.

It would not seem likely that these two quiet occurrences might
alter the course of human history, upset the balance of economic
power in European countries, set Vesuvius to spouting again, put
a Radical-Socialist in the White House, cure the common cold,
and fertilize the American desert from Middle Texas to the California shore.

On Friday of that same week I telephoned Asia Battle about the
long-delayed plan I had for going horseback riding with her new
hired hand, Jefferson Cordee. Following which I spoke to Mungo
Oldbuck, asking if he could put me up that night and lend me a
fiery horse with the speed of light for my expedition next day.

All was in order. I sat down with Gene Shallow and began going
over those high-level matters he'd need to handle during my absence. He let on he understood every word I said. If I seem to be
conveying the impression that Gene is not overly bright, that is
the impression I mean to convey. It is told around town that my
assistant went into Irving Susann's store one day to buy a sports
coat. Irving slipped a powder-blue job on him and stood him before the three-way mirror. Gene inspected himself in each of the
mirrors and then said, "I like them. I'll take all three."

"Now," I said to him, "I may be back Sunday evening, and I may not get back till some time Monday. You think everything will be all right?"

"Things will run smooth, Grady," he said, "just as long as we got them good fine men runnin' arr affairs up there in Austin and long as we got a wise and pewsippient public to keep the right Christian element in the legislature."

"You are *so* right," I told him. The less larcenous of the right Christian element up there in Austin steal only State-owned postage stamps in five-thousand-dollar batches and, when caught, justify the act by crying out, "Dad blame it! What'sa matter you people? I didn't steal no *money!*"

Gene Shallow then began telling me about something he had heard during breakfast at Kohlick's.

"Claude Boggy was there," he said, "and some other men, and they got to talkin' about chili. Claude said that up in Denver they are now claimin' that chili wasn't made to be eat at all, that it was used as a sorta corn plaster on Wyoming sheep dogs. I find that a little hard to bleeve, Grady."

He stroked his mustache vigorously, waking up three billion microbes, and gave me a questioning look.

"Wyoming," I told him, "is a much stranger place than the geography books make out."

"I don't think I'll eat any more chili," he said, as if I had endorsed the corn-plaster postulate. I swear I don't know why I would go away and leave him in charge of a sandpile.

Half an hour later I gassed up Old Blue and lit for the tules. As I sailed down El Highway of the Buzzard, that long lonely stretch of pavement set me once again on a course of clear and pewsippient thinking, and I found myself meditating matters of a literary nature.

I gave some thought to that term paper I ghosted for Leopard Callahan at West Texas Anabaptist, a project that entailed some serious research into the life and letters of Owen Wister. I could remember that I saved my notebooks, together with a copy of the essay, and that this material was probably in my old footlocker. I'd check on it when I got a chance.

Then I got to ruminating on the weird workings of the time-space conjunctures which we call coincidence. During my P. G. Wodehouse phase there was an aspect of Old Plum's novels that sometimes gave me the yaller whim-whams and took away some of the beauty from his books. Coincidence. There was just too much of it, and it detracted from logic and from credibility. Lord Chumley has a chance encounter with a certain Cynthia Threepwood somewhere along the Strand, and they get into a bit of a dustup, and along comes Freddie Psmith to espouse the cause of Miss Threepwood, brandishing his furled umbrella and chasing Lord Chumley clean down to Fleet Street, colliding with and knocking down Stiffy Spode during the mad pursuit; and then a week later, downcountry at Blandings, Cynthia Threepwood turns up as a houseguest of Lady Chumley, and Freddie Psmith comes along to the castle under contract to catalogue the contents of the li-bray, while Stiffy Spode is rattling the front door knocker to report that his blawsted Daimler has broken down a quarter mile up the Little Wabbsley Road. It's that way all through the Wodehouse novels, and a bleedin' shyme, you might say. Yet here I was, light-years away from Blandings, facing into the biggest series of linkages and concatenations known anywhere in literature. One of them being that same term paper I wrote for The Leopard.

Things were happening too fast. I was well aware of the fact that when all the ragged ends had been pulled together and all questions resolved, I would have in my lap a story of some consequence to the American literary world. It would be the literary afterclap of the year, perhaps of the decade; it would likely be the biggest literary disturbance in Texas since Edna Ferber wrote *Giant;* and it would surely rank as the second most sensational literary happening in the annals of Blackleg County.

The first needs recounting. On a morning in the spring of 1936 two prominent citizens of Caliche found themselves in a discussion of *belles-lettres* on the sidewalk in front of Mary Jane Canary's Beauty Salon. One was Hummin'bird Woke, then mayor of the town, and the other was George Bernard Lubbock, member of an old Texas family and proprietor of a shoe-repair shop across from the courthouse. Mayor Woke had a book under his arm which, he informed Mr. Lubbock, he was returning to the library. Mr. Lubbock remarked that he was a book reader of parts, and asked if he might inspect the volume. It turned out to be *The Five Furies of Leaning Ladder,* by B. M. Bower.

"Well, I declare," exclaimed Mr. Lubbock. "I didn't know you were a B. M. Bower reader."

"Must've read forty or fifty of them," Hummin'bird Woke replied. "Been readin' his things since *Chip of the Flying U.*"

"*His* things?" Mr. Lubbock inquired archly.

"Never miss a one."

"B. M. Bower is not a man, Hummin'bird. B. M. Bower is a woman."

"Don't be a fool, Lubbock."

"I'm not being a fool, Mayor, but you sure are. I've been a B. M. Bower reader all my life. I know about B. M. Bower. She was from Minnesota and her name was Bertha Muzzy and that's where them initials come from."

Mayor Woke exploded a sardonic burst of laughter. He called Mr. Lubbock's sanity into question. Mr. Lubbock should consult his physician and have his head palpated. No female woman, snorted the mayor, could have written a single one of those B. M. Bower books.

These acidulous remarks did not set well with Mr. Lubbock and soon the affair had turned into a shouting match.

"You are a slosh-burned whod-whammed idiot!" cried Mayor Woke. "I demand that you come around right now to the library and we'll settle this thing once and for all!"

Mr. Lubbock, whose southern bloodlines were fairly pure, was in such a rage that he couldn't speak. The two men stomped their way around the square to lay the question before the town librarian, Edna St. Vincent Poteet.

His every hair abristle, the mayor spoke loudly to Miz Poteet: "Is B. M. Bower a woman, or is B. M. Bower a man?"

Miz Poteet was startled; nay, she was shocked. More than that, she was agape, and for a few moments her tongue clove to the roof of her mouth. When she could find words, she spoke:

"Well, I never!"

"Woman or man?" shouted Mr. Lubbock, still crimson with anger.

"Have you two min bin imbibing?" the librarian asked, looking from one to the other. "How could B. M. Bower be a woman?"

"She *is* a woman, by God!" came from Mr. Lubbock.

"Watch your language in here!" warned Edna St. Vincent Poteet. "And don't go coming around here giving me any advice about books and authors. B. M. Bower a woman? Ridiculous. In the first place, what woman would ever give herself the first name of B. M.? In the second place . . ."

"Hold everything, you country-jake numbskulls!" cried Mr. Lubbock, now near the breaking point. He strode into the adjoining room, probed around on a shelf for a bit, then came up with a chunky volume titled *Twentieth Century Authors*. Swiftly he turned the pages, and then came his shout of triumph. He hurried back to the desk, the book cradled on his left arm, his right index finger jabbing at the biographical sketch and photograph of B. M. Bower.

"There!" he yelled straight into Hummin'bird Woke's face. "Look at that! Is that a man? Read what it says! Go ahead! Bertha Muzzy! And you set yourself up for a B. M. Bower reader! Oh, Lord, why did I ever settle in such a town? The mayor and the town liberrian both numbskulls!"

In majestic disbelief, Mayor Woke had been inspecting the sketch of B. M. Bower intently, and staring at the photograph of the handsome lady in the cowboy hat. It took some time for the hard truth to penetrate, but at last he came to the conclusion that B. M. Bower was in truth a female. The effect was both shattering and traumatic. He went out of his head. His eyes widened, his face twisted with rage, he turned slowly around, and punched George Bernard Lubbock right in the nose.

Mr. Lubbock staggered back, the heavy book thudded to the floor, and he fell against the Dewey Decimal System card index, striking his head against a corner of the cabinet. Then this proud and knowledgeable man dropped unconscious to the floor.

It was a skull fracture, and Mr. Lubbock lay near death for ten days, but then he recovered sufficiently to be interviewed by newspaper people out of Houston and Dallas, for the quarrel and the clouting had attracted Statewide attention, and was given whimsical coverage across the nation by both the AP and the UP.

This Wister entanglement I now found myself facing, with all its developing tangents and tentacles, was dramatic enough, but it couldn't compare with the B. M. Bower affair for sheer soul-stirring sensation.

Unless . . . and I shuddered even to think the word . . . unless it ended in killin'.

Let us now attempt a reconstruction of the principal events attending upon Rustler Smith's assumption of power as ramrod at
Rancho Traseros.

It was still early on that Monday morning when The Rustler
and Holly Ann chugged up to Mungo Oldbuck's pueblo-style
residence and sat for a few minutes staring at the big house itself
and the congeries of dwellings and courtyards and outbuildings
and corrals on beyond.

"Well, by God," said Mean Smith, "this I don't bleeve. I never
see anything to beat this setup in Wyomin' er Montana er Idaho."

Mungo's house was built for him by an El Paso contractor and
is very likely the most striking residence on any ranch in West
Texas. Some people might say they prefer Asia Battle's home, but
Asia's establishment is to Mungo's Pueblo as Marie Antoinette's
Petit Trianon was to Louis Sixteen's Versailles.

Ten years back Mungo slept overnight at Indian Lodge, a handsome State-owned motor hotel just outside Fort Davis, Texas,
and he had been taken by the gleaming architectural beauty of the
structure, copied from the pueblo of the Acoma Indians over in
New Mexico. He took his contractor to Indian Lodge and said:

"Build me this in a smaller version, with twelve to fifteen rooms
so there will be enough setbacks to give the place the look of a
pueblo. Give me *vigas* the way they have them here and get me
some Mexicans who know how to make adobe bricks, and use
adobe and fieldstone for the walls. I want walls two feet thick and
windows set deep, with selenite panes in the smaller ones. Put a
big arched fireplace in the main room downstairs, and smaller ones
in the master bedroom and in my office. Plaster everything white,
inside and out, so the house will stand out in this drab country
during all seasons of the year."

He got it as he commanded it, and now Holly Ann Smith gazed

at it and murmured, "It's beautiful . . . an Indian palace. I think, Daddy, we both must have been born on the sunny side of the hedge to finally arrive at a windfall as grand as all this. It's just pure luck."

"Luck's got nothin' to do with it," rejoined her father. "I busted a chair over that dude's head and this Mango saw me do it and he says to himself, he says, I want this chair-buster in my *imm*ploy, so he can bust a few chairs over a few heads fer me. That's the way it was, girl. No luck."

"Well," said Holly Ann, "maybe it was luck that brought the young man into Kohlick's restaurant. He could just as easily have gone to the Sangre de Cristo for his dinner, or to Esperanza's."

Mungo greeted them in the cactus garden and made them acquainted with his housekeeper, Sabina Orinal. The two men went at once to Mungo's office while Sabina took Holly Ann for a tour of the guesthouse.

When the men got comfortable in chairs upholstered in tan leather, Smith asked his first question.

"How many head you runnin'?"

"Cattle? None. Hasn't been a cow on this place since I bought the land."

"In that case," said Smith, "it looks like I got my work cut out fer me. I'll git you some of them Charlie Rays I mentioned back at the bank. I never dealt in any Charlie Ray stuff, since they didn't have them up in my part of the country. They don't want 'em around, but I won't rest easy till I've wide-looped me a few. They must be great to work with—white all over like that—show up good in the dark."

"I'm afraid," said Mungo, "that if you want to get back into the rustlin' game, you'll have to be satisfied with cactus. That's the only kind of rustlin' we have around here. They come down from Dallas and San Antonio and Austin and out from Houston and even New Orleans—cut the fence at night and sneak in and dig out the expensive plants like staghorn and fairy-duster and claret cup. No, Mr. Smith, we . . ."

"My babtized name is Henry but people always call me Rustler. Call me Rustler."

"Fine. I'm Mungo."

"Up north," said Rustler, "I was give out to be might near the best in the business. Did better than the men I rustled offa. Now,

you tell me you got these cactus rustlers. That gives me an idea.
Just fer one single time in my life I'd *inn*joy bein' on the other side
of the bob-warr fer a change. Just one time I'd like to have the
pleasure of dealin' with the lowdown polecat that'd try to rustle
offa *me*. I happen to know how a rustler's mind works, how he
plans things out, what his next move'll be, and now that I've
reached the prime of life, I'd like to match myself up against a
whole regiment of the thievin' sons a bitches."

"They work at night, usually, with hooded lights," said Mungo.
He was beginning to wonder what he'd got himself into.

"No matter. I'll ketch 'em. I'll git me some prickly pear and
strip the britches offa the bastards and take that prickly pear and
rub 'em all over in the crotch, and when I git through with them
they'll look like they been married thirty years to a bobcat."

Mungo suggested rather nervously that Smith go on over to his
new home and take it easy for a while, get acquainted with the
house, and the other people around the premises. He hoped Old
Smith wouldn't be clattering around the ranch all hours of the night
looking for cattle rustlers. He summoned Idaho Tunket from the
kitchen and suggested that the cook stroll over to the guesthouse
and speak some words of welcome, and issue a formal invitation
to lunch. Mungo had a feeling that, no matter how great the odds
were against it, Idaho and The Rustler would get along together.
That, or kill each other.

It may be remembered that in Kohlick's Cafe, Idaho spoke his
opinion of Old Smith, and it was not flattering. Neither was it
adulatory. Still, the cook was a man of peace and, for all his occasional bluster, lived his days in a serene enjoyment of superior
eating and sound sleep. He was determined to shy away from dis-
putation, brabblement, fistfightin' and manslaughter.

In the front yard of the guesthouse he introduced himself to
Rustler and Rustler grunted and then spit. He spoke friendly words
of welcome to Rustler and Rustler scowled.

"You and your girl," said Idaho, "are sposed to come up to the
big house for dinner ever day at noon. You're sposed to fix your
own breakfast and supper in your own kitchen. So startin' right
now, today, be up there at twelve sharp. On the nose. Mr. Oldbuck
he don't like to be kep waitin'."

Smith glared at Idaho half a minute and the frown-creases in
his forehead were washboard deep. Then he spoke.

"Listen, coosie," he said, using the old-time cowboy term for cook, "you tryin' to give me orders?"

"Course not. I'm just passin' the word. Twelve, on the dot. Mr. Oldbuck says twelve. High noon. If you have fell off a horse and fractured your skull he will maybe allow you to be ten minutes late. And don't call me coosie."

Old Smith twisted himself into a posture vaguely representing old-maid prissiness.

"I swan!" he exclaimed. "A big dumb sop-and-taters tryin' to boss the boss-man around. Tellin' the boss-man how to speak proper. Now, you git this, coosie. You are a coosie. A coosie is a cook and a coosie is likewise a Chinee, and that makes you a Chinee, and I don't want you flabbin' yer mouth when I'm in the same quarter-section with you. You speak when you are spoke to."

Idaho decided to temporize. "Be a nice fella, old man," he urged, "and come on over at noon. We're havin' *choucroute d'Alsace Monique.*"

"We're havin' *what?*"

"It's one of the things I do best. Maybe I don't pernounce it right, but I sure as hell can cook it. You'll love it. What it is, is smoked pork loin with . . ."

"Hold on, coosie. I got a delicate stummick. Fer my dinner I want a dish of red beans cooked with sow-bosom and a little onion."

Idaho stiffened. "That don't go with *d'Alsace Monique.* No beans today, buster."

"You git a move on, and cook me that dish of frijoles the way I said, er I'll take an ax handle to you."

This was war, Idaho sadly concluded. "You want frijoles, cook 'em yourself. And don't come near my kitchen."

Smith took two threatening steps toward the cook, paused, and then issued his ramrod's decree.

"Pack!" he ordered. "Go git yer duds together. Git offa this ranch, you Chinee doughbelly coosie!"

Now it was time for Idaho to bristle up. The appellation *coosie* offended his sensitive soul; someone had told him not long ago that the word no longer means cook, but is used nowadays to designate something else. So he summoned to his tongue a dozen or so juicy epithets he had acquired in his years as a rodeo rider. He spoke these epithets straight at the old man, and when he reached the zenith of his withering philippic, referring to his adversary in terms of gaseous eruptions out of a camel's sigmoid flexure, Rustler Smith lost all control. To use Elmer Kelton's graceful and sensitive locution, he felt as if someone had hit him in the face with the afterbirth of a turkey buzzard. He stood transfixed, staring at Idaho, and then he let out what was meant to be a jungle roar. It emerged from his larynx as a harsh and strangled gurgle. Following which, with fists bunched, he charged upon the opprobrious coosie. I wish to God I had been there to see it! Old Smith couldn't weigh more than a hundred and two with a plate of cherry pie in each hand, whereas Idaho Tunket was a Texan of tall brawn.

Idaho played the old man like a bull, sidestepping the furious charge and, as Smith's body hurtled past, throwing out his right arm and wrapping it deftly around The Rustler's middle. He then whirled his captive about, and Smith's arms were flailing the wind, and Idaho was able to grasp him in the armpits and lift him a foot off the ground and hold him there. Smith was now screeching with rage and beating his heels against the shins of the cook. These backward kickings were turning painful and Idaho solved his dilemma by hurling Rustler to the ground, on his back. Then quickly he seized Smith's ankles and before the old man could gather his breath, he began flogging his ancient buttocks against the hard ground. The Rustler was howling bloody murder but Idaho had him, and continued bouncing his butt against the turf as if he were shaking a pair of reins.

At length Old Smith hollered calf rope, and Idaho lifted him to his feet.

"Don't talk," ordered Idaho, fastening his right hand over the old man's shirt collar and Spanish-walking him off toward Mungo's office.

Señor Oldbuck was surprised at the rapidity with which his new foreman could go to war. And Smith was by no means playing it contrite. His chin was thrust forward and his eyes were blazing and his buttocks were smarting as if branding irons had been applied to them.

Idaho recited his bill of particulars, saying Rustler had called him a coosie, had ordered him to prepare a special serving of beans and sow-bosom, had threatened to shatter his skull with an ax handle, had fired him off the ranch, and, worst of all, had impugned the quality of his cuisine.

At which point the old rustler wrenched free, whirled, and threw a punch at Idaho's chin. It missed by a yard and a half and in a split second Idaho had him in hand again. The cook pulled back his arm as if preparing to cuff the old man one across the chops, then thought better of it and turned back to his employer.

"Turn him loose," Mungo said, "and go on back to the kitchen and proceed with lunch as you had it planned. No beans. No sow-bosom, whatever the hell that is. And don't coose up the sauerkraut." He gave Idaho a flicker of a smile with the final order.

As the cook departed Smith's beady eyes followed him, and as he went through the door, he yelled: "You . . . have . . . gone . . . too . . . fur . . . with . . . a . . . Smith!" The accents were measured and menacing and fraught with sudden death.

Mungo invited the old man into a chair and asked him to state his case against Idaho Tunket, if he had one.

"He pounded my ass against the ground," said The Rustler. "Up whirr I come from nobody pounds a foreman's ass against the ground, especially no coosie don't, and in puh-*tick*-ular nobody pounds a Smith's ass against the ground. And he kep' talkin' about how I had to eat some kind of cowzass manicure he was fixin' fer dinner, and when I told him to take his manicure and shove it, and fix me some beans, he told me to go cook my beans myself. That tooken the rag offa the bush."

"Rustler," said Mungo with a placating smile, "I want you to know that Idaho Tunket is the best French cook I've ever met and, further than that, he was once a champion bronc rider on the rodeo circuit. I want to show you exactly what kind of a sweet and considerate man he is, even against the lowly and downtrodden. He came to me one day and said something had been worrying him, and I advised him to get it off his chest, and he said, 'Who is it that says a lobster don't feel anything when you throw him in a pot of boiling water?' How about that, Rustler?"

"I don't like lobster. Never did. Gotta fight 'em too hard to git at the meat."

"Let me tell you how Idaho got to be an expert at French cooking."

"I don't think it would inna-rest me, but you're the boss."

Mungo then narrated the way in which Idaho, as a young man

out of Eagle Pass, had shunned the sinful life usually associated
with traveling the rodeo circuit—no whiskey, no gambling, no
broads, no little boys—and how he had won large sums of prize
money and banked most of it. In the seventh year of his rodeoin'
he had gone to France with an American Wild West Show and in
Paris a horse named Tailwind flung him against the arena wall and
broke his hip.

Idaho was in the American Hospital for months, Mungo said.
One day a calf roper named Bradshaw, who had made Idaho into
his personal hero and who knew how handy the bronc rider was
at a kitchen stove, came to the hospital and presented the bed-
ridden cowboy with a copy of Brillat-Savarin's celebrated book on
eating, *Physiologie du goût,* rendered into English. Idaho read it,
over and over, until he had a feeling that all of France's proverbial
one hundred sauces were squirting out of his ears.

"What we have here, Rustler," Mungo said, "is a man who has
trained himself in the French school of cookery, which is the best
on earth, while retaining the knowledge and skills and taste he already possessed for chuck wagon grub. I happen to be partial to
French cooking, so we have a lot of it here, but Idaho makes the
switch to Tex-Mex two or three days a week and that usually satis-
fies all concerned."

"It won't satisfy me none," Smith insisted. "I got to have my
beans and bacon. You come at me with French cookin' and I'll
throw it to the dogs. I'll take beef like we used to call machinery-
beltin', a man could git his teeth inta, and some gun-waddin' bread
with skid grease smeared onto it."

Mungo gentled him down with additional words of praise for
Idaho, and then tried to talk him into coming over an hour later
and having a go at cowzass a la Tunket. Rustler stood firm, being
a man of lofty principle, and Mungo was unable to sway him.

Holly Ann was. When her father returned to the guesthouse
and told her about the quarrel and his decision that the Smiths
would eat all their meals in their own dining room, she blew her
cork. Two or three times in her life she had been fortunate enough
to meet up with true French cuisine, and she too was partial toward it. She had tried her hand at it but in wide Wyoming it seemed
out of place to sprinkle kirsch on strawberries, to *flambé* prairie
chicken with Châtelaine Armagnac, or to poach eels in Vouvray
wine.

She now berated her father for his blundering, came close to hysteria, wept some, and then announced that she would not fix his *frijoles con sow-bosom,* she would not cook for him *ever.* He soon surrendered.

Half an hour later they were at the big house, feasting on cowzass manicure. The Rustler ate every bite that was served to him and did little complaining, except to say that it was too damn German fer his taste.

Chapter Thirteen incorporating an account
of a cussin' contest in the town of Salida,
Colorado

13

Friday evenings it was customary for the people of the rancho to assemble on a second-floor *terraza* to chew the rag and drink beer and look at the sunset. On the Friday evening of my visit those present were Old Smith and Holly Ann, Idaho Tunket, Spiro Keats, the Lord of the Estancia, and, to my surprise, the Ultimate Englishman, Ian Christchild-Muckeridge. I was there in the guise of visiting dignitary—representing the vast political clout of The Thunderer of North Leakey Street. The beer and the Monterey Jack were served by one of Sabina Orinal's daughters.

A bit of mystery intruded upon the calm twilight ambience of the terrace when Holly Ann arrived with her father. As the two walked across to a wicker settee they passed close to Spiro Keats and I heard the wrangler speak to Holly Ann.

"Good evening," he said in a quiet tone. "I see you got here without banging your head against a clothespin factory."

The young lady halted for a moment, a flustered look on her face. She stared at Spiro, who was smiling, and then walked on without a response. During the remainder of the time she was on the terrace I noticed that she would glance in Spiro's direction from time to time, always with perplexity in her eyes. I know there was perplexity in mine, but then I had to decide that I was making too much of too little. It was simply some new Texas expression, a piece of regional slang unknown to me. Clothespin factory? Maybe a tree. I let it go, at least for the time being.

I was pleased that The Rustler appeared to be on friendly terms with his two recent antagonists, the cook and the wrangler. Idaho Tunket had on a brand new pair of blue tennis slippers and brand new tennis slippers always look brand new, so Old Smith passed a compliment on this pair. He did not, however, commit himself whole hog.

"That's a real purty blue," he said to Idaho, and then, ashamed of his descent into cordiality, he added, "that is, in case you happen to favor blue on your shoes, which I never did."

The Smithian backspin whipped right past Idaho, or he chose to ignore it, possibly because it gave him an opening. He went straightway into a moral discourse, directed against people who torture their feet by wearing western boots. This was one of his hang-ups, and he had a short set speech on the subject, which included such observations and conclusions as:

"I always wear tennis slippers durn workin' hours, and I got three pair of different-colored Hush Puppies I keep fer formal, like goin' into town or when I'm watchin' the Dallas Cowboys on TV. It sure aggervates my soul to see all them Caliche businessmin wearin' high-heel boots and yammerin' all day about how comfortable they are, how their feet set easy in them. Bull roar."

He paused and turned toward Mungo. Idaho had a mind capable of dealing with two disparate subjects simultaneously. "Sundy dinner," he said, "is tarrnados bare-nee with whipped potatoes." Mungo nodded.

"These businessmin, they tell me," Idaho shifted back to his main topic, "that ordinary shoes hurt their feet. Only way they can walk any more is by wearin' cowboy boots. Bull roar and sass-eye-frass! Cowboy boots was never made to be walked in. They kill a man's feet. Go ask the boys that ride in the rodeos. Minute they finish the day's work they take off them boots, you can hear them groanin' first and then you can hear them sighin' with relief, and they set there a while wigglin' their toes, and grinnin' all over, and then they rub this foot-ease and Doctor Shawl's all over their feet and say man-oh-man-that-sure-feels-good, and I mean it does when . . ."

"I agree with you a hunderd per cent," put in Smith, who was wearing the same pair of sodbuster work shoes he had on the day he arrived in Caliche. "By the way, Idaho, they was somethin' I wanted to ast you about the way you . . ."

Mungo flung in an abrupt interruption, addressing himself to Christchild-Muckeridge, who didn't mix well with people.

"Ian, I wish you'd tell the folks about the visitors you've been having. I want everyone to be on the alert in case any more of them turn up."

"Yes," said the Englishman. "Quite. Indeed." He had a pale tannish mustache fastened onto a long upper lip, so characteristic of overly muddled Britishers. Whenever he was absorbed in conversation he was inclined to perform little fingering and plucking operations on this hair-thing.

"Bloke came across the moors yesterday afternoon, about five-ish," he said, flocculating the fuzz. "Had a fat manuscript under his arm, this fellow. Jacket and trou all ripped from climbing through the fences. Cawn't understand how he knew I was in residence here. Wanted me to read his bloody manuscript and find him a bloody publisher. Rotten sort. Said something about wanting to get in on the sex market, grab a quick million. Book was about some vague relationship between men and sheep. I told the . . ."

"Hold it, Ian," broke in Mungo. "Are you sure it wasn't our friend Grady here who came across the moors?"

Christchild-Muckeridge twitched his mustache, possibly to denote his recognition of a keen jocularity.

"I thought you said there were two of them," Mungo added.

"Decided-leh. Quite. Second one bagged me an hour later. I have a suspicion they were working in concert, though in England we would never do it that way. This one was carrying his memoirs. Said what so many of them say. Said, 'I've really lived.' It is my impression that most people, most Americans, have really lived. In any case this second bounder wanted me to find a publisher for his work, and then to collaborate with him on a second book stripping the tinsel from some individual named Wyatt Europe. Had a frightful time getting rid of the bugger. Tell me, Grady, don't you people in the village have anything better to offer in the way of lit'ry people? These two were somewhat on the scabby side."

"We're in short supply," I told him. "I can't even seem to place either one of your characters. We do have a poet in Caliche. Flat Hat Irene. Last name Wickett. I'll try to line her up for you, have her bring some of her poems down. She is runner-up for town harridan, always wears a flat hat like a Spanish stomp-dancer. Her poetry is largely about Jesus the Christ. She is on his team, and she is said to be the only female water witch in this part of Texas. She hates all men and cusses them out in public places. People go around her like she was a swamp. I could send her down with a sheaf of her Jesus poems."

"My dear fellow, I'd be most appreesh-tuhv if you'd keep her locked up whenever I'm in town. Better yet, tell her to go to

Hanover and hoe turnips. Ha! A thing we used sometimes in the Gog Magog Hills. Jolly, what?"

I was still curious about the two vagrant authors, and asked Ian to describe the one who seemed interested in an exposé of Wyatt Europe.

"Average height," said the Englishman. "Weight about average, I should guess. Ord'n'ry-looking blighter. No distinguishing marks or blemishes. Voice much like that of your everyday man in the street. Human look about him. Attire . . . let me think, now . . . undistinguished."

Old Smith spoke up. "Sounds a good deal like a man I used to know by the name of Carruthers. Couldn't of been Carruthers, though. He was a railroadin' man, come from around Rock Springs. Only man I ever met that could take off his long underwear without takin' off his pants. Seen him do it once. I still don't understand how he worked it, but he did, and he won ten dollars."

"You said he was a railroad man?" put in Idaho, excitement in his voice. "Are you certain about whirr he come from? Could it of been Salida, Colorado?"

"Nope," said Smith. "Rock Springs, Wyomin'. Union Pacific town. Never liked the place—right in the middle of sheep country. But this party I mentioned, this Carruthers, he . . ."

"You mentioned he was a railroad man," Idaho persisted. He was ready for a launch, a blast-off. I knew the symptoms.

"This Carruthers," The Rustler said loudly, unwilling to give up the ball, "him and I got to be purty well acquainted and drunk a good deal of whiskey together around Laramie, and *there* was a railroadin' town fer you, back in the days I'm speakin' of, and one day this Carruthers—he could take off them long johns without even *unbuttonin'* his pants—one day he told me I was the snottiest individual on the face of the earth, and the way he said it he made it sound convincin', so later on I set down and took a kind of inventory on myself, and tried to figure out why I got this undeserved reputation."

Spiro Keats had an opinion to contribute.

"You're mean," he said to The Rustler, "but I wouldn't exactly call you snotty."

"I appreciate that, wrangler. But I got it all figured out, the reason I am give out to be onnery. The reason is, I got it built into me. It's in my bones and in my gristle . . . somethin' I ain't rightly responsible for. Oncet I killed a rattlesnake, somewhere like around Gunnison, Colorado, and this . . ."

"God amighty you're gettin' close!" exclaimed Idaho Tunket. "What I had in mind was this time I was in the town of Salida, Colorado, I was workin' at . . ."

"*If* you will be so kind," said The Rustler in a stern and admonitory tone, "I do bleeve I was in the mist of tellin' a story about a rattlesnake. Well, *if* I may have the floor, I have killed manys a rattler in my day and cussed ever one of them to hell and perdition. This time I was hangin' around a big spread in that Gunnison country—don't remember what I was up to, but I wasn't sellin' Iv'ry soap—and this snake come at me and I grabbed him by the tail and bullwhipped him and snapped his head off, which is on account of his neck vertibrate bein' the weakest vertibrate he's got in his backbone. About three arrs later I happened to come back to the place whirr that snake was layin' on the ground—only the body part—and it was movin' around, wriggelin' and jerkin', still alive without no head on it. So I walked over and retch down and that bloody stump whirr the head had been *struck at my hand*. As God is my judge, that stump struck . . . at . . . my . . . hand. It was built into that snake to strike at humans when they come around, and it's the same with me—it's built into me to bark and snap at people because I always know they're up to no good. I'd even do it with my head snapped off."

Mungo was in a chair next to me. He leaned over and spoke to me back of his hand. "Two of them now. It's difficult to tell which one would be able to talk the other one down. Grady, it looks as if I'm fated to be monologued straight to the Stygian shore."

"It would be my guess," I answered him, "that Smith could take Idaho in the sprints, but Idaho would triumph in the distance events."

As if he had heard us, Idaho flung up heavy sail and shoved off, determined that no sticky-rope from Powder River was gonna outtalk him. He entered upon his recitation with the air of a seasoned professional.

"Mr. Smith," he began, "speaks about a railroad man and he speaks about a town in Colorado and these great events remind me of a town called Salida up there in the Colorado mountains. I wasn't much more'n a button when I worked at the Perkin-Peckham ranch near Salida. I was a puncher then, and couldn't of boiled green beans. 'Member one Saturday I went into town with some cowhands and we got in a saloon whirr they was a gang of railroad workers outa the Denver & Rio Grande shops, and bless my soul if they wasn't havin' a cussin' contest. Reg'lar champinship with a nice prozz put up. In that parta Colorado they got an old sayin' nobody on earth can out-cuss a railroad fella . . ."

He paused and shifted his eyes over to Mungo, but there was no sign of disapproval in that quarter. Idaho was always apprehensive about Mungo when he was telling one of his stories. The cook seemed to feel that his boss just plain didn't favor long-winded first-person narrative. The truth was, Mungo was sometimes annoyed by the grating sound of Idaho's voice. It was a Texas voice and people meeting the cook for the first time, people from other sections of the country, were startled to hear those harsh and high-pitched noises coming from such a ruggedly attractive man. It sometimes provoked even me, Grady, brought up as I was among bluegrass people whose talk is as gentle as moonbeams falling on white magnolia blossoms. It never bothered other Texas men and it never annoyed Texas women—they all, for the most part, speak the same way. And as for The Rustler's manner of speech, which was Midwestern crow-caw mildly diluted with old-age cackle, it usually had the sound of a butter knife caught in a garbage disposer.

Idaho resumed his Colorado narrative.

"They was machinists and boilermakers and gandy dancers for the most part and knew all about railroadin' and whorin' and politics and whiskey drinkin'. Oh, excuse me, Miss Holly, for that rough language. I didn't . . ."

"Go right ahead," smiled Holly Ann. "It's in the dictionary."

"Well sir, even a D&R wheeltapper could cuss better'n inny cowhand I ever knew, and they was a little guy from Orkansaw got up and stood there and cussed for twinny minutes by the clock, and you could feel the ee-ternal snows a-meltin' on them mountain peaks out there. When the little fella got finished and set down, a peaceful-lookin' man from Kentucky got up on his hind laigs and he says, 'Boys,' he says, 'I got to admit that was right smart of a job of cussin' and I don't know if I can beat him er not, but by the bald-headed Jesus and the cream-colored Christ I aim to give it a try.' Then that man from Kentucky cussed some cussin' that out-duganed anything I ever heard. Turned loose avalanches down them cliffs fifteen moll away. Wiped out whole towns. Never ferget that man long as I live. Name was Cap Monahan. He . . ."

"What part of Kentucky did he come from?" I, a proud native of the state, interposed. We got little enough to brag about, once you get past the Derby.

Idaho gave me a forbidding glance. Someone had once, in his presence, described him as a master storyteller—a poisonous thing to do to any man—and he had given careful consideration to that judgment, deciding at last that it was adequate and honest, and in consequence of all this he did not cotton to interruptions. He returned to his tale.

". . . and this Cap Monahan won the first prozz which was a bottle of homemade Leadville whiskey. I had a long swaller of it and except for a little zinc taste, it was better'n Shivvas Wriggle. He was a sarr-lookin' fella with a kind heart, the winner was, but he knew railroadin' and whorin' purty good."

Rustler Smith was futzing around, picking imaginary lint off his pants, and I judged that he was searching his mind for some rich and extended anecdote that would keep him in the running, but the little hand had moved up to whirr it says ten and Mungo decided to send the company off to bed.

I had the same room I always occupied in the big house, but I felt like stretching my legs and I walked out with Spiro Keats, filling him in on my plans for early next morning when I'd be riding a cock-horse to Asia Battle's ranch.

Spiro was almost always good company. He was a graduate of Clutie Hump College, where he took two years of American Lit and then someone told him that the average plumber makes five times as much money as the average writer, and that he should study plumbing. He said that under normal circumstances he had nothing against toilets, but when they got plugged up they brought on fright and torment in his soul, and he hated them. So he abandoned his plan to become a writer and enrolled for two years of Farm Animal Anatomy and Introductory Veterinary Medicine. He could talk intelligently about Willa Cather and knew who Konrad Bercovici was and he knew what to do for a horse afflicted with a bowed tendon.

As we strolled back toward the square 'dobe house where Spiro lived his bachelor life, I made bold to ask him if the expression "clothespin factory" was a slang term for something I didn't know

about. He didn't seem to remember using it, and then I reminded
him of the remark he had passed to Holly Ann.

"Oh, that. I was jostling her mind a little, giving her a start.
Maybe I'd better tell you about it, Grady."

We had come to his place and we sat down on the front steps.

"Yesterday afternoon," he said, "I saddled up and rode out
north to look for a stray pony that's been missing a couple of days.
I got clear to Rinderpest Creek and then followed the stream west
till I came to a big patch of live oaks that hug up against the bank,
and I thought that the pony might have gone into the trees to avoid
the sun, and so I went in on foot and wandered around and then
I heard voices. I took it easy and moved in toward the creek and
finally pushed aside some shrubbery, and there sat Miss Holly,
and stretched out on the ground beside her was that new boy at the
Two Cross T—the one who pulled a gun on Holly Ann's pappy."

It took a few moments for the portentous implications of his
words to come clear in my mind.

"What were they doing?" I asked Spiro, trying to keep my voice
calm.

"They had a blanket spread out on the ground and there were
some books scattered around and Holly Ann was doing most of
the talking. It may sound daft, but I do believe she was trying to
teach school."

"With one pupil?"

"One full-grown student. Of course, Grady, I want you to understand that I would never eavesdrop on people, never snoop on
them, but here she was talking about the books and the people
who wrote them and I decided I could use a little brush-up in
American Lit, so I stayed in the bushes and listened. I might just
as well have gone back and got my horse and headed for home. I
couldn't understand a thing she was saying. This kook Mailer
figured in it—I've read some things about him and I tried to read
one of his books, which was about Vietnam, except that it wasn't.
It was mostly about a bear hunt in Alaska, with a lot of dirty talk,
and some people said it would rank as a classic long after Shakespeare and Hemingway are forgotten."

Spiro interrupted his discourse long enough to go to the kitchen
for a couple of bottles of beer.

"I remember," he resumed, "that she talked about this John
Barth, and Faulkner, and then she explained what those two are

driving at, telling that cowboy that in the end analysis Barth and
Faulkner are saying the same thing, and then she explained the
thing they are saying which adds up to the same, in the end analysis, and she said this parallel is downright enchanting, but she
never did get around to saying what the thing is that Barth and
Faulkner think the same thing about. It was weird. That boy just
lay there flipping pebbles toward the creek and I was positive that
he wasn't even listening, and even if he *knew* what she was talking
about, *he,* of all people, wouldn't have been able to nail down
that thing of Barth and Faulkner. Am I getting through to you,
Grady?"

"No. But, you lead me into a question. Do you think those two
have a thing going?"

"I'm coming to that. I could tell he wanted her to stop with the
book jazz, because he suddenly asked her if she'd like to hear
about life in West Virginia, and then he went into a story about
how when he was a kid he spent quite a bit of time visiting his
Uncle Gatlin somewhere in West Virginia, and he said that . . ."

I had to break in. "Your interest, Spiro, was still literary—this
talk about West Virginia fell right into that category?"

"Geography," he answered. "Always one of my favorite courses.
I wouldn't have continued the eavesdropping if the subject had
been malnutrition or silkworm culture or Big Bend Folkways. So
he told her that whenever he went out for a walk in West Virginia
he invariably banged his head against a clothespin factory—he
said there were clothespin factories every direction a body looked
—and if it wasn't a clothespin factory, he was forever bumping into
people who were eating a kind of vile onion called a ramp. He said
that the people of West Virginia divided their time between making
clothespins or standing around chewing on ramps, and that he
couldn't recollect a single person in the whole state who didn't
smell worse than a wood pussy."

Holly Ann Smith, I thought, and Jefferson Cordee! Clothespin
factories and ramps and wood pussies! What in Christ's name was
going on?

I said to Spiro, "It doesn't sound to me as if they had a thing
going."

"Wait. Soon as he got through with his boyhood recollections
of West Virginia, she tried to get him back on American Lit, and
she began talking about Hemingway—something concerning the

heartlessness and self-deception with which Ole Ernest acknowledged his instinctual life, notwithstanding the ironic linkage of his transparent insubstantiality. Whereupon this boy crawled right over to her and grabbed her and said something about liking *Mad* magazine and *Sports Illustrated* and then he dampered off the literary criticism with a great big luxurious kiss."

"Did they . . . ?" I began.

"I didn't stay. When they ride out that far and hide themselves in the forest, I feel they're entitled to a little privacy. I wouldn't have stayed any longer anyway. When I was at Clutie Hump we had a boy from Alpine, Texas, who had a thing about playing with himself. The only way he could score was if somebody was watching him when he was lopin' his mule. He used to beg me to help him out, but I never had much of a taste for the sport known as *watchin' it.*"

So I went to bed with a variety of worries nagging at my mind. And with a fine new Texas metaphor added to my vocabulary.

Lopin' his mule.

Chapter Fourteen embracing an account
of how a Choctaw brave went a-pigging
in a lavender pickup

14

My blaze-face sorrel and I skirted a small mesa and rode up to Asia Battle's main barn, where we found Jeff Cordee busy at some kind of a carpentry job. He was building what looked to be a doghouse, styled roughly in the manner of those ugly New England habitations known as saltboxes. A profound thought crossed my mind, to wit: the dashing cavalier life of a cowboy has degenerated some from the way it used to be, if it ever used to be the way they are always saying it used to be.

The handsome young Virginian was bursting with good cheer as he put down his hammer.

"A man's got to be a carpenter and a plumber and an electrician on a place like this," he said. "I've done a little ridin' fence already, and checkin' water tanks and windmills, pullin' sucker-rods to change the leathers, checkin' the force pumps . . . otherwise I just been a-settin' around on a stump."

He picked up his tools and stepped inside the barn with them and I took note of the fact that his doghouse was furnished with wall-to-wall shag carpeting. When he came out he said:

"I'll have the horses ready in about ten minutes if you want to stop by and see Miz Battle." He glanced up the path leading to Miz Battle's residence just in time to see Rosa Chupador, the pretty Mexican girl, bouncing toward us in a jeep. This was the girl Asia had told me about, the one that oily gigolo had been after before Jaybird Huddleston gave him a pistol-whipping. She pulled up alongside the barn and got out and approached Jeff with an aluminum pitcher in her hand.

"Is for Emily," she said with a beautiful glistening smile. I knew instantly that the young man had made another conquest. I could almost see the goose pimples standing out on that girl's considerable body. She was playing it both bold and bashful, a provocative faculty inherent in woman. I quietly cursed the fate that had stacked the years onto me. Jeff took the pitcher from her—I could see that it contained milk—and he neglected wrapping an arm around her and giving her a hug and perhaps a feel, as I would have done.

I got out of the saddle and turned Midnight over to Jeff.

"We'll be takin' a pack horse," he said, his hands now full of sorrel and milk.

"To tote the milk?"

"No. This is for Emily." As if I knew who Emily was.

Rosa drove me to the house and I was soon in the presence of Asia, who sat working at her desk in the high-ceilinged living room. She had on female clothes, a dark blue skirt full of swirly little pleats like they wore in the thirties, and a creamy white blouse that fair took my breath away on account of its unbridled contents.

I looked her up and down audaciously and said, "You must be workin' roundup today, mam."

She smiled and said, "Welcome to Central America."

"Hey, I never saw you before in girl clothes. You getting married, or is it a church supper?"

Now she laughed, that handsome head thrown back, the glow from her face penetrating every sinew in me.

"About once a week," she said, "just to keep my hand in, I put aside the dungarees and the double-knits and play woman. I did it especially for you today, Henry. I like to play woman."

"You're equipped for it," I ventured. I moved back a couple of steps, cocked my head to one side, and gave her a fresh inspection.

"Stand up a moment," I said.

She did.

"Now turn around, slowly."

She gave the skirt a pleaty twist and then followed orders.

"Like it?" she asked. She thought she was modeling the costume.

"I love it," I said, feeling arrogant and insolent. "And I don't mean the skirt. I wanted to look at your bottom. Do you mind?"

"Yes," she said, turning quickly back. "It wasn't put on me for that."

"The hell it wasn't." Then I changed the subject. "How's Jeff working out?"

"To perfection. He's strong and willing and decorative and so far he hasn't taken down drunk."

"Thanks for letting him ride with me. I've got some things I want to talk to him about. We'll be leaving in a few minutes and I'll get him back here some time tomorrow afternoon unless the panthers eat us. He's down at the barn, performing the basic chore of the hard-ridin' western buckaroo—building a doghouse."

If she had been at all offended by my inspection of her bottom, her attitude was changing and I detected a certain coquettishness in her manner.

"It's not a doghouse. It's for Emily."

"Who's Emily?"

"She's our new pig. A little pinkish baby pig. She came walking in one day last week, right out of the blue, and she's quite the sensation of the old homestead. You'll love her, Henry."

I wouldn't. I didn't say so, but I can prevail against the awful rigors of living without a pig at my side. I don't like their looks, the noises they make, or their indifference toward me.

I set down my inimical, contrapiggish feelings by way of introduction to the story of Emily's origin, and of how she came to the Two Cross T ranch in lower Blackleg County.

Any definitive family-authorized biography of Emily has to begin in the Choctaw Indian country around McAlester, Oklahoma. Here on a small farm devoted to the raising of pigs and chickens and garden produce lived a well-spoken Choctaw named Victor Standcabbage and his wife Pushy (short for Pushmataha).

In the short while I have known him Victor and I have become friends and through him I am able today to narrate his part in this gripping saga of lust and derring-do and unbridled passion and malefactors of great wealth and sneering lechery and dry-land piracy . . . all in luscious and picaresque detail.

Victor Standcabbage had been through high school and at thirty retained an interest in improving his mind and advancing the welfare of his people. Up to the moment we first encounter him, he had nursed no ambition to break away from his Oklahoma farm. There were dreams, but Victor recognized them for what they were. His solid concerns were insular—the weather, his small accumulation of books, his pigs, his chickens, and his wife. And now something had happened in the head of Pushy to set her to acting crazy.

Word had filtered through to her that the white women of the nation were rising up against the men, asserting their independence, telling the men, *"You* go wash the dishes! *You* go make the beds! *You* go have the babies!"

Pushy Standcabbage was both shocked and amused when she first heard about the Revolt of the Women but as time went along and she gave continuing thought to it, she came to realize that justice had been a long time coming. And she began to snipe at her man. She'd put down her hoe out in the turnip patch, march resolutely to the pigsty, and say to Victor, "I am tired. *You* hoe the turnips!"

He ignored her. Some kind of female sickness. But he was worried when she failed to get over this strange affliction, when it worsened. She began rephrasing her commands, saying, *"You* hoe the fucking turnips!"

Victor was somewhat of an inscrutable Indian, lacking scroot, not given to demonstrative acts, soft-spoken, and easygoing. He tried to find out what had brought on his wife's aberration and he was surprised to learn that it was not Pushmataha's sickness alone; other Choctaw women of the neighborhood had come down with it.

When Pushy and the other women reached the point of refusing to cook, and when they began ganging together for frivolous trips in to McAlester, the men held little meetings out in the woods. Their wives were having jolly picnics in Tent Store Meadows when they should have been home scrubbing floors and taking care of the chickens and the kids; they were gathering in the Ohoyahoma Clubhouse to drink strong coffee and chatter disrespectfully about their clodhopper husbands.

Victor and Pushy Standcabbage had no children and this fact made it possible for him to reach a mutinous decision. Those dreams . . . he had sometimes indulged himself in fantasy, involving travel to far places, and the kind of adventure that befitted an Indian brave and . . . who knows? . . . perhaps something in the way of a pretty maiden. His wife had lost her youthful attractiveness and become a frump, and now this senseless revolt against the sacred inviolable laws of Nanih Waya, laws that had held their force since the Choctaw Nation was founded on a mountain in the present Neshoba County, Mississippi.

Victor's toleration at last vanished altogether; his stoic manner of meeting a crisis turned to lemon jello, and he ordered himself a new life, the kind of life he had dreamed about.

In the middle of the night, while Pushmataha snored and herself dreamed of becoming County Agent, Victor hoisted six of his younger pigs into his pickup, an aging vehicle which he had painted an engaging lavender. Up front he put two suitcases and a box of books. Then he lit out.

The noble redskin was on his way. He rode a purple pickup into the maelstrom of history. He drove unflinchingly straight for the dizzy vortex of Man's Fate, knowing aught of the Absence of Assignable Cause. The Earth would shake. Tidal waves were poised in the Middle Seas, eager to sweep down on peaceful lands and lay waste entire nations. Kings would abdicate. The golden throats of songbirds would wither and strangulate. Kokernot Mountain would erupt and destroy some of the finest people on earth. Vast schools of the deadly piranha would leave South American waters and swim northward to settle in the Mississippi, the Ohio, and the Missouri rivers. Victor Standcabbage was headed for deep Mexico to do his thing, the thing he knew best how to do . . . raise pigs.

The Mexican people are high on hogs; one of the great delicacies of the world is the stuffed *cochinita*—a pig no more than three weeks old, choked with walnuts and roasted whole with a mantle of fine herbs. Victor had heard of such things and his plan was to set himself up as a Mexican pig farmer, maybe develop some new breeding procedures, spend five or six years accumulating a stake, and then set forth to see the world.

As he headed south he entertained no qualms about deserting Choctaw country. He felt no compassion for Pushy, whatever her plight might be. Now she had the damn independence she had been slavering about.

He crossed the Red River into Texas and at Denton bought shelled corn and some jugs of water for his pigs and a sleeping bag for himself. He veered west to avoid the traffic snarls of the Dallas-Fort Worth complex, and made for the Rio Grande.

He felt happy and free and eager to get to work. He was a man liberated. He moved southwestward out of Abilene and on the third afternoon he was rambling down the highway that skirts the two ranches which figure so importantly in our narrative—the highway known to Mungo Oldbuck as El Camino del Zopilote.

On this roadway, about a quarter of a mile north of Asia Battle's cattle guard, is an abrupt DIP—a topographical configuration widely known through the American Southwest. A DIP is a sudden depression in the highway marking the route of a dry stream or draw, and it is dangerous for two reasons: a speeding car might enter a DIP and upon emerging, take off like a skyrocket; or a sudden thundershower could send a wall of water crashing down the draw and catapult an automobile into the next county. DIPS are generally marked with warning signs which say, simply, DIP. This one was so marked. And let me mention, parenthetically, that one of the greatest of the movie cowboys, Tom Mix, was killed hitting an Arizona DIP at blazing speed.

The characters involved in this history add up to a near multitude, and yet this specific, inanimate DIP—five and a half feet below the surrounding ground level—might be considered the leading actor in the unfolding tale, for it figures importantly in two of the most impelling and motivating episodes contained in the narrative. This DIP, as we shall see, just may outshine Mungo Oldbuck, Asia Battle, Jefferson Cordee, Rustler Smith, and even Idaho Tunket, as foremost character of the drama.

Victor Standcabbage was woolgathering and castle building as he approached the DIP and he was late in braking the pickup down to a sensible speed. The truck leaped maybe ten inches off the pavement and no harm done except . . . one small pig bounced out and onto the highway.

Victor knew nothing about it. There were no witnesses, except possibly five other pigs, but by way of hindsight it is my guess that when she fell on the pavement from the moving truck she stretched out her back legs and doubled her front legs under her and twitched herself into a posture where she would hit and roll, breaking no bones. We are dealing with a smart pig.

Her owner drove on another forty miles and picked a spot to camp for the night and then discovered he was shy a pig.

The lost one was the smallest he had brought along, and he chose her for Mexico out of compassion—she always seemed to carry an air of helplessness about her, and she was consistently affectionate toward Victor, nuzzling his ankles, trotting and prancing after him like a puppy. At the last minute back home when he was putting the other pigs in the truck, he happened to glance at her and she was gazing into his eyes as if she knew he was going away for good. He figured her for a weak character, a pig who would never attain to intellectual maturity.

How wrong can an Indian be?

He had forgotten the small bounce he took in that DIP and he had no inkling of where he might have lost the little one. The chances were strong that the fall killed her if she hit solid pavement and so, in view of the uncertainties, he decided not to go back looking for her. He was anxious to get across the river and into Mexico.

Another pickup, this one with a gooseneck trailer, came down the highway thirty minutes after the Indian hit the DIP. Its occupants were Jaybird Huddleston and Jeff Cordee, returning from town with a ton of horse feed, mostly oats and hay. Jaybird, foreman for Asia Battle, was a hard-bitten man in his forties possessing more knowledge of Hereford cattle than would seem necessary. He is the same man who pistol-whipped the prowler on the terrace outside of Asia's bedroom.

There were four bump-gates in the thirteen-mile drive from the highway to Asia's hacienda, and the Two Cross T pickup was approaching the second when Jeff spotted the young pig.

"Pull up," he said, putting a hand on Jaybird's arm and pointing ahead.

"It's a pig," observed Huddleston.

"I believe," said Jeff, "he's tryin' to open that gate."

"Horse manure," said Jaybird, a true cattleman with a low regard for the hog family.

The two men sat quietly in the truck and watched as the animal sniffed along the bottom rail of the gate, then transferred its attention to the second board, tilting its head to glance upward to the top. Suddenly, as if on spoken direction, the pig trotted over to the left end of the gate, brought itself up on its hind legs, and hit the wooden panel with both front hooves. Obedient to the laws under which it was constructed, the gate swung quickly inward, the pig walked through, and the counterweighted gate moved back into place.

Neither of the two men spoke for a moment. Then Jaybird slapped his large hand against his thigh, shook his head vigorously from side to side, thumped the heel of his hand against the side of his skull, and said:

"Up to now, boy, I've had twenty-twenty. But the old orbs have begun to fail. It's either that or I have just looked at a mir-

acle in the desert. A pig that knows how to open a bump-gate!
No . . . it couldn't be . . . my eyesight is shot!"

"I saw it," said Jeff.

"I am well aware," went on Jaybird, looking a mite dazed, "that
the pig is widely considered to be the most intelligent of all domestic animals, but I refuse to believe that a baby porker can figure
out the mechanism of a bump-gate. I refuse to believe it even
though I saw it done."

"Let's go on up and see what he does next," Jeff Cordee
suggested.

They hit the gate with their bumper and went on through and
drove slowly until they caught sight of the pig again. It was trotting
merrily along, glancing from side to side as if it were enjoying the
scenery.

At one point the animal changed pace and cantered off the road
to look at a patch of fragrant limoncillo in full blossom, standing
off and admiring the colors and then approaching for a sniff at the
blooms. Returning toward the roadway, ignoring the men in the
pickup, it took notice of a claret cup—the most spectacular cactus
in West Texas—and veered off to have a whiff at its deep crimson
flowers. Poking its pinkish snout in close, the pig encountered
the vicious stickers surrounding the blossoms, felt the sting, and
leaped backward with the grace and agility of a cat.

"My God!" Jaybird exclaimed. "That's got to be a human being
in pig form!"

Returning to the road, the little shoat hurried along to the next
gate, bumping this one open without any preliminary sniffing and
probing. The pickup nudged through, in turn, and followed along
slowly. Jaybird and Jeff watched the opening of the last gate
and then saw the pig head on up toward the big house.

They found the little creature standing on a strip of grass near
the entrance to the inner courtyard, staring thoughtfully at the
splendors of the place.

"If he goes in there and takes a swim in the pool," said Jaybird
grimly, "I aim to surrender and go get myself examined by one of
these shrink doctors."

The pig now switched its attention to the two men. Jeff got out
of the truck and walked slowly toward it, speaking softly, holding
his right hand out. In a few moments he was sitting on the grass,

petting the animal, and the animal showed signs of enjoying it.
Then suddenly Asia Battle appeared in the entrance to the patio.

"A pig!" she exclaimed. "Where in the world did you get a pig?
And why?"

"We didn't get him, Asia," said her foreman. "You'll deep-six
me off the premises for a liar, but I've got a witness. This pig came
in from the highway and opened four . . ." Jaybird had been
walking up closer to Jeff as he talked, staring at the shoat, and now
he interrupted himself.

"A Mulefoot!" he almost shouted. "Look at the hooves! Solid.
No cleft. This is one of the rare creatures of the earth—probably
rates today as an endangered species. Jeff, remember I said back
yonder that the pig is the smartest of all domestic animals. Well,
the Mulefoot is *twice as smart* as the ordinary barnyard pig. This
is the first one I ever laid eyes on. A Mulefoot! That explains why
he . . . hold it!"

He leaned in closer for a moment.

"Jeff," he said, "you'd better watch your language. We've been
calling it a *he*. It's a she. This is a lady Mulefoot."

Jeff turned to Asia. "Would we be able to keep her around,
more as a pet than anything else?"

"I don't see why not," said Asia. "So let's give her a name."

A half minute of silence and then Jeff spoke.

"Back in Virginia," he said, "I grew up on a pig farm. I know
about pigs, and like them, and pigs always seemed to like me.
Would you let me name her, mam?"

"Go ahead—give it a try."

"I'm real thankful to you. If it sounds all right to you, I'd like
to name her Emily."

"Emily it is," said Asia, smiling.

Chapter Fifteen in which the true name
of The Virginian is at last revealed to
the world

15

When I got back to the barn Jeff had the pack horse loaded with
enough stuff for a week and a half on the Mendenhall Glacier.
Everything but a cabin tent and a motorized rotisserie. There were
two sleeping bags, a first-aid kit, a skillet, two saucepans, a dutch
oven, a jar of instant coffee crystals processed in Kansas City, a
dozen cans of beans and chili, and a six-pack of Coors. We were
to be in the wilderness about thirty hours.

My own equipment consisted of one pillowcase tied to Midnight's saddle with whang leather and containing a full quart of
Kentucky sour mash. In some respects I am a dedicated patriot.

We rode northwest toward Hollohorn Flats, always with the
Doble Traseros peaks on the left and the Chinga tu Madres far off
to our right. Jeff would have the assignment of finding the Vinegaroon Highway, and I'd take it from there to Big Jim Deehardt's place.

We talked a blue streak. That is, Jeff did . . . under my steady
prodding. I had a lot of questions I wanted answered and I hit him
with the biggest one before we had been ten minutes on the trail.

"I know about you and Holly Ann Smith," I said.

"So?" My abrupt shot didn't seem to unsettle him a bit.

"You move pretty fast. You must know who she is."

"Sure. I know."

"So you've found your man."

"I haven't met up with him yet, but I knew right away."

"How'd you happen to meet her?"

"Some folks would call it fate, Mr. Grady."

"Don't call me Mister. Just call me Grady."

"Okay, sir."

"And don't call me sir, for Christ's sake."

"Okay, Grady. Do you recollect that frog-strangler we had about
a week ago? You must have got some of it up in town."

"I remember it. Inch and a quarter up there."

"I had been out ridin' fence, with the sun shinin' and the ground squirrels gallopin' around, and there she come. It was like solid water. Right out of nowhere. I was over near the highway so I raced toward our road and I came over a knoll and saw the girl trapped in the draw. You know that big DIP in the road about a quarter mile south of our entrance?"

"I know it."

What I didn't know, at the moment, was that he had reference to the same DIP that bounced a little pig into our lives.

"A wall of water had come poundin' down that draw and there was this station wagon stranded right in the middle of the DIP, and on top of the car was this girl, just standin' up there lookin' down at the flood. It was up to the door handles and still risin'. She wasn't hollerin' or anything but I jumped off my horse and went over the sheep fencin' and waded in and got her and carried her out."

"You hadn't met her somewhere before? Like in town?"

"Never. God, she was purty. Soppin' wet, but beautiful. She was little and had this tan hair and big blue eyes and . . ."

"I know her."

"Oh." He seemed surprised that I should be acquainted with the young woman, then he realized that she and I had been residents of the same small town for a couple of years.

"Well," he went on, "she was too scared to talk much. The thing I remember best is that when I was carryin' her out she had her arms around me and it seemed like she was holdin' me a little tighter than was needful, and had her face pressed up against my chest, and I . . ."

"Love at first sight," I said.

"How'd you know, Grady?" he demanded, excitement in his tone.

"I'm psychic," I said. "She told you her name then?"

"Sure. I stayed with her till the water started goin' down and we talked some. She told me first that her father was the new foreman at the Oldbuck ranch, and I asked her where they came from, and she said Wyomin', and naturally I wanted to know where in Wyomin', and she said a little town named Buffalo, and I swear it nearly knocked me off my feet. Smith. From Buffalo, Wyomin'. I'd found the man I'd been lookin' for."

"And Holly Ann knew who you were?"

"No. When the water begun to settle I waded back in and got a rag and wiped off from all around the plugs and all, and got the engine started by some kinda miracle, and then she said she had the mail for the ranch and she'd have to hurry along. So I told her there was something I wanted to talk to her about that was important, and we made a date to meet the next afternoon at a place out where our two ranches come together. Out on a crick."

"Rinderpest Crick," I said, riding along with his pronunciation. "You knew her grandfather was Trampas, and you didn't tell her who *your* grandfather was?"

"I didn't have time, and I didn't want to . . . right then."

"So you told her later?"

"I haven't told her at all. It's got me sorta nervous."

"But you met her the next day?"

"Sure. And, Grady, I've got a confession to make. I've done ape with that girl."

"You've *what?*"

"I've done ape with her."

"It's *gone* ape, Jeff. Gone ape . . . *for* her. Not *with* her."

"Well, that's what I've gone."

We hadn't paid a bit of attention to the scenery. Two cowboys riding side by side on a lengthy journey don't commonly do much talking. They might speak briefly of the quality of their horses, or the brand of beer they favor, or what a horse turd the foreman is, but otherwise they exchange few words. They generally just ride along in silence, each man thinking his private thoughts. There's a reason why they seldom talk. They don't have anything substantial to talk about. And when they think their private thoughts, those thoughts are of such a poor quality that they wouldn't be worth talking about.

I said to Jeff, "Tell me about that meeting out at the crick."

"There's this big clump of trees, and there was water in the crick, and it was nice, and she was still purty as a picture—but not as purty as the first time I saw her, when she was up on top of that wagon lookin' like a drownded rat."

"Out there at the crick," I hammered away, "did you tell her who you were, and that you had been trailing her old man?"

"No. I decided it could wait. Things had changed, right smart."

"Jeff, just what the hell is it you want with that old man?"

"Old? How old is he?"

Then it dawned on me . . . Jeff still didn't know that the old man in the soggy hat, eating the cherry pie at Kohlick's, had been Henry Smith from Wyoming. It was time somebody told him.

"That mean old man you pulled your gun on in the restaurant— that was your guy, Jeff. That was Holly Ann's Daddy."

It came in on him slowly. "Judas . . . Priest!" he murmured.

"He knows who you are. And he's convinced himself that you followed him all the way down here to kill him."

"*Kill* him? What on earth for? He's never done anything to me!"

"Then why have you been shagging him across half the United States of America?"

"I just wanted to ask him two or three questions."

"What questions?"

"I don't think I'd better tell you, Grady. They might sound crazy to you. It's just that I've got this hunch that Henry Smith could clear up a couple of things."

"What did you tell Holly Ann about yourself?"

"I didn't lie to her. I told her I was from West Virginia, and that's where I was when I started out. I've got to see her father first, one way or another, let him know I only want to have a little talk with him."

"He might take another chair and knock your brains out this time."

I don't think Jeff heard my last remark. The solemn look had vanished from his face, he flashed me a broad grin, and then he began to laugh.

"Grady," he said, "I just happened to think. This is like in a movie."

"Also like in Shakespeare," I responded. Actually I was inclined to think of it in terms of a newspaper story. And to run from it. All old newspapermen, the legend says, adore to watch a story develop right under their noses, see it blossom and spread out and get itself complicated and snarled up, and find themselves all personally involved in it, watching it as it snowballs along, growing into Page One meat.

Not me. There's none of that old firehorse blood surging in my veins when the bell rings. I'm for the easy chair, the middlin' highball, and the good book.

Old Ral Rock is a boulder twice the size of Chug Peavy's bank building and has long been a landmark in this flattish part of Blackleg County, lying between the two mountain ranges. It was in sight when we crossed Assáche Creek and we hurried the horses along because this was the spot where we would camp for the night.

Jeff, having been a country boy all his life, located an overhang where we could retreat in case of bad weather, and then he set to work gathering wood for a fire. The creek was flowing well, from the recent rains, and I walked the horses over and let them drink themselves stuporous.

We argued playfully over the supper menu, Jeff contending for the Argentine corned beef with Colorado pinto beans, and his elderly companion favoring the chili canned in Austin, Minnesota. The good life is made up of happy compromise, so we settled on the chili.

Off to the west we could see the serrated lines of the Canalla Escarpment and we watched the sun descend behind its gray undulating facade. Then it was time for more talk. There were things about The Virginian—events that took place after Owen Wister closed his story—that I wanted to know. His grandson was eager to satisfy my curiosity; he was almighty proud of his six-gun ancestor.

Wister ends his book with The Virginian taking his family and his cattle out of Wyoming. Why? Because the rustlers had triumphed over the honest cattlemen and made life unbearable for them.

"A dam-ned lie," said Jeff, making two distinct syllables out of the cussword.

Wister said The Virginian and his Vermonter wife Molly and their children found happiness in Montana.

"A puddin'headed untruth," declared The Virginian's grandson.

"You don't seem to have much faith in Mr. Wister's book," I said. "So what did happen?"

"My granddad left Wyomin' because his brother Frank died and left him a farm back in Virginia."

Thus, by the testimony of Jefferson Cordee, The Virginian vanished into the obscurity of a small farm, and Molly Wood traveled to Virginia with him, and they had children, including a girl who was to become Jeff's mother. She grew up to marry a pig farmer named Cordee, and here was old Forsyte Grady from the Kaintuck Pennyrile, sitting beside Old Ral Rock in the western mountains, listening to their handsome son talk family history.

"I heired some money," he said, "from my uncle Gatlin Cordee —he was a bachelor and conducted a general mercantile store over in Randolph County, West Virginia, close to Elkins."

"Is that," I interposed, "where they have all the clothespin factories?"

He gave me a long inquiring look.

"You've been in West Virginia?"

"Never. I just heard somebody say once that clothespins are big in West Virginia."

"You heard right. At least they were big when I was a kid visitin' Uncle Gatlin. He died when I was about twelve and his money was put in a trust for me, but I couldn't have it till I was twenty-one. I didn't even know about it till I was twenty and then my folks told me. Soon as I got it I decided I'd had enough pig farmin' to last me a while, and I went out to see the world."

He got up and put some sticks on the dying fire, and I took time to fetch out my corn-squeezin's. We each had a good stiff belt and then I wanted to know which direction he took when he left home.

"I always dreamed of goin' out West the way my granddad did," he said when we had settled down again alongside the big rock. "So I spent a couple of years wanderin' around in Nebraska and Colorado and Wyomin'. I stopped from time to time to work on a farm or a ranch because I like to work. I still got most of the money Uncle Gatlin Cordee left me, something in the neighborhood of eighty thousand dollars."

I remembered that back in Caliche he had mentioned Medicine Bow and I asked him about it.

"I passed through there when I first started bummin' around," he said, "and spent a day or two lookin' at Granddad's old stampin' grounds. I told a man in a drugstore who I was and he cussed me out and called me a G. D. liar and said the tourists were gettin' rottener every year, and turnin' into con men, so after that I just kep' my mouth shut. It was a year and a half later that I went back and spent a year in the town, mostly workin' for a well driller."

"What's Medicine Bow like now?"

"They got signs all over town that say, 'When you call me that, smile.' The hotel is called The Virginian, and next door to it is The Virginian Motel, and there's a sign on the hotel wall for the tourists, says on this spot The Virginian killed Trampas, and across the street at the Union Pacific depot is a monument to Mr. Wister made out of hunks of petrified wood, and on up . . ."

"Sounds suitable and appropriate," I said. "Mr. Wister was himself a hunk of petrified wood. A snob of the worst kind."

"I just wish he hadn't said my granddad turned his back on his best friend. He wouldn't have stood by and let them lynch his pal Steve."

"It was a little before my time," I said, "so I won't venture an opinion."

We had another go at the Kentucky loddnum and then crawled into the sleeping bags and I lay there looking up at the stars and trying to absorb what I had learned about Jeff and his family and his romance. There was still a faint glow from the fire and the only sound was the slight burbling of the creek.

Then something came to me. *I didn't know The Virginian's name.* At no point in the book did Owen Wister ever call him anything but The Virginian.

"Hey!" I called out to Jefferson Cordee. "It just occurred to me that I don't know your grandfather's real name. What was it?"

"Cyril Tharp."

I let it sink in a minute.

"Did you say Cyril Tharp?"

"That's right."

"Thanks, Jeff." I turned over in my sack and spoke in low tones into the starlit Texas night.

"Cyril Tharp," I said.

"Jesus," I added.

"Henry," I went on.

"Christ!" I concluded.

And then I went to sleep.

Chapter Sixteen touching on the fate
of Milly Erne, who was drug to hell by
the Mormons

16

We got organized early and hit the trail before six, traveling almost
due west. By sunup we were beyond sight of Old Ral Rock and
winding through the foothills, and Jeff pointed to a pinnacle on
the far horizon, saying it was Dead Mule Peak. It would serve as
our landmark the rest of the westward journey.

We creaked along for another ten or fifteen minutes and then
we suddenly encountered human life.

Coming from behind a small grassy hill were two riders. One
was a chunky man of advanced years and the other was a smallish
boy who turned out to be, on closer inspection, a smallish girl.

As they came up to us the man, whose clothing was made of
tattered black leather and who wore two black Colts slung low
against his leather britches, let his right arm drop into drawing
position. He had on black gloves with cuffs made of cracked patent
leather, and there was something deeply menacing about his
manner.

"Howdy do," he said.

I looked into his face and saw beyond the furrows of age, caught
a glimpse of the man as he must have been in the long ago—the
fictive range rider of ten thousand adventures, lean features dark-
ened by the sun, possessed now of a stern and disciplined change-
lessness that came with years of silence and solitude. But it was
not this momentary vision that held me; it was, rather, the intensity
of his gaze, the strained weariness, the piercing wistfulness of keen
gray sight, as if he were forever looking for a thing he would never
find. There was steel in those eyes. Cold steel. Occasionally turning
hot.

"Hidy, good folk," said the little girl. She looked to be about
twelve or thirteen, very self-possessed and sure of herself, wearing a faded gray blouse and a gathered skirt of a dull reddish color

that might have been made from sacking. Her hair was in pigtails, tied at the ends with little red ribbons.

"Air they any waterhole up ahead of us?" the man in black wanted to know, his eyes darting from Jeff to me and back to Jeff again. I told him he was but a short ride from Assáche Creek and pointed back east.

"Assáche," he drawled. "A Injun name. Tell me this, stranjuh. Did you come from that dye-rection?"

I said we had.

"You see anything of a purty little ole woman name of Milly Erne?"

"We didn't see a soul. Who is Milly Erne?"

The piercing wistfulness of his keen gray sight turned to hard questing intensity. He spoke now with an accusing voice.

"Is either one of you Maw-muns?" His black-gloved left hand dropped onto the black butt of a Colt. "Speak up! Has either one of you seed Milly Erne?"

Before I could answer, Jeff Cordee leaned forward in the saddle and challenged the dark stranger.

"Now you hold your horses, mister!" he said. "And take your fist offa that gun. Take . . . it . . . . off!"

The man in black slowly moved his hand away from the gun butt.

Then Jeff spoke to the girl.

"Who is this man?" he asked her. "Is he your Paw?"

"Oh no! I just encountered him on the trail day before yesterday. He is a good Christian gentleman, and knows his Bible, and he is looking for his sister by the name of Milly Erne. She was drug to hell by the Mormons."

"I will find the cur," growled the man in black. "I will find the low dawg Maw-mun that drug Milly Erne to hell. I will ram one of my pistols down his throat and the other up his behind and farr them off soze the bullets will meet in his low Maw-mun gizzud."

The contrast between the man's aura of fire and strength, and his kentry-and-western style of talk, was as sharp as the contrast between himself and the pigtailed girl. No single-gallused rube out of Pike County, Kentucky, ever twanged such a twang as this man twung.

The little girl addressed us again through her braids.

"He is looking for the polecat who drug his sister to hell," she said with great juvenile solemnity. "I, too, am looking for someone, and I only got this . . ." She withdrew an old dragoon cap-and-ball pistol from beneath a bundle which was strapped to her horse. "It is my hope," she went on, "to find another weapon such as this one, so that I may do the same to my man, when I find him, as my new friend plans on doing to the Mormon who drug Milly Erne straight to hell. One barrel shoved into each end of Tom Chaney so the bullets will meet in his sinful murderous gizzard."

"What did this Tom Chaney do to you?" Jeff asked her.

"My father, Frank Ross, was killed by Tom Chaney in front of the Monarch boarding house in Fort Smith, Arkansas. I am going to find Tom Chaney and kill him in return. I once engaged the services of a fine man named Rooster Cogburn, who had but one eye, to help me find Tom Chaney and send him to hell. I shot him once, when Rooster and I went after him in the Choctaw Nation, and Rooster caved in his head with the stock of his rifle, and we thought we were done and finished with Tom Chaney, but somehow he survived, and Rooster Cogburn passed away of the night-hoss disorder and the early summer heat of Jonesboro, Arkansas, and now I must seek out Tom Chaney and kill him anew. I have headstrong ways that lead me into tight corners, but I have now found a new staunch friend who will assist me in my search."

"The Lawd will show us the way," said the man in black, and he nodded to the girl, indicating that it was time for them to be off. The two lifted their hands in farewell and rode off toward the cottonwoods of Assáche Creek. As they moved out on the trail I heard the man chanting a little ditty. The words, which he repeated over and over, were:

The sun's done riz
An' the sun's done set,
An' I ain't found
Muh Maw-mun yet.

Impulsively I turned my horse and trotted out in pursuit. Coming abreast of the black-leather man, who hadn't slowed the pace of his mount, I said:

"Would you mind if I asked you a personal question?"

"Not at all. The Lawd abideth a frank and honest hommbry."

"Would your name by any chance be Lassiter?"

"Kee-reckt, brother."

"Good hunting," I said, out of politeness, and rode back to re-join Jeff Cordee. I decided not to try telling the grandson of The Virginian anything further about the man in black. Things were fucked up enough.

Chapter Seventeen treating of a mountain
eyrie more startling than Adolf Hitler's
Berchtesgaden

17

An hour later we came to the Vinegaroon Highway, which winds southward through the mountainous country of lower Blackleg. I had my soundings now and we bore left and rode until we came to Leydigs Duct, a small spring-fed stream with a nice pastoral air about it.

Perched on a rise midway between the creek and the highway was Big Jim Deehardt's grotesque shanty. It did not quite fit the personality of its owner; his customary posture was one of fallen aristocracy, but not such a total collapse as was suggested here. Big Jim strove always for an elegance of speech in the midst of trying conditions, and one tended to associate him with dinner clothes and vintage wines and shiny *fiacres* spanking along through Central Park.

It would require this entire page to enumerate the materials with which the Deehardt *maisonette* had been constructed. Basic in the architecture, however, were rumpled sheets of flattened-out tin that had once been cans containing coffee and fruit juices; scraps of mismatched lumber, clods of caliche that appeared to have been loaded into a bazooka and fired at the more glaring cracks, and a roof made entirely of discarded auto license plates.

The whole structure had been intertwined and dovetailed and convolved higgledy-piggledy by the Hermit of Leydigs Duct himself, in a time when he could not afford cement and siding and hardware. He had come up with but one single item of quality in building his country seat. Set near the middle of the crazy quilt facade was a striking, anomalistic fixture—a carved Mexican door painted a deep brownish red, such a door as would not have been out of place on the finest whorehouse in Ciudad Juárez or the residence of an Arizona realtor. The first time I visited Big Jim in his chalet, something over six months earlier, I had hesitated about asking how he had come by that majestic door; I felt certain he had stolen it, probably from some splendid house of ill repute.

As we rode up the carven door was thrown open and the proprietor of the establishment stood on the threshold waiting to welcome us. He was clothed in casual attire, a sports outfit of the type he customarily wore around the house: an ancient denim shirt that hadn't been laundered at any time during the Christian Era, and a pair of pants ostensibly clawed off at the knees by relays of mountain panthers. On his feet were disreputable sandals which he wore without socks, and surmounting all this, that rugged head with all those whiskers and the single glittering eye . . . that deceptive eye that was forever lively, though no one could say for sure whether The Hermit was glaring out of it in bitterness, or permitting it to twinkle with delight.

The whiskers bothered me, as almost all whiskers bothered me. I tend to equate beards and long hair with moderate but unquestioned insanity. This predisposition dates possibly from my early years in New York City, where I spent much of my time in the general area of Times Square. During those years a beard was the badge of a nut. The wackeroos in dirty white robes and messianic whiskers paraded the streets carrying placards proclaiming that the world would end next Tuesday at daybreak, crying out for the populace to repent. Or the hirsute crackbrains were down on all fours inscribing their messages on the sidewalks with varicolored chalk, urging all to Get Right With God, Revere the Flag, or Quit Playing Cards.

I hasten to say that I am not imputing mental unbalance to the Hermit of Leydigs Duct. Far from it. He is every bit as alert and as level-headed as I am.

"Welcome to my humble hearth!" he cried out, and on the instant, leaping from his doorsill, he launched himself into three whirling handsprings, fetching up directly in front of our horses. A remarkable display of agility for a man of his years.

We dismounted, and he shook hands with us both, and said to Jeff, "I was not expecting company, else I would have tidied up. Come into my house. It isn't much but I have a great affection for it. It is so much more attractive than the country hotels I lived in during my years as Lightning Rod King of the Middle Border. My territory, if you didn't know it, was Illinois, Missouri, and Arkansas, and my monument is to be found in those provinces—thousands of steel fingers pointing heavenward from lonely farmhouses and barns, protecting the occupants from the justified Wrath of God. Grady, my friend, you look weary. Come in. The coffee's on the giant electric range, the bourbon's on the Hepplewhite sideboard—circa 1791—and the branchwater flows yonder in my own private brook. There's a pot of the gopher burgoo ready for warming, and, to top everything off, I have glorious news for you—*not,* let me caution you, *not* for your distinguished journal, no, not for publication, because it is a great secret. Grady, you are looking at the new Croesus!"

While this recital was filtering through his jungle of whiskers, he was escorting us back to his Mexican door, and Jeff paused once to stare at the prehistoric truck which stood beside the house— The Hermit's only means of conveyance. He never was one to apologize for the shabby look of his possessions.

"A beauty, isn't she!" he boomed to Jeff. "Take a good look at her, boy. You are contemplating history. Touch her, if you want. A very famous vehicle—belongs in the Smithsonian. I call her Alice, for the wife of Theodore Roosevelt. This truck, young man, was used to haul the first load of dirt shoveled out of the big ditch that became the Panama Canal. Theodore Roosevelt himself, and William Jennings Bryan, and Diamond Jim Brady, and Thomas A. Edison—all four of them, wielding solid silver shovels, turned the first dirt and loaded it into this truck. And Teddy himself took the wheel and drove her through the mire and the muck, drove her with his own two hands!"

Jeff cast a surreptitious, questioning glance at me. He wasn't real sure.

Inside the shanty . . . well, it was a pigpen, but a neat pigpen. The giant electric range was a wood stove with one leg missing; the Hepplewhite sideboard was a battered deal table (circa 1942) that probably had been discarded by wetback Mexicans, and the whiskey was a brand I'd never encountered before.

"So you're a newcomer to these starry precincts?" Big Jim said to Jeff. "You've come to a great country. Let me introduce myself more adequately, in case we get into . . . well, in case we get into a deal of some kind. I'm an Illinois Deehardt, a remittance man out of the Sucker State. They call it the Inland Empire these days but it was always the State of the Suckers to me, sometimes with a graceful prefix, and I am proud of it, and the next Texas moron

I hear referring to it as Illi-*noise* will earn himself an ass-kicking he will remember to the grave. Fairest of all the Commonwealths! Godmother to Texas! And they call it Illi-*noise!*"

As if to settle his angered blood he fluffed his whiskers with both hands and then clapped Jeff on the shoulder and said:

"I am loyal to Illinois, though my people gave me a hard time in my childhood. Dickens never wrote anything more touching. When I was born they put me under a tub and after two days they lifted it up to see if I cried or swung by the tail. I remember when I was about three, I asked my parents where I came from, and they said a crow brought me. Yet I . . ."

"Big Jim," I interrupted him, "just what do you mean that Illinois was the Godmother of Texas?"

"Plain truth. Grand and glorious men out of Illinois have come out to Texas and made this State into an acceptable member of the Union. Think on them! Stephen J. Austin. Big Footed Wallace. Ike Eisenhower. William Jennings Bryan. Honest Sam Bass. J. Frank Dobie. Diamond Jim Brady. Henry Wadsup Longfellow. Harry Truman . . ."

"Maurice Chevalier," I added. "And you forgot Lyndon Johnson."

"Hell, Lyndon never set foot in Illinois."

"I know," I said. "I was just testing you, Big Jim. Lyndon was a Kentucky boy."

"Of course. I like Kentucky. I also like Nebraska, although I can't remember why." He turned again to Jeff. "Where'd you say you came from, boy?"

"Wyomin'."

"I've traveled Wyoming."

"A notion crosses my mind, sir," said Jeff. "By any chance, in your wandering, did you ever run into a man named Cyril Tharp?"

"Cyril Tharp," Big Jim murmured. "Tharp. Tharp. Cyril Tharp. Wonder what his folks had against him to name him Cyril Tharp." Jeff Cordee stiffened slightly but The Hermit didn't notice.

"No," he said. "Knew a sheepherder once, name of Cal Thorpe. Wise in the astrological sciences and could horoscope a man right down to his heel bone. Took hold of my birthday once—August the second—and put his pencil to it and figured out, quite accurately, that I was . . . could that have been in Nebraska? No. That was Joplin . . . figured out that I was fond of animals, honest as the day is long, generous to a fault, a good judge of character, given to charitable works, not a selfish bone in my body, magnanimous toward my fellow man, and then he borrowed twenty dollars off of me and that's the last time I ever saw him. Joplin, Missouri. A sheepherder named Cal Thorpe. A party I will kill the next time I come up against him."

Big Jim freshened up Jeff's coffee and replenished my whiskey.

"Can't remember for the life of me," he continued, "what in the condominium hell I was doing in Nebraska, or why I like Nebraska. Let me think. Could have been a pilgrimage I made once to a town called Beatrice, which is the place Benjamin Franklin installed the first lightning rod in the history of the civilized world. Big frame house painted a sickly green, with pink shutters, can't imagine how old Franklin could have got within half a mile of it without throwing up his guts . . . thing I'm getting at"—he returned his attention to Jeff—"is that you need to embrace the scientific posture. Go to the beasts and the wing-gud creatures. Study the ant and the honey bee. Observe the delicate way a yellow-crowned night heron eats a crawdad. Did you know, my boy, that a bighorn sheep can jump off a one-hundred-foot cliff and if he lands on his horns he won't be hurt? A Christ's fact, lab tested by *Good Housekeeping*. One hundred feet straight down, onto the rocks. And not even a headache!"

I, Grady, the peripatetic iconoclast, chose to throw in a question.

"Just what could Jeff learn from that bighorn sheep?"

Now it was clearly a twinkle in that single eye.

"Grow horns," said Big Jim, "or stay the hell off the cliffs."

"Mr. Deehardt," said Jeff, who was becoming more impressed with each passing minute, "one thing we forgot to ask you about. The last time we saw you, up in town, you were on your way over to kill the mayor."

"That," said Big Jim, "brings us right up to the big secret. I'm sure you heard that I actually didn't kill that worm, though I may do it yet. Meanwhile, Jefferson Cordee, in order that you may get the picture firmly in your mind, with background materials and forecasts of the future, I must tell you about . . ."

Chapter Eighteen in explanation of why
Big Jim Deehardt cannot avoid becoming
a millionaire

18

Big Jim stepped to a corner of the little room and dragged out a carton. He fumbled around inside it and emerged with a black wooden box about the size of an automobile storage battery. There was a dial on it, and a couple of tuning knobs, and two little levers, and a metal post with a red label that said "Positive." Hitched to this post was a length of jumper cable with red clamps at either end.

He set the box beside his chair and then embarked upon a glorification of American Enterprise in Action, demonstrating how commercial mind can triumph enduringly over industrial matter, treating of his own career as an exemplification of the genius inherent in American Know-how. If I tried to set down the lecture in full, it would take another complete book, so I'll attempt to boil it down as best I can. This is a tough job, like trying to put the Pacific Ocean into a beer can.

First off, a few paragraphs of Deehardt history. When he came to Blackleg County about five years back, and after I'd heard stories about him and then made his acquaintance, I decided to try him for my most unforgettable character in *Reader's Digest,* where I've heard they sometimes go clean out of their minds and pay a man as much as two thousand bucks for an article in that category. (I even got around to writing it and sending it in, but Pleasantville responded with a pleasant note saying it was wrought in beauty, loaded with wisdom, unforgettable as the dickens, the kind of writing that the world sorely needs, but not suited to *their* needs.) I had done a lot of earnest digging on the Deehardt story, and spent about fifty dollars on telephone calls, talking to a couple of Big Jim's brothers in Illinois, and to several sheriffs and newspaper editors in other localities. In his time The Hermit had been run out of his native state, out of Missouri, and out of Arkansas.

In those regions he billed himself as King of the Lightning Rods.

It was his custom to wander along the rural routes and peddle his rods to the farmers, doing the installation work himself. Once he had them rigged he would get out his magic black box, clamp the jumper cable onto the ground wires and then, with ceremonial flourishes as spectacular as those attending the initiation of a new member into the BPOE, he would throw one of the levers. A great buzzing and clanking and whirring would come from the box, continuing for thirty clamorous seconds, and the farmer's new lightning rods had been charged.

Deehardt set up a one-man industry, patterned after the procedures of a life insurance salesman. There was more blood to be squeezed from the turnip. Every six months Big Jim would travel back over his territory, visiting those farmers who had bought his rods. Once again he'd hook up his black box to the ground wires, set it to buzzing and clanging, and when the noise had subsided he'd turn to the farmer and say, "There you are, my friend, all lines reactivated . . . you're protected for another six months, safe as the Pope in Rome. That'll be three dollars and a half."

Time after time Big Jim was obliged to flee before the law.

"They hit me," he recalled, "with bench warrants and encumbrancer judgments and mechanics liens . . . true bills and *nolle prosses* and *nolo contenderes* . . . subpoenas duces tecum and mittimuses and mandamuses and the law of supply and demand and . . . it got so, friend Grady, that I was beginning to talk like a law book. And so I came to Texas, never more to grub and grovel for the abominable dollar."

There in his shack beside the trickling waters of Leydigs Duct, after he had shown us the basic controls on his lightning-rod charger, Big Jim finally got around to his encounter with Mayor Ford Winkler, and the Winkler story led in the end straight to the great secret The Hermit was so eager to reveal.

"As you must know," said Big Jim, "that weasel Winkler makes more money out of water witchin' than he ever takes out of City Hall, if you overlook what he steals. Well, he was driving down this way one afternoon and he stopped off to inspect my landed estates, and I gave him a bowl of gopher burgoo—just the thing to cure the tic he has in that right eyelid—and I showed him this little box of mine, and I even threw the lever and set the machinery in motion. He sat right in that chair and gave off little jerks and jumps and then when the siren sounded he was really shook—I estimated that the precipitation probability in his pantaloons was eighty per cent."

The fire siren, Big Jim explained, was a recent addition to the mechanism and was activated after all the clanks and whinnies and buzzings had run their course.

"I made a grievous mistake," said our host. "I told that squirmy little son of a bitch about my latest enterprise. I told him that I had turned my genius to water witching. But I employed no silly rods, no limbs cut off of peach trees. I adapted my lightning rod techniques to the pursuit of underground water. I tried to explain to your mayor that he and all his associate witches were on the wrong track, using rods and wands. I tried to explain to him that a rod is a phallic symbol and that by using their rods he and his friends were loading sexual connotations into their work, and that every time he waved a rod over a piece of ground he was indulging in hard-core pornography and thereby offending the One True God. You know what, Grady? He didn't understand a word I was saying. He had never in his life heard of a phallic symbol. If I'd have searched him on the spot I doubt if I'd have found a single one."

Mayor Ford Winkler, said Big Jim, went back to Caliche and with the help of Cee Minus Hoffelinck, constructed a magic witching box of his own.

"He started traveling around with a *silver* box," said Big Jim, "the same size as my black one, with the same kind of gadgets and gimmicks on it, and layovers to ketch meddlers. The minute I found out about it . . . that was the day you saw me in town, on my way to kill him. Before I went into his private office I had to talk to his old-maid secretary. I told her I had heard about his magic box and she said, oh yes indeedy, the mayor had . . ." Big Jim now went into prissy maiden-lady talk, accompanied by effeminate twists and fidgetings. ". . . she says, yes indeedy, the mayor had doubled his witchin' business and this was jest peachy keen because ever one knew he had always been the most sot-after water witch in the whole county and now that the Lord had give him the dee-sign for his silver box . . . get that, Grady! The Lord give him the dee-sign! The Lord showed him how to *steal* it from me! Christ over El Paso! Wye, goddamn it to neverending hell, if they would let me back into Arkansas or Missouri for ten minutes, I could get affidavits that I was using that box thirty years ago. And your own *mayor!* It's just getting so a man can't trust a single soul any more, even people in high places."

"But," I reminded him, "what did you do to the mayor? There wasn't a word on the grapevine. What happened?"

"I told him that if I ever heard of him using that box again, I'd come back up to town and get hold of it and tear it into pieces and I'd take the pieces, wood and metal and glass and wire and cogwheels and everything else, and I'd cram them one by one straight past his hemorrhoids, and then I'd worm the seven-foot jumper cable right in behind everything else, inch by slow inch. Don't put these details in your paper, Grady."

"I won't. But what did he say?"

"He knew I meant it. He hemmed and hawed and elasticated and said he had his police force to protect him from ruffians and jailbirds, and that the Lord had put a hand on his shoulder and spoke the words, and so *I* placed a hand on his shoulder and spoke several of my own, and then I took him by the neck and lifted him off the floor and shook him a little bit and then he promised he'd throw his box away, and I said, no, I'd take it with me just to make certain. So now I've got two witchin' boxes, one black and one silver, and the silver one operates with the endorsement of the Lord God Himself."

He went back to the carton and got out the contrivance which the mayor and Hoffelinck had put together. It was much neater and more efficient-looking than Big Jim's old lightning-rod charger.

"Now," he said, "we come to the secret. This one . . ."—he indicated the black box—". . . this one I use for witchin' water exclusively. I could get rich with this one alone, confining my endeavors to witching wells. For example, two days hence I take off for some witching in New Mexico, around Deming and Lordsburg, and I'll come out of that trip with a net of better than five hundred dollars. Three days' witching—five hundred simoleons. Got more jobs than I can handle. But that's just the beginning. Here . . . this baby . . ." He reached down and gave the silver box a loving pat. "This baby will put Big Jim Deehardt up there with the Rockefeller boys and J. Paul Getty and Jackie O. and that old man with the finger-lickin' chicken. This silver box—I have torn the Winkler guts out of it and replaced them with a brand new installation. I got my inspiration from that marvelous Dixon woman back there in Washington, D.C. She's now going into a new field—outerspatial medicodynamics. I hear she's drawing a bead on the common cold. Now, get this straight, gentlemen. I wouldn't steal from Dixon. She's got her side of the fence, I've got mine. Tell you what I've done with this little box. I've devised a chemokinetic attachment that works off the reciprocal pulsion thrust, and this gives me a voltaic pile made up chiefly of blunted megacoulombs. Know what it does?"

Jeff Cordee had been bending forward, a boyish eagerness in his manner.

"What?" he asked.

"Cures cancer."

"Now, Big Jim . . ." I protested.

"Just one minute, Grady. This whole idea comes straight from Dixon, and she's not walking around with her head in the clouds. She told about it in one of the scientific journals I take—*National Geographic,* maybe, or *Architectural Forum.*"

He let this substantial information have time to settle in. Then he went on:

"Note these two little holes here, right in front. Once I turn this son of a bitch on, the megacoulombs are radiated out through those holes, straight into the patient's body, and *whambo!* Away goes the cancer."

"Now, Big Jim . . ." I said again, a little more forcefully this time. "That box is not about to cure any cancer and you know it."

"Well, I suppose I shouldn't call it a cure. All it does is *prevent* cancer. That's even better. One shot of irradiated megacoulombs every six months and any cancer cell that tries to raise its stinking head anywhere inside your body, that cancer cell will die like a dog. On closer consideration, I believe it could be called a cure. If my silver box makes it impossible for you to *get* cancer, then by God I call that being *cured* of cancer. I've already serviced thirty-eight customers right here in the southern part of Blackleg County, without ever setting foot in town. I intend to pick up a new batch over in New Mexico."

"How much do you charge, Mr. Deehardt?" Jeff wanted to know.

"Ah!" exclaimed Big Jim, as if the very mention of money brought fresh blood surging into his veins. "It's duck soup, lead pipe, dead certainty, ipsy-dixit. One hundred kroner for the first shot. Fifty bucks after that, every six months. And you know what the whole deal costs me? Three dollars and sixty cents. Two six-volt lantern batteries, and they last damn near forever."

Exhilarated with the curiosity of youth, Jeff had another question.

"Does the cancer machine set off bells and sirens and all that?"

"God yes. It isn't at all necessary, but the customers like to hear that noise. It reassures them. It's like drums and trumpets, proclaiming victory. All I'd really need would be a small beep to signify that the megacoulombs have found the target—but I give them a fanfare that damn near takes the roof off. Just think what all this means, Grady! Think what it means to the cigarette industry alone! Millions who quit in terror will now start smoking again!"

"You'll really get rich," Jeff concluded. "You'll be able to move out of this packin' crate and get yourself a big house in town."

"Son, don't say that!" Big Jim was crushed, devastated, wounded to the quick. "You are suggesting that I would elevate money to a position above principle. I love this little home of mine. I really do. It suits my needs, and it suits my economic philosophy. I don't suppose you know that I am the last of the Single Taxers. The last disciple of Henry George and his great formula. Finest thinker we ever had in this country, Henry George. Beat out TR for President but then got jobbed out of the White House by that rascal Harding. Henry's idea—and mine—was to slap a tax on land. Nothing else. Soak the landowner. No taxes of any kind for working people, none on bosses, not on Texas oilmen, not a penny levied against barbers or university professors or water witches or newspaper editors. Thus, young man, this little chalet of mine represents a great and shining principle, just as my truck yonder, Old Alice Roosevelt, represents a sentimental attachment to our glorious American past."

By this time we had edged our way slowly to the door, and then out to the tree where we had tied the horses. Big Jim followed right along, talking steadily, scattering his wisdom to the mountain winds. We were in the saddle and ready to ride away when Jeff called out:

"What would you say, Mr. Deehardt, if I told you that all the water witchin' business in this part of the country will soon be taken over by one little old pig?"

"Son," Big Jim responded, "nothing surprises me any more."

We gave him a wave and turned our horses and trotted off toward Hollohorn Flats and the Two Cross T ranch. We jogged along for half an hour or so, satisfied with silence, each of us holding enough conversational ballast to last a week.

Then I had to speak.

"The pig," I said. "What's this about the pig?"

He straightened in the saddle and his white teeth glistened back of a big grin . . . and he told me.

Chapter Nineteen containing a bowdlerized
account of how ape is done in an intensive
care room

19

I wanted to see that pig.

As a metropolitan newspaper wretch I always enjoyed stories
about animals whose owners claimed the dumb beasts were en-
dowed with psychic powers. I remember wheedling myself an assignment which took me to Richmond, Virginia, where I became
personally acquainted with a horse named Lady Wonder who
could predict the stock market, announce floods in advance, advise
people to stay out of flying machines during September, and spell.
She performed her clairvoyant duties by thumping out words on a
crude keyboard twenty feet long, and thousands of mortals traveled
to Richmond from all over the land, seeking surcease from their
troubles.

A water witchin' pig? Hardly. Yet something told me I ought to
have a look and so we hurried the horses and got back to the ranch
by midafternoon. We went straight to Jeff's cottage and he took
a one-gallon graniteware bucket out of the refrigerator, unclamped
its lid, and briefly inspected its contents, a gray-brown sickly-
looking porridge. Then he dropped two red apples on top of the
porridge.

"Emily's mush," he said, and replaced the lid.

He put the bucket in the pickup and we drove over to the big
barn. Up against the barn wall Jeff had built a neat pen and inside
the small enclosure was the habitation which I thought was a doghouse. This was where I had my first look at Emily. She was a
pinkish gray in color and as we approached she gave off a series of
soft baby grunts by way of salutation. Her eyes were steadily on
Jefferson Cordee.

He began uttering a sickening kind of baby talk, directed at the
pig, while he was reaching for a dog collar and leash which were
hanging from a nail on the wall of the barn. He buckled the collar
around Emily's neck and then lifted her into the back of the truck.

We followed wheel-track trails toward the north sections, where the land lay dry as a chip. About a mile from the barn Jeff pointed out the spot where Emily had witched her first water. He had taken the pig with him while he checked a windmill and the presence of tank water apparently had made her thirsty. She had simply sniffed around a bit in the sandy soil, settled on a likely spot, then rooted down a foot or so and brought up water.

We bumped on northward and I said, "What's with the bucket of mush?"

"I'm trainin' her," he said. "Pigs are a lot easier to train than dogs. That mush is a special mixture me and Jaybird worked out. When we get to a place where I want her to smell us up some water, I take the mush and . . ."

"Hold it, cowboy. Smell it up? Smell underground water?"

"Sure. You'll see her do it in a little bit. I feed her the mush when we're ready. It makes her thirsty and she goes after water."

"What's in the mush?"

"You wouldn't want to eat it, Grady. I start off with one package of Grape Nuts. That was Jaybird's idea. He said he had seen a commercial on TV where a man named You-All Gibbons ate some Grape Nuts out in a pasture and then said they tasted like wild hick'ry nuts. Jaybird said a pig was bound to go for anything tasted like hick'ry nuts, so the next time I was in town I got half a dozen boxes. I take one fifteen-ounce can of Crown-Prince brand Norwegian sardines and two cans of Crown-Prince anchovies, come from Portugal, and mix ever'thing up together, stirrin' in half a bottle of Hick'ry Harry's Liquid Smoke—that was my own idea, I happen to favor it on things. And there you have the mush. I scatter some chopped apple over the top of it before I offer it to her. The mush itself is too tangy for her but she'll eat it if the chopped apple is sprinkled on."

"I noticed you brought two apples."

"She gets a whole one as a reward after she finds the water."

He chose a stretch of desert with a close resemblance to Death Valley as the site for the demonstration. It was an area lumped up with small sand dunes, and while I'm no hydrologist I would have bet good money that you could have drilled straight through to Hunan Province without encountering moisture.

Jeff took the leash off Emily and set her on the ground and she watched him dump the mush into an old tin washpan. Then he used his pocketknife to cube up the apple, and set the pan down in front of the pig. She went at it rather daintily, for a pig, and when she was finished she raised her head, glanced around the gritty landscape, and began sniffing the air.

At which point Jefferson Davis Cordee, a Hercules in cowboy clothes, committed an act bordering on degeneracy. In a strong commanding voice he spoke to Emily as follows:

"Go . . . git . . . wah-wah!"

"St. Anthony of the Desert, preserve us!" I cried, flinging up my hands in antic despair.

"Go . . . git . . . wah-wah!" Jeff repeated, and Emily took off.

She moved quickly across the sand, pursuing a zigzag course, her nose close to the ground and moving from side to side, making me think of the disc type mine detectors we used in World War II.

"She's thirsty as the devils in hell," Jeff observed, "and she oughta be. I put in three cans of the anchovies this time."

We followed along about a hundred feet behind Emily, watching her closely. Sometimes she'd break abruptly to the right or left, like a broken field runner, and always that little head was wagging back and forth and the snuffling was clearly audible to us. We had covered the best part of a mile and the pig was keeping to her steady pace and Jeff was showing signs of nervousness.

"Miz Battle told me," he said, "that this country up here is the dryest part of the ranch. Maybe we better take her down toward the south bound'ry."

"Give her another few minutes," I said, feeling the time had come for application of the famous Grady needle. "Could be she'll miss on water but discover gold or oil or uranium or paregoric or vodka-and-tonic or ketchup or . . ."

Emily hit.

Her uncloven feet stopped moving. Her head no longer swung from side to side. There was a slight trembling in her pinkish body. The snuffling was louder and punctuated now with little grunts of anchovy-induced desire.

"I've been tryin' to learn her to . . ." Jeff began.

"Shhhhhhh!"

I was more excited than the pig. Emily stood there, her front legs spread apart, her snout down against the sand, and then she started rooting. She moved sand faster than I could have done it with a Fresno. Jeff and I edged in quietly, not wanting to distract her but anxious for closeup observation. She had a hole about eighteen inches deep when she hit the rock. It turned out to be no bigger than a grapefruit, and she used her hooves to loosen it and then nudge it upward and out of her excavation. She returned to her eager grubbing and at a depth of two feet and three inches she struck her vein. She backed out as the water came seeping into the hole and she stood watching it intently for a minute or so until the well was about half filled. Then she leaned in and drank. Drank like Henry the Eighth having a beer.

"Be god damn," I said.

Jeff was exultant.

"That's the deepest she's ever gone," he said. "For a minute there I thought she was gonna fail me. She's still battin' a thousand."

I stood for a while in thought. There was something wrong, something out of kilter, but I couldn't lay my finger on it.

We got Emily back in the pickup, rewarded her with the second apple, and returned her to her pen. From there we went to Jeff's house to shower and get ready for dinner. Asia had invited both of us to have drinks in the patio first, and she wouldn't hear of my sleeping on a couch in Jeff's cottage. I was to be installed in her best guest room, and no argument please.

Twilight was coming on when we entered the patio and found the mistress of the tropical plantation waiting for us. A three-quarter moon was riding in from the east and I felt a series of nebulous twinges tugging around somewhere in my epigastric regions. It could have been the moonlight falling on the white-and-red planes of that desert mansion, with the two graceful lines of yuccas bending out to the stone gateposts where the roadway began. It could have been the leathery green foliage of the stately madrona tree which stood near the pool—a living legacy from Uncle Crawford Battle's long tenure. Clearly, a soft guitar playing *"Noche de Ronde"* was needed.

What in the name of God was coming over me?

The Mexican girl Rosa served the drinks and we talked some about the pig. Jaybird Huddleston came in and said he'd settle for a beer, and I began fishing for his judgment. He's the kind of a man you would trust on sight.

"Jaybird," I said, "do you believe in dowsing?"

"Certainly," he responded. "I'm one of these Nature Boys. I

was brought up on a farm in the civilized part of Texas. No high
heels on *us*. We always had . . ."

"Wait a minute. What part of Texas you referring to?"

"East Texas. God's Country."

"You are living in a dream world, Jaybird. Go back some day
and have a second look."

"My old man called in water witches twice that I can remember,"
he continued, unabashed by my slur against his homeland. "And
we always had pigs. I'm up on pigs. Not Mulefoot in particular,
but I know a few things about them. I know they come from some
island out in the Pacific. A good deal of the readin' I do is about
animals of one kind or another, and I know that the Mulefoot is
the smartest of all the pig family. If any pig on earth could witch
water, the Mulefoot could do it. But understand one thing: there's
not much of a trick to smellin' up water at a depth of a foot or
two. I expect I could get down and crawl around and do it myself.
'Specially if I'd just eaten a peck of anchovies. A true water witch
has to locate a vein or stream or dome or whatever maybe a
thousand feet down if he expects to collect his pay."

It was apparent that Jaybird had divined the direction of my
thinking.

"You know about Bedichek?" he asked. "He was a good old
Texas naturalist, close friend of Dobie and Webb. In one of his
books he told about makin' camp somewhere in the Monahans
neighborhood, and it was out there that he saw an old sow
witchin' for water, saw her root up a bubblin' spring out of all that
Monahans sand. I've got that book in my bedroom and a few
nights back I looked up that part about the pig, and there it was,
and Bedichek mentioned how Dobie had seen coyotes dig up water
in the Sonora desert below the river."

"The thing is," I said, "I don't want to see old Jeff here disillu-
sioned. I don't want to see him get his heart broken by a pig." No
laughter from Jeff, no smile. "What Emily is doing, so far, is not
much more than I could do with a grub hoe."

"You'd have to smell it up first," Jeff challenged me.

"Maybe. What I'm after, Jaybird, is can you think of any way we
could get this pig to smell water way down deep?"

"Tough order."

"I know. I've been puzzling over it."

Asia had been sitting quietly with her drink, but now she had something to say.

"If she's as smart as Jaybird claims," she offered, "then maybe she could be trained to go for deep water. As it is, she's smelling out water for herself, for her own use. I'd recommend that we do away with the anchovy goozlum and concentrate on the reward she gets if she can come up with deep water."

"You mean, mam," Jeff asked, "not get her thirsty?"

"Right. Eliminate the goozlum and concentrate on the reward. An apple is not enough. Find out what type of food a Mulefoot pig likes better than anything else . . ."

"You're talkin' about slops, mam. Table scraps and skim milk. That's what we slopped the hogs with back home. Garbage. It's all right for hog type pigs, but not for Emily."

"Nevertheless," Asia argued, "it might turn out that she preferred slops over anything else you could give her. On the other hand, you might find out that she has a passion for chocolate malteds. If I were a pig I imagine I would kill for a bucket of chocolate malteds."

"Suppose," said Jeff, "I experiment a little and try to find out what she would like best. You may be on the right track, mam."

"Yes," I agreed. "In fact, Asia, you are a plain marvel. Straight to the heart of the matter. I'm just astonished that I've let five long years slide by without getting better acquainted with you."

She didn't respond to that, with words. She did respond with another of those little lingering smiles.

Both Jeff and I were tired from all that riding, and curfew was sounded early. My room in the east wing was a trifle on the girlish side, but stylish beyond belief for this desolate part of the country, and my bathroom was as big as Jeff's whole house.

There were copies of *Newsweek* and *W* and *Texas Parade* on the night table, plus two books: *The Desert Year* by Joseph Wood Krutch, and Elroy Bode's *Texas Sketchbook*. I chose the glamorous world of the Parasite People as doxologized in *W* but inside of three minutes I had had a surfeit of Rosemarie Bogley and Dear Truman and Lily Auchincloss and Art Buchwald's see-gar and Babe Paley and Estee Lauder's Bronze Sparkle.

I turned off the light.

From the time I grew to young manhood in Kentucky I've always considered myself backward and loutish in my approach to sex. Every woman I've ever ached for has appeared to me to be immediately and forever unattainable. And yet somehow I've nearly always blundered into the right move, the correct approach. It's almost enough to make a man believe in that Omniscient Governing Force that people talk about so knowingly.

The right move on this occasion was for me to climb out of bed and walk down the hall to her door. I stood there a long moment and then turned the knob and gave a gentle push. I was trembling a little.

The room was dark, but she was wide awake.

"Welcome to the intensive care room," she said.

I dislike the detailed account that has become so popular, the clinical report complete to the last gasp and gurgle. Yet I can't resist setting down a judgment. How different it was! No gymnastics, no double-jointed acrobatics, no whooping and yelling of the type I had grown accustomed to in Caliche bedrooms.

With Asia it was quiet. Tender. Exalted.

There was nothing remotely comic about it, yet, afterward, as I lay there with my arms around her, I caught myself smiling. I had suddenly remembered Jeff Cordee's misuse of a locution common among young people these days, and my mind spoke . . .

What I think we done is we done ape.

Asia and I had *huevos rancheros* beside the pool early the next
morning and no reference was made to the joyous moments of
the night just ended. I had to get moving—as matters stood I was
missing a full day at the office—but I did bring up the question
about the commercialization of Emily. It hadn't once been mentioned but I was certain it was in everyone's mind.

She didn't want any part of it.

"In the first place," she said, "I consider this water witching to
be a sort of game for people with infantile minds. Pure nonsense.
The same as recasting the letters in your name to assure yourself
a place in heaven. The same as calling on tea leaves to send you
off on a journey to the Khyber Pass or . . . or Kentucky. I'm doing
fine with my cattle and don't even have to bother with hunting
leases to balance the budget. The pig belongs to Jeff."

"Last night," I reminded her, "you seemed to be developing an
interest in Emily's future as a witch. You were beginning to get
all involved in the new training program."

"I like to play games," she said.

"I know." I got out of my chair and went round the table and
put a half nelson on her and kissed her, but she failed to respond
in a manner commensurate with my standing in the community.
In fact, she pushed me away.

"Hey," I said. "You forgot something. I love you."

"You've got the eagers," she said.

"Of course I've got the eagers. I love you."

"It's too early for the eagers," she said.

"You mean too early in the day, or the month, or . . ."

"In the year. The eagers aren't good for you. They'll give you
acne."

"Oh, come on, Asia!"

But she had turned cold biscuit on me, even in the face of my noted charm and physical allure. Still, she quickly let me know she wasn't sore about anything. She gave me her warmest smile and put her hand on my arm and then told me that Jeff and Jaybird probably had my horse ready.

"Call me up sometime," she said. "Maybe we could have a date. Walk out with one another. Go to the picture show."

"I'll do that," I said, knowing now that she was merely exercising the perfectly reasonable and despicable and horrid prerogative of setting her own time.

I rode Midnight out past the wooded trysting place on Rinderpest Creek and on through the sand and cactus to Mungo's stables, where Spiro Keats took the horse off my hands.

"Did he buck on you?" Spiro asked with a big grin.

"Nary a pitch."

"I suppose you already know," said the wrangler, "that he's kin to the original Midnight the way I'm first cousin to William S. Hart."

"I suspected it."

"Mungo wants to see you up at the house before you leave. He said it's important."

I walked to The Pueblo and found the proprietor in his den— a paneled cubbyhole with just a little less acreage than the Gregory Gymnasium at the University of Texas in Austin, and with approximately six thousand books lining the walls. He asked me about the trip and I gave him a synopsis and suggested that if he ever turns to collecting bizarre human beings he should not overlook Big Jim Deehardt.

"You've acquired a fine specimen in The Rustler," I said, "and you already had Christchild-Muckeridge."

He asked me if I remembered a book he had given me, the Englishman's latest production, called *Descent into America*. I remembered, but, I said, I must have misplaced it.

"It has some pretty fair stuff in it," he remarked offhandedly. "A change of pace for Ian."

"To be truthful, Mungo, I've never cracked a Christchild-Muckeridge book in my life and in fact I never heard of the man till he landed in Blackleg County."

I recalled that the first time I met the Englishman I professed ignorance about his work and asked him to enlighten me concerning it. He replied, "Frederick Locker-Lampson is my god." He said the line rather rapturously, the way cubs around the news-paper offices used to say, "Hemingway is my god." I had never heard of Frederick Locker-Lampson and I was equally ignorant of his work and made immediate plans to remain in that condition.

Mungo went to a closet and returned with another copy of *Descent into America*. He laid a finger on some blurb copy on the back of the jacket. I read a couple of lines and my eyebrows went up. They went:

He's surely the reincarnation of Bernard Shaw—*Manchester Guardian*.

Christchild-Muckeridge is Britain's answer to Mencken—Chicago *Tribune*.

"They forgot to throw in Mark Twain," I said. I simply couldn't conceive of Christchild-Muckeridge ever composing a zestful and exciting sentence. He was so nothing, so numb, so candy ass. The most profound thing I ever heard him say with respect to Life and Love and Energy and Futility was a crisp "Quite! Quite!" He never seemed to stroll about in a thoughtful fog, rubbing the bowl of his pipe against his nose, as substantial English authors are required to do.

In his own way he was a bigger freak than the one-titted cow of Snow Hill. Almost alone among novelists he never talked about the work in progress; he never mentioned the titanic struggle he was having with Chapter Twelve; no one ever had a hint of the locale or the theme or the plot twistings in the novel he was labor-ing over at the moment. He offered no evidence to the world (be-yond a general air of stupefaction) that he was an author. The only complaint he ever uttered about his accommodations at the ranch was a whisper that the blosted commode in his cabin had to be jiggled.

This was the new Mencken? The risen Shaw?

"I'm sure," I told Mungo, "that the other copy is kicking around my house somewhere. But I'll take this one along."

"Right now," he said, "I hope you can spare me a few minutes. It's not important. It's simply that I've taken over the direction of your life and ought to tell you about it. Sit down."

I took a chair opposite him.

"You may hate me for this," he began. "You are this moment sitting in the presence of a man who is now your employer. I have set up shop as the Lord Beaverbrook of West Texas. I am the new owner of the Caliche Weekly *Mud Dobber*."

"Come off it!" I was fairly aghast. "What in the name of God would you want with that crummy thing?"

"I don't want it, and I agree with your evaluation of it, and I wouldn't even use it for bathroom daintiness. But I caught fire when she let go at you with the rocks. Don't forget, one of those damn rocks almost took an ear off of me. So I sat down with Chug Peavy and we put Lawyer Childers to poking around. We found that there was a forty-thousand-dollar note standing against the paper. I acquired that note, Grady, and I took possession of the lien, and I connived toward an immediate foreclosure. How do you like them apples?"

"So why in Christ's name didn't you let *me* in on the secret?"

"I like to surprise and confound people. Are you surprised and confounded?"

"You damn right. I'm not a lawyer, Mungo, and I'm not a business head, but you can't just walk into a courtroom and foreclose on a person unless you have some grounds."

"I had 'em. The person we are alluding to was in arrears. Delinquent by four monthly payments."

"You still can't foreclose without giving her a chance to pay up."

"Ah, Grady, that is where you demonstrate your ignorance of small-town life in this great Land of the Free. There's more chicanery, more dollar villainy, more flagrant dishonesty in Caliche, Texas, than you'll find at the Annual Convention of American Highway Contractors. Ponzi himself could walk into the town of Caliche tomorrow and lose his fine Italian ass in fifteen minutes."

I was truly confused and thrown out of joint. I dislike the former Fern Mobeetie intensely, but I doubt that I really hate her. I don't hate anybody. It's an emotion that fouls up the Purkinje cells in the cerebellar cortex and causes people to walk into trees.

I asked Mungo, "What'll you do with the miserable rag now that you've got it?"

"I'm making you a present of it, and if you tell me you don't want it, then I'll make you the editor, with any and all profits going to you, and you can write thunderous editorials that will sway the sheep and topple the government in Washington."

I told him I'd have to think about it, and I did, in the Pontiac driving the long smooth highway back to town.

Suppose I did want to own the *Dobber?* One tempting notion ran through my mind. I might cut loose and make a real newspaper out of it. I realized instantly that it couldn't be done. If I so much as mentioned in print that Catherinella (Bubby) Goodnight's boy Kicker got a summons for riding his bicycle on the downtown sidewalks (fourth offense) his muscular Mama would invade my office and spit in my eye and then have me boycotted and ostracized by all the decent people in Caliche.

It wouldn't work. So I let my mind dwell on the curious evil in Fern Mobeetie's heart, enumerating the tribulations and the embarrassments she had brought me over the years. It made a long inventory. Still, I have some shreds and tatters of integrity left.

Don't get the wrong idea about me. I ain't noble. I'm no hero. My sword doesn't glint and glisten in the sunlight of Camelot. Yet neither am I a thirty-third-degree son of a bitch. I gave the whole thing a long think, including that recent scene she had made in the office—the rock bombardment.

I shuddered to think what she might do now, on finding out that she had been given the old dry-shave. It might be bombs. Highmegaton stuff. I reminded myself that the next day I should get with Cliff Childers for a legal briefing on the foreclosure and for one other thing—a divorce.

With all these matters roiling my mind it wouldn't seem likely that any book could hold my attention for more than three and a half minutes on that particular evening. I had a glass of cold milk and then took *Desent into America* to bed with me. I looked again at the quotes on the dust jacket. I opened to Chapter One and began reading. I read without lifting my eyes from the pages until I had finished seven chapters. Then I borrowed a phrase from Big Jim Deehardt and spoke aloud to the empty room: "Christ over El Paso!"

Both the *Manchester Guardian* and the Chicago *Tribune* had been right . . . up to a point. There were, in addition, echoes of Voltaire and intimations of Swift and overtones of Ambrose Bierce and flavorings out of Norman Douglas and Saki. This was my kind of book. The feel of Shaw and the thrust of Mencken were there, and yet the author was his own guy—Ian Christchild-Muckeridge. Bitter, derisive, slashing, ironical, witty . . . a hundred pungent adjectives might be applied to that prose. And mortifying to me was the certain fact that here was a stuffy Englishman—a wispy, woolgathering guy who venerated somebody named Frederick Locker-Lampson—knowing far more about America than I do, understanding my people better than I do, and writing as if eighteen of the wickedest demons in hell were guiding his hand.

I made it halfway through Chapter Eleven before I fell into exhausted sleep. I didn't even turn off the light.

Chapter Twenty-one incorporating the
complete lyrics of The Ballad of Rustler
Smith

21

It takes an advanced intelligence to qualify for manic-depressive but The Rustler made it with ease. The next word I had of his creative schemings came from the lips of Idaho Tunket at noon-time on a Tuesday, the week following the concerns and contrivances narrated in the preceding chapter. It was possibly the worst day I ever went through in my life. Dreck Tuesday.

Let's take the affairs of that day in order and begin with the story of the shattered typewriter.

At 6 A.M., having slept like an on-duty deputy sheriff, I went straight from the house to Kohlick's, aching a little for the superb lady of the Two Cross T (as I ached every day now, especially in the early morning hours) and I joined Cee Minus Hoffelinck at a table-for-two and ordered buckwheat cakes con Grandma's Natural Unsulphured Molasses.

Cee Minus, whose title derived from his scholarly achievements at Caliche High twenty years back, was asking me if it were true that Mungo Oldbuck really has the exact same gun that Bob Ford he used to bring down ole Jesse James while Jesse was standin' on a chair and hangin' up a framed picture . . . and I was about to respond that Mungo *claimed* he had the very same pissoliver, when my trusty assistant Gene Shallow came through the street door, moving somewhat faster than his customary pace, which is precisely the speed with which a hookworm larva travels through the gristle of a sharecropper's big toe.

I had not downed more than three bites of my breakfast when Gene spotted me and came rumbling and puffing over to my table.

" 'Mergency!" he gasped. "I been to your house. You wasn't there. Figgered out you might be here. Come on. To the office. Big 'mergency! Where the dickens was you last night? For heaven sake! I looked ever'where!"

"Well *say* it!" I all but yelled at him. "What the hell is it?"

"You won't bleeve it with your own eyes. Come on. Your poor typewriter. Total wreck. Hurry up."

He continued this kind of disjointed talk as we hustled along the street.

"It was Fern," he finally revealed. "Brought her own hammer. Musta been close to six, after you left last night. Busted it all to the dickens. Just stood there and whaled away . . ."

"Busted *what* all to the dickens?" I demanded.

"It was a ball peen, Grady, and she kep' turnin' it around and usin' both ends. I mean both ends of the head part."

We whammed through the front door of the office and there it was, my beautiful Royal—the instrument through which I disseminate my wit and wisdom to a race of beings thirsting for knowledge . . . busted all to the dickens.

"I don't care what kind of a hammer it was," I told Gene Shallow. "Get to the details. Start at the beginning. When did you say it happened?"

"It was a ball peen hammer, Grady. I thought I told you that."

I was prodding around in the shattered carcass of the Royal. A total loss.

"I'll have her thrown in jail for this. She doesn't own one stick of this joint any more and she can't . . ."

"You cain't have her arrested, Grady."

"Why the hell not?"

"The judge was with her, and helped. The judge had a hammer, too."

"The judge? What judge?"

"Miz Whipple. She got in a couple of licks herself."

"My God, Gene, they must have been drunk!"

"You're approachin' motty close to the truth, Grady. They had been ebbryatin'. Dear me! Just look at that poor typewriter! This is what we call something like A Visitation. You reckon this was A Visitation?"

"You're goddamn right it was A Visitation. With ears on. They must have said something. What did they say, Gene?"

"It was hard to make out, the two of them was so ebbryated, and most of it was takin' the name of the Lord Thy God in vain and even worse. Only thing I could make out, made halfway sense, was Fern kep' yellin' that you blank would'n be writin' out your blankin' life story on *this* blankin' typewriter . . . I declare, Grady, I do believe it was A Visitation . . ."

"But not from on high," I said. I couldn't bear to look at the wreckage any longer. I had to sit down and think. Nothing made any sense, certainly not this violent vengeful eruption of my estranged helpmate. I was perplexed by Daff Whipple's participation in the raid, but then I remembered that when she got to fooling around with a jug of wobble-jaw she sometimes took on the guise of an avenging angel with profane tongue. And I always had a feeling that she had a bug up her ass on account of my refusal to call at her house for a second helping of chicken-and-dumplings.

There were two aspects of this drunken invasion that I couldn't have known about until later: cause, and then effect. In time I learned about the letter from Bertha Wollenschlager. Of all the letters that might come to me in Caliche, this was the one the post office people chose to deliver to the wrong place—to the sagging homestead of the Mobeetie clan, where I had once been a tenant in good standing.

Bertha Wollenschlager was a girl who did woman's work on the New York *Times* when I was there, and we dated a lot. She was stacked, and blond, with a Dutch complexion, and just as loving as a girl can get—she could throw off her clothes quicker than hell can scorch a feather.

Bertha did occasional reviews for the Sunday book section and knew her way around amongst the lit'ry crowd. Eventually she quit the paper and established a small-caliber literary agency. She was still at it and her agency continued small but well respected. In our time together she gave me everything but the heartbreak of psoriasis, right up to the moment of my fatal meeting with Fern Mobeetie in the lobby of the Broadhurst.

Fern knew that Bertha Wollenschlager had been my girl friend and the two met one afternoon at the *Times*. Mobeetie's behavior contained all of the saccharine gentility that is reputed to characterize the southern belle. Later on, after I married her, she always remembered my ex-bedmate with Lone Star understanding and tolerance, speaking of her as Horsefrau Wollenschflucker, The Limburger Cesspool, That Four-Cornered Crotch, and, in a burst of lovely creativity, That Tub of Dutch Snot.

Slight flashback:

About ten days before the assault upon my typewriter, I had

begun reflecting cautiously on the Wister-Virginian story that was unfolding before my eyes in Blackleg County. I had no idea which direction it might take but it had to go somewhere, and there was bound to be a dramatic culmination of one kind or another. So on impulse I sat down and wrote Bertha in New York, hinting around at some of the angles and asking if she thought I were capable of putting the whole thing together in a book. My idea was not so much concerned with the literary aspect of the drama, but with the impact, if any, it would have on an isolated village in the West Texas cattle country. Something, perhaps, on the order of Ruggles coming to Red Gap.

Bertha's response was in the letter delivered at Fern's house and swiftly slit open by Fern herself. I should set to work at once, said Bertha, on a book about *all* my adventures in Caliche, turning out an honest portrait of the town and its people and, threading in and out of this picture, the story of the modern-day confrontation of The Virginian and Trampas.

I still don't know if the prospect of my Telling All in a book was the triggering element, setting off the Mobeetie explosion; or if it could have been the complimentary close Bertha had tacked on her letter, to wit: "I really miss Big Charlie." You guess.

So Bertha's letter had been The Cause. And The Effect? Grounds for a divorce. Now I could get myself unshackled. It is said that the Texas divorce laws are sharply slanted in favor of the wife; but not when the wife is stoned to the adenoids and wielding a ball peen hammer.

End flashback.

I got out my camera and took several shots of the battered typewriter.

"We gonna run a picture of it in the paper?" Gene Shallow wanted to know.

"No, we gonna show a picture to a judge. Grady is gonna get himself a divorce."

"This is kinda sudden, ain't it?"

"Twelve years ain't sudden, Gene."

At twelve o'clock I weltied around to Kholick's and invited myself, as was my news-gathering custom, to sit in with a couple of dynamic civic leaders. Almost all the gentry take their noon meals at home, where they can climb on a couch and have a twenty-minute nap after shoveling in a four-pound bolus. At table with me were Caddo Pope and Cliff Childers, whose wives had gone to San Antonio to shop and catch up on dirty shows.

"Welcome to the club!" Caddo sang out.

I think I have indicated elsewhere that juicy news travels with the speed of light in the City of Caliche and these two gents were already acquainted with every detail of the assault on my type-writer; the story, in fact, was already current in San Antonio. Cliff Childers said that Veenie had phoned him and told him how Fern had got red-assed when somebody in New York tipped her off that I had written a book spilling the beans on the whole town of Caliche.

"I'd like to have an autographed copy when it comes out," said Cliff.

I got down on my knees and begged for news items and Caddo said his sister-in-law from Beeville was spending a few days in town, and gave me her name and identified her as a person who knows everything in all the encyclopedias and has been every place mentioned in the atlases and once shook hands with Lyndon John-son at Love Field in Dallas.

Burdened with this great scoop I prepared to depart and on my way out spotted Idaho Tunket sitting at a table by himself, com-mitting assault on a breaded catfish fourteen inches long.

"Come in to pick up the mail and buy some butter," he told me when I sat down. "Supprizes me the Boss will let me set butter on the table the way he has it against cows."

"So what's been going on down there?"

"I'm fixin' to make some onion soup the way they do it in a place called Norman's in the town of Nice, and I don't have a speck of Gruyère, and that's another item I got to pick up, except I won't be able to find any. I declare one of these days I'm gonna load a pickup fulla freezer chests and drive to Houston and get me a thou-sand dollars worth of supplies." He paused for another forkful of catfish, then continued, "You mean to say you ain't heard about Rustler and his antics? That man is about to drive me clean outa my mind. What he did was he got himself a lenth of one-inch rope and made a hangman's noose and now, once er twice a day, he goes out to that tree back of the house, you've noticed it, Grady, must be forty foot high. Old Smith has located a stout limb on that tree that would be suitable fer hangin' somebody, so he stands out there ten er fifteen minutes ever' day, throwin' that noose over the limb like he was practicin' up fer a hangin', and he keeps singin' a little song he's made up to go along with the practicin'."

I persuaded Idaho to sing The Rustler's song, begging him to keep it low, and so he furnished me with the words of the ballad, fitted to a melody that I'm sure was out of true. It went something like this:

Innybody on this here ranch,
Gits smort with me-ee,
He's gonna stand aw-awn
Nothin' a-tall, a-tall,
An' he's gonna kick at
The Yew-Nided States of,
Ay-MERRR-ee-kuh,
Till he cain't kick,
Inny more.

The rendition was praiseworthy by reason of Idaho's skillful impersonation of Rustler Smith, both in voice and in facial contortions. Yet Mungo's cook didn't enjoy my laughter.

"Nothin' funny about it," he objected. "That oak tree is in plain view when I'm standin' at my choppin' block in the kitchen, and Old Smith's carryin' on out there makes me nervous."

"Oh, now, Idaho. You don't think he's got you in mind for a lynching, do you?"

"That ain't the point. Look, Grady. I grew up in a mean town called Eagle Pass, where inny ole piece of rope, even a lenth of clothesline, will give a man a case of the nerves. He keeps throwin' that noose over that limb and I git to shakin' like a dog passin' peach seeds. I told the Boss yesterdy if he don't put a stop to it I'll have to quit. He said he'd talk to Smith some time today and order him to git rid of the rope. And I says, 'Order him also to quit singin' the fuckin' song—that's even worse'n the rope.'"

I disagree with Idaho's disparagement of the song. In any compendium of stirring western ballads, The Song of Rustler Smith belongs right up there alongside "The Streets of Laredo" and "High Chin Bob with Sinful Pride."

Thus Dreck Tuesday—another slumberous and serene day in Our Town. Yet it was not quite over. I had to tell Asia about The Visitation. I got her on the phone and gave her the story in detail.

I even confessed to my long-ago affair with Bertha Wollenschlager and told her about the exchange of letters, and how Bertha's response led to Fern's coming unglued. Through this narrative Asia offered no comment beyond an occasional non-committal "Mmmmmmm." When I got through the whole cruddy story I said:

"What do you think?"

"All circumstances taken into account," she said, "I don't think I'd better comment."

"Come on, Asia!"

"Your wife doesn't want you to write the book?"

"Apparently not."

"I want you to write it, and I think you *could* write it, and it would be a good book."

"I love you."

"And I have a dandy title for it. *Peyton Place West.*"

"Asia, you ring my chimes."

"Really? When?"

"Usually in the morning, more often in the afternoon, always at night, and later in my dreams. And I would like to say further that you are a consummation devoutly to be wished."

I said that, being fifty-seven years of age and an orphan.

I don't apologize for it.

Chapter Twenty-two devoted largely to
an exposure of another great literary
hoax

22

At the close of the tranquil day we've had under discussion I
propped myself up on the pillows and went through Ian
Christchild-Muckeridge's book from beginning to end, this time
taking notes. I had a reason for this second scrutiny of the book,
over and beyond the pleasure I got from its spirit and form and
language. There had been a line that evoked a vague response—
something having to do with anti-Semitism.

Between nine and ten the next morning I telephoned Bertha
Wollenschlager in New York.

First off I gave her a résumé of the donnybrook touched off by
her letter having fallen into the hands of my precious wife.

"Great!" said the Hun. "Put it in your book!"

"I'm not writing a book, Dutch."

"Well then, get the hell busy. Pile it all in. You may turn out
to be the Sinclair Lewis of the seventies."

"I have a word for that," I said, "but I always suspect some
old-maid telephone company lady is listening in."

"Then I'll say it for you." She said it.

"I didn't call you about *my* book, Bertha. What do you know
about a bloke who calls himself Ian Christchild-Muckeridge?"

"Only everything. You mean the pony express hasn't got through
to you yet with the news about Ian? He's all of a sudden something
of a sensation in the trade, on account of a book called *Descent
into America.* It won't be on sale for another two weeks but people
are talking up a storm. It's going to . . ."

"I've read it, Dutch. I agree that it's brilliant. What I want to
know is: where has this guy been?"

"Up to now he's been a colossal pipsqueak. A limey drudge.
A hack straight out of Grub Street. A scribbler of . . ."

"That's almost a physical description of the guy," I said.

"What do you mean, Grady? What do you know about him?"

"He's out here. Living out here."

"Out where, for God's sake? In Texas?"

"I see him all the time. You remember Mungo Oldbuck, don't you?"

"Of course. Everybody remembers Mungo Oldbuck. He's in Texas too, I've heard."

"Certainly he's in Texas. He has a beautiful ranch about sixty miles from where I'm sitting. He's become a good friend of mine, and your limey drudge is living in a cabin on his place."

"My God, Grady. Everybody in New York has been searching high and low for the lug. His publishers say they think he's hiding out somewhere in Mexico. I'll tip the *Times* gang the minute I hang up."

"Hold it, Dutch. Don't tell anybody yet. I didn't realize this Englisher was making a big score with anyone but me."

"He'll scrape down a million dollars."

"Listen, kid. I'm working on something that may be real important. I mean more important than a nobody Britisher making a million. I've got to know a little more about Christchild Et Cetera. What's he written before?"

"C-R-A-P. Cheap novels. Stories about true and undying love, with intense suffering, in mildewed castles and on the moors of Midlothian and Flodden Field and all that slow drip. Nobody has ever figured out why Mungo Oldbuck took him on. Mungo published his last novel, a passable story that some reviewers said was a direct steal from Ivy Compton-Burnett or Edgar Wallace or one of the Bronte broads or somebody. Then *bingo! Descent into America!* Listen, Grady, I've just got to tell the *Times* where he is."

"Promise me you won't and I can almost guarantee you a better story. I've got to get ahead with my newspaper drivel today and then I'm heading for the ranch to have a talk with the blighter."

She gave me a few additional bits of information. Christchild-Muckeridge had been in this country maybe ten years. He had been the only author in the entire Oldbuck stable with whom Mungo would break bread. Consequently there was talk. "Homo talk," was the way Bertha put it.

I worked like a dog to get ahead on the aforementioned office drivel and then lit for the tules again, driving straight for The

Pueblo and averting my eyes from Asia's gateway as I went past it. Moonstruck over a cattle guard!

I rapped on the door of the cabin and the Englishman responded. He had on a bathrobe and slippers and was unshaven, presenting the appearance of a hung-over Leslie Howard, yet he was courtly in his greeting as he led me into his little living room, which served also as his workshop.

I told him that the Caliche *Mud Dobber* had never carried a line about his distinguished presence in Blackleg County and that I wanted to compose a sketch about him, the nature of his work, and including by all means his opinion of his adopted home and the people of the area.

"Of course," he said agreeably. "Quite. But it is nawt my adopted home, old boy. And I regard the people of Blackleg County to be boorish peasants whose armpits smell."

I changed course.

"It's common knowledge, Ian, that Mungo Oldbuck gave up the publishing business because he has an intense distaste for authors, and yet you are an author whose company he seems to enjoy. How do you explain that?"

I was carefully hiding the fact that I had read his new book and I had no intention of telling him what Bertha had said about it on the phone.

There was something of a glint in his drab brown eyes as he answered my question.

"One nosty bounder in New York," he said, "a colyumnist as I remembuh, implied that Mungo and I were quee-uh. How *do* you newspapering chaps go about it, turning up everyone's secrets, cawn't keep a bloody thing from you, New York *Times* and Washington *Post* and Caliche *Mud Slopper* all in the same bossket! Tell me, old boy, haven't you observed me hanging round the sheepfold? Hah! A good one, wot? Capital!"

I broke in to advise him that I was being quite serious.

"Dash it all, Grady," he went right on, "you must let me spread the wanton truth before you. I am thinking about emulating that cinema fellow you have in Hollywood—the one who plays at light housekeeping with nanny goats."

"Ian," I said firmly, "I really came here to tell you that the jig is up. I know that you didn't write *Descent into America*."

His watery eyes bulged and he began some fingering operations on his lip hair.

"You have gone out of your bloody mind!" he finally stammered.

I just sat and stared into his face. I was throwing a bit of a bluff, don'tcha know, but I was fairly sure of my ground.

He suddenly bounced out of his chair.

"If you'll be so kind as to excuse me for a few minutes," he said nervously, "I need to run up to The Pueblo and get some aspirin. Please make yourself comfortable. Shawn't be a mome."

And off he went.

I was convinced now, more than ever, that this clod could never have composed a single page of *Descent into America,* even with Shaw and Mencken and Anatole France standing by to give him pointers and tell him where to put commas.

This conviction was sustained by a quick inspection of the dozen or so books scattered around his workroom. Novels by people with such names as Coningsby Allingham, Enid Bottomley, Basil Bagshawe, Pamela Sitwell, Clive Cutliffe, A. A. Wyndham-Mitford, and Nigel Beerbohm. In the entire lot I spotted only one volume written by an American, *And Then We Moved to Rossen-arra,* by Richard Condon. I picked this one up and flipped through the opening pages and my eye fell on the word *pudibundous* and I quickly put the damn thing down.

So . . . fraud established. Swindle certified. Larceny laid bare. Imposter exposed. This guy hadn't the slightest interest in America or Americans.

Next step . . . find the true author. Already done.

Christchild-Muckeridge returned looking as if he had been caught between a hawk and a buzzard (which he had) and said:

"Mungo would like to see you in his office, immediately."

I got up and started for the door and then turned back.

"I say, old chap," I sang out cheerily, "I do want to thank you for putting my crusading journal right up there with the *Times* and the Washington *Post.* Decent of you."

He tried to grin.

"I believe," he said, "that I have slid on a banonna."

Mungo had his back to me when I entered. He was standing strangely in the posture of an English gentleman, gazing out at his swales and his swards, feet wide apart, hands fastened across his rump. He turned around and tried to wither me with a glare.

"All right, you nosy bastard," he said. "How did you find out my Englishman didn't write it?"

"I respond, Mungo, with a question of my own: who *did* write it?"

"Another party. I'm not willing to tell you. I won't even tell you the other party's sex. I thought you were my friend."

"I am your friend," I assured him, "and I'm also your admirer. More so than ever now. I know who wrote *Descent into America*. And I've been on the phone to New York and they've told me that everybody's talking about the book."

He looked at me a long time and I sensed surrender.

"If you hired a dick for this job, Grady, I'll strangle you where you stand."

"I didn't need a dick." I pulled my little brown notebook out of my pocket. "It's all right here. The clerk will mark the notebook for identification and enter it in evidence."

"Quit futzing around, Grady. What's in it?"

I was ready to begin citing chapter and verse, but his manner suddenly changed.

"Wait a minute," he said, eagerness in both his tone and his posture. "You were mentioning something about the reaction in New York. What are they saying? Come on, out with it."

"*Descent into America* is already a sensation, two weeks before publication. People are nuts about it. And, Mungo, you old son of a bitch, you've got more author-hambone in you than Jacqueline Susann and Truman Capote working as a team."

The bastard actually smirked.

"The truth is, Grady," he said, "that I don't know a frigging thing about writing a book. But first, tell me how you nailed me."

"In this notebook," I told him, "I've copied down ten or twelve passages from the book. They are things I have heard you say at various times during the last few years, word for word, in precise Oldbuckian language. The one passage that set me on the trail was something I heard you say that day we were in Chug Peavy's office. You were arguing that you cannot be called a misogynist merely because you despise a handful of women. Remember? And in the book, on page thirty-six, a character named Jason speaks the same words."

"All right," he said. "But let me finish what I started to tell you before you began quoting great philosophic truths at me. So I've written a book. That is, I scribbled notes for it, and dictated most of it to the Englishman. Anybody could do it. Idaho could write a book. Put your finger on any person here on this ranch and that person could write a book. Any idiot at the idiot farm could do it. I just wanted to prove that all these insipid jerks who write books and then go around acting as if they were superior beings, every damn one of them is a flabnoggin, because even an insipid jerk like me . . . I can write a book, and a better book than they can write."

"Damn right you can. But why didn't you just sit down and write it and slap your name on it and send it off to market?"

"Grady, there exists only one slight flaw in my character. I like to bamboozle people. Look," said Mungo, "I'm still not convinced that you deduced my authorship of the book on the strength of those few quotations."

"No. There was a clincher, Mungo. The ideas in the book were palpably your ideas. They were also pretty much my ideas. Now, if Christchild-Muckeridge had written the book, that would mean that here in Blackleg County there were three of us holding the same violent off-key beliefs. It couldn't be . . . three different men with such an astute grasp of the realities, all living within the five thousand square miles of this Texas county."

"Baker Street couldn't have done a better job," said Mungo.

"One thing more. How'd you happen to pick the limey to serve as your alter ego?"

"Again, for the sake of confusion, and because of his glorious name. Mungo Oldbuck sounds like a cockney coal-heaver. I wanted a name that had the smell of Oxford and Cambridge in it, with a slight theological odor for the sake of irony, and Christchild-Muckeridge kept popping into my head and so I fetched him over from London. Worst British import since we brought over the English sparrow. Somehow I found myself stuck with him—he alone knew my secret—and so I've kept him on. But now, if you insist on spilling the beans and telling the *Times,* I'll be able to get rid of the clunk."

Chapter Twenty-three containing proof
that cattle rustling is the very same thing
as free enterprise

23

Among the three hundred and eighteen essential requirements of
a competent newsman are acute hearing, the firm conviction that
Nothing is Sacred, a passion for snooping, a firm grasp of Frederick Locker-Lampson's personal mystique, and a stomach lined
with galvanized iron. Of these five prerequisites, let us consider
the middle one.

The average small-town editor engages in very little eavesdropping; he bugs no telephones and hires no call girls to entice secrets
from politicians and preachers. The fact is, snooping is a delicious
art that belongs to the general public in the villages of our land. It
is the province of the common man.

I snoop out of long habit, and for the pleasure involved, and
because I am licensed to do it, and I am pleased to report that my
eavesdropping during the period under review turned up certain
facts which could bulk large in the literary history of the United
States. These facts concern the sublime humanity residing in the
most celebrated of our Western villains—the obnoxious Wyoming
cad known as Trampas.

Walking from The Pueblo to my car after that session with
Mungo, my path led along a whitewashed 'dobe wall, maybe six
feet high, and as I skirted this gleaming structure I heard voices
coming from the other side. I couldn't see the people, but I recognized the voices; they belonged to Holly Ann Smith and her
hangman-father. As I came to a halt Holly Ann was just finishing
off a sentence, this way:

". . . just have to be ashamed of him, just have to live with the
knowledge that he was a criminal of the worst sort, and if he hadn't
been shot he'd likely have been lynched. My own grandfather!
And everybody knows about him! I hate bringing it up all the
time, Daddy, but some day I may want to get married and even
have children, and it's an awful curse over my head."

"He wasn't no criminal," came Old Smith's voice. "He was a good man. He could lick his weight in mountain lions and he must of been orry-eyed to let that Virginian outdraw him. I had a great likin' fer him but I didn't git to know him very long. I was a little runny-nose kid when he was shot down, and the best thing I remember is standin' alongside of the coffin and lookin' at him. He whupped me once and a while but he never spoke a mean nasty word to me. After he went over the chilly hill, that undertaker he did me a big favor. He didn't know he was doin' it fer me, but he did it."

"Daddy, there really is something weird about you. Saying your best memory of him is when he was lying dead in the coffin."

The Rustler trudged stubbornly on down the road he had cut out for himself.

"I stood there and looked at my daddy," he said, "and I looked at him a long time, layin' there, and it wasn't him. It wasn't him a-tall. Some other man was layin' in that coffin. I didn't know who he was but he wasn't my daddy. You know why, girl?"

"You're talking in circles, but go ahead."

"I'll tell you why it wasn't my daddy. I don't remember I ever saw him without three things in his mouth. First, he'd load in a good dose of snuff, lined under his lower lip, made it puff out sorta, the lower lip. Then he'd shove in a could of Brown Mule chewin' tobacco in the left-hand cheek of his face, a good-size could."

"A what?"

"A could. A could of chewin' tobacco. Size of a jar of mentholadum. When he got the snuff in and the Brown Mule, then he'd stick this big cigar in the right-hand side of his mouth and most of the time it wouldn't be lit. Mornin' to night. All the time. Like I say, fer all I know he maybe slep' with all three of them items in his mouth. So I walked up to that coffin half-dead from grievin' because he was my daddy and I admard him, and there he laid. Lower lip flatted out. No Copenhagen. No Brown Mule could in his face. No cigar. It wasn't him. It was somebody else. I said, hell, my daddy ain't dead."

The Rustler paused as if reflecting back, and I stood my ground. Then Holly Ann spoke.

"Tell me some more about him. Something about his family background."

"Sure, girl. Let me see now. Well, he couldn't read ner write ner even sign his name, but he always kep' a pencil around the house, and told me to keep my goddamn hands off of it, and whatta you spose he kep' it for?"

"Did he sketch with it?"

"Wrong. He used it to make a mark on a board soze he could saw it straight."

That didn't seem to satisfy Holly Ann's thirst for family background.

"What made him want to become an outlaw?" she asked.

"Now, you listen to me, girl. He wasn't no outlaw. He was only a rustler, the same like I become when I grew up. I follered in my father's footsteps—took up his line of work—the American Way. It's what they call free entaprise. Ever' man for himself. You go out with a runnin' arn and change the brand on a cow and that takes a lot of savvy and hard labor and stayin' up late, and things gotta be planned out same as a bank robbery, and maybe you burn the bejezus outa your hands. For what? You're entitled to a profit, ain't you? So whirr you gonna git it if you don't take the cow? It's as simple as that. If the former owner ain't got any more sense than to leave his cow run around loose like a wild animal, if he don't look after that cow, then it's what we call tough tiddy."

Holly Ann mumbled a vague protest against his use of business English and I decided that the day's lesson in rangeland economics was over for me, and I departed. I would be a better man for it. In the future I would be able to handle myself better in commercial transactions, to hold my own in the marketplace. I headed out for Asia Battle's house.

I didn't stop to see her, it being a regulation in the game of love, Kentucky style, that if one side plays coy and hard to get, then the other side should assume an attitude of indifference . . . for a little while. So I drove airily past the *palacio* and pulled up at Jeff's cottage. I had to go looking for him. Jaybird Huddleston was at the big barn, shaking the hell out of a bottle of cow paregoric or somesuch concoction and he said Jeff had gone out to pull more sucker rods and change more leathers and do various other things a cowboy needs to do to a windmill to keep it from running backwards against the breeze. So I returned to the cottage to wait, and to glance over some books I found stacked on the floor in a corner of the living room. They were books, I soon decided, that Holly Ann had given to Jeff in her heinous plot to educate him.

There were seven or eight books in the pile. I had tried to read a couple of them when they first came out and I'd heard of the others and seen pictures of their goat-faced authors in journals of the New Criticism. Please understand that in literary matters I insist upon granting the other fellow his point of view. There's room for all kinds in this great polyglot democracy of ours. I shall assume no posture of intolerance toward the authors of those seven or eight books, no position of parochial fogyism. I shall be content to say that their authors represent as ratty a crew as ever stunk up the back alleys of Manhattan Island since the Canarsee Indians lived there and each day anointed their bodies with sulphur water and vulture spit.

When Jeff came in from the windmill fixin' he caught me with the books and he forestalled anything in the way of a fatherly lecture by saying they belonged to Holly Ann and that he hadn't been able to make any sense out of them. I delivered my lecture anyway, cutting it way down, saying simply that the books in the pile added up to a large crock of waste material, and I cut that last expression down from thirteen letters to four. And of their authors, I only said that we should try to be broad-minded toward them, except for their hairiness and their life-style and the waste material that flows from their typewriters.

Jeff passed over the book talk. He was almost frothing with excitement, and had big news for me concerning the progress of Emily's training program. He led me into the kitchen and opened the freezer compartment of his refrigerator and waved a hand at a dozen quart containers of ice cream: Cherry Vanilla, Banana Nut, Chocolate Chip, Fro-Zan Neapolitan, Verdant Pistachio, and some other exotic flavors.

"You're gonna have to help me eat this stuff," he said. "Emily's already made up her mind what she likes best. Come on out here."

We stepped onto his little back porch and he pointed at a chest type freezer.

"Got it at Fugglin's," he said. "On sale." He lifted the lid to expose a solid phalanx of half-gallon containers.

"Big Dish Strawberry Swirl," he said. "The first time I got out a carton of it, before I could take the lid off, she smelled it and stood up on her back legs and knocked it outa my hands and tore it open and gobbled down the Swirl and then tried to eat the carton. She really does ape for Strawberry Swirl."

"*Goes,*" I muttered. "*Goes* ape!" There's a difference.

"Emily," he now told me, "is smarter than childern. She knew that I was trainin' her to change her way of findin' water. Soon as I got her on the Big Dish Strawberry Swirl, and let her know *that* would be her reward if she did her work, she was easy to manage. When I tell her to go find wah-wah, she sniffs along the ground the way she always did. Then when she hits the spot she lets out a little squeal, followed by three grunts, and just stands there."

"She doesn't root?"

"No. She just stands in her tracks and gives me a mournful look, which means she wants her ice cream."

"Do you think there's deep water where she squeals and grunts?"

"I'd stake my Uncle Gatlin's money on it."

"Well, Jeff," I said, "we've now reached the point where we've got to prove up our pig. We've got to drill a well. I want you to take Emily out and let her witch water in some unlikely stretch of sand, and then we'll get Billy Yewclid down here with his drilling rig. Let's go up to the house right now and phone him. You could run Emily over the ground tomorrow and maybe we could get Billy down the next day."

We used the extension phone in the kitchen and I located Billy at his house, where he was working at his hobby: watching soap operas. I gave him the rundown, complete and entire, and he demonstrated no eagerness over the project.

"Did you say a pig?" he wanted to know, shouting the words into the phone—the "connection" is always thought to be bad between town and the outlying ranches, and people yell.

"A pig," I assured him.

"And this pig witched the well?"

"Right."

"I wouldn't touch it with a ten-foot pole, Grady," he hollered.

"Why the hell not?"

"It'd ruin my reputation. I got enough common horse sense not to set up and drill a well that has been witched by a pig. I wouldn't be able to hold my head up in public, anywhere in Texas. No sirree bob, sir! You put a pig to doin' the Lord's work and you might as well pick up your things and move to Paris, France."

"What do you mean, the Lord's work?"

"That's what it is. Darn near every switcher I've ever met tells me The Power is not his. It comes straight from the Lord. You can't fart around with a thing like that, Grady. It's dynamite. *Dyne-uh-mite!*"

"Then you won't drill this well for us?"

"No, Grady. I'm sorry. But my mama didn't raise no idiot children."

"Then you know what you can do with your rig."

"I won't do that, neither. Too much arn on it."

I hung up and sat and thought for a minute or two. Jeff interrupted my ecclesiastical meditation to ask what the man had said. I told him. Then I got Directory Assistance, which I still call Information, and after a lot of backing and filling on the part of Directory Assistance, a well driller named Smiley Kock was on the phone. Mr. Kock operates out of Uvalde and just to intimidate him a little I asked if he uses a cable rig or a rotary and he said cable and that his equipment was the best—Bucyrus-Erie stuff out of Milwaukee. So I said we had this job for him down in dry country south of Caliche.

"We've witched it," I said. A feeler.

"Good. Who you usin'? I know a heap of witches around your part of the country."

"This one's a female," I said, cautiously.

"A woman witch? They're purty rare. It ain't Flat Hat Irene, is it?"

"This one's name is Emily."

"Emily what?"

"Dickinson," I said.

"Sounds real innarestin'," said Smiley Kock. "When you want me?"

"Any time you can come." I gave him the location.

"Motty fine, Mr. Grady," he said. "Be seein' you."

That was it. I turned to Jeff. He wanted to know if the driller was comin'.

"He's comin'," I said. "Everything seems to be motty fine."

Chapter Twenty-four in which we contrast
the witching techniques of Flat Hat Irene
and Cee Minus Hoffelinck

24

The question of money was now riding into view and so we called an immediate conference beside Asia's pool. Jaybird Huddleston didn't attend; he told us he was getting ready to retire himself away from all human endeavor and he wasn't about to get himself involved with anything so time-consuming as a conglomerated pig.

Asia had changed her mind, out of a growing fondness for Emily, and now she asked me to blueprint the proposition for the board of directors.

First, I said, I felt the need of hiring at least two water witches of the human variety. This would mean that Smiley Kock would have to drill at least three wells. The witching and the drilling were necessary in the production of corroborative evidence.

"It costs a lot of money to ram a hole in the ground from five hundred to a thousand feet deep," I explained, "and Smiley Kock will have to ram three such holes. I move that we split the overall cost three ways."

"Overruled," Asia spoke up quickly. "I'll let you guys pay for the witches. I'll foot the bill for the drilling. Keep in mind that we may get some water, and that's something I can use."

"My guess," I said, "is that Smiley's bill will run to about ten thousand dollars."

"Overhead," said Asia. And that settled it.

Back in town I went to Flat Hat Irene Wickett, the poet of heavenly redemption, and asked her if she'd be willing to go out to the Two Cross T and witch a well for Asia Battle.

Flat Hat Irene is adroit in the use of innuendo.

"I don't like you, you son of a bitch," she said. "But God gave me the gift, The Power, and I wouldn't turn down that Jane Fonda creep if she needed water."

The pig had not been mentioned to Flat Hat. From the reaction of Billy Yewclid I knew that we were venturing onto dangerous ground. Human water witches would give short shrift to a pig water witch.

By the time Flat Hat Irene and I arrived at the ranch, Jeff had put Emily through her paces and the pig had selected a spot in the northern part of the ranch. She had squealed and grunted and cast the imploring eye on Jeff and he had given her the half gallon of Big Dish Strawberry Swirl. I told Jeff to mark the spot with a rock and he had done so with a boulder weighing about twenty pounds. Anything under twenty pounds would be blown away by the zephyrs which waft steadily across the sands of West Texas.

Jeff and Irene and I jeeped out to the site where Emily had performed her chore. It was a dry and desolate landscape, but Flat Hat exhibited no sign of displeasure. She had, in fact, developed an interest in Jefferson Cordee.

"Boy," she said to him, "why in hell didn't you drill Old Smith right between the eyes while you had him at your mercy? If you'd a done that and then killed this newspaper creep, you'd a made Texas a better place to live."

Jeff just gave her his wry charming smile.

Flat Hat's wand was a fork cut from a peach tree. She carried it in an old violin case and after we dismounted from the jeep she got it out and showed it to Jeff, ignoring me.

"Peach," she said. "No other kinda stick is worth a shit." It looked like an oversized slingshot and she grasped it by both prongs. I quickly pointed to the boulder and said we had a feeling there was a dome of water in that area.

"Try your wand about where that rock is," I said, and she promptly struggled down to her knees and began mumbling a prayer.

She got to her feet and began cocking her head around, surveying the entire prospect. Then she settled her gaze on the spot we wanted dowsed.

"Did somebody say right under that old rock? I get the message says that's an unlikely spot. That rock, that's palladium oxhide. Any time you see palladium oxhide, you ain't likely to find water. Less see what the old peach tree has to say about it."

She started walking toward the rock, slowly, looking first at the ground, then up to heaven, then back to earth.

"Don't make noises," she said. "Don't talk none. If I fall down on the ground, don't touch me. If there happens to be a powerful body of water underneath me, sometimes I throw a fit. Most of the time, though, it's only a splittin' headache and a nauseous feelin' in the gut. Mind now. Quiet."

She came up to the palladium oxhide rock, holding the forked stick straight out in front of her overorganized chest, and now she was mumbling and muttering biblical incantations. Her head was thrown back and her body was tensed, but she continued walking forward and one foot hit the edge of the rock and over she went into the sand, right on top of her magic wand.

"Son . . . of . . . a . . . bee . . . ITCH!" she howled. "Why didn't you bastards *holler* at me!"

Jeff and I helped her to her feet and she used a forefinger to ream the sand and gravel out of her mouth.

"Min!" she snorted. "More like little childern! Well, there's one thing I know for goddamn sure. No water. A body can always depend on palladium oxhide formations. Not a drop anywhere near it. Now what you want me to do?"

"Head away from here," I said, "in any direction you feel like going, and see if you can locate any trace of water."

"If it's here, I'll find it."

She glanced around at those directions available to her and chose one, I guessed, where the footing would be easy and where there were no palladium oxhide boulders. To me she presented a spectacular appearance as she zigzagged across the ground in her piebald green-and-yellow dress, the peach stick thrust forward, her face wreathed in which she believed to be an expression of sanctified grace.

Ten or twelve minutes passed and then she began to grunt and gurgle, and her footsteps were faltering, and we could see the peach stick jerking and twisting in her grip, and then it dipped sharply and pointed toward the ground. Flat Hat Irene let out a shriek as if labor had set in, dropped the wand, and clasped both hands to her stomach. The nauseous feeling had set in.

Her indisposition was of short duration, passing away in a flash. She raised her head and announced:

"Eighteen hundret forty gallons per minute. You want me to tell you how deep? That'll be another fifteen dollars."

"Go ahead."

She retrieved her peach stick, took hold of the prongs again, and went into a squat. The most beautiful woman in the world

looks hideous in a squat; Flat Hat Irene resembled nothing so
much as a giant toad. Once again she stuck the wand straight out
in front of her body.

"How far down?" she sang out, speaking to the stick. It began
to move in her hands, bobbing up and down, and with each bob
she counted. The rhythmic jerking continued until she hit seventy
and then the wand steadied itself. She strained her heaven-sent
faculties and in the doing her squat failed her and she tumbled
over on her side, as if in slow motion, the wood still gripped in
her hands.

The thought crossed my mind that life is no bed of roses for
those blest with The Power, those tetched ones who have more
sensitized souls than the rest of us.

Flat Hat echoed my thought. "Wear a body out," she gasped.
"Wake up in the night sometimes, countin' and countin' and my
hands jerkin' up and down, countin' how far down it is to Hell."

"Seventy feet," I said, thinking of the drilling expense. "It could
have been worse."

"It's not seventy feet," proclaimed Flat Hat Irene. "It's seven
hundret. When the water's over a hundret foot down, the rod dips
once for every ten foot. If I had to squat down there and count
up to seven hundret with this peach limb dippin' seven hundret
times, you'd have to take me straight to the hospital because my
hands would come right off at the wrist. That'll be twinny-five for
what I call the house call and fifteen for depth and the day you hit
water you'll owe me another sixty."

I paid her the forty.

The next day I hauled Number Two Witch out from town. Cee
Minus Hoffelinck. Cee is a retired carpenter and scientist and says
his witching is not divinely inspired.

"I pursue the ordained scientific principles," he told me. "These
people who claim that God guides their hand, or their puny little
sticks, they are ridiculous. Pure superstition. What I get from God
is my ordained scientific principles. He gives me them and then
he leaves me alone. I take it from there. He told me in a dream
that twigs off of peach trees and willow trees and the like, they are
no good. He said brass. Brass rods. I fell asleep in a chair, setting
in front of television, and I had this vision, and He says to me,
He says, 'Like Likes Like.' He says Brass is like Water, and in

the final analysis, Brass will locate Water. Makes good sense, don't it? What I say is piddle on peach tree sticks."

I told Cee Minus that I had heard how he had used his talents to help Mayor Ford Winkler construct a silver box for witching water.

"He paid me for it," was the answer.

We started Cee Minus off at the palladium oxhide rock. His brass rods were about a foot and a half long and he held them parallel and pointed straight up. I had a feeling he was getting ready to knit himself a coat of mail. He was more resolute and purposeful in his movements than Flat Hat Irene had been. He marched straight up to the boulder, keeping the rods erect. They remained erect.

"Nothing here," he said. "Not a whisper."

"When you hit a good spot," I asked him, "do you feel sick?"

"Course not. That's superstition. If it's a good find, sometimes I get shooting pains in my bunion." He reached in his coat pocket and pulled out a small medicine bottle and showed it to me.

"Water-miscible benzote," he said. "My own formula. I don't trust druggists. This is the best thing you can put on a flaming bunion. I'll mix you up a batch soon as I get back to the house."

"I don't have a bunion," I assured him.

"I'll see you get a bottle," he said.

Jeff now suggested that Cee Minus go it on his own, and the ex-carpenter lit out briskly through the cactus. He'd walk in a straight line a distance of perhaps thirty yards, then make an abrupt right-angle turn like a soldier on the drill field, proceed another thirty yards, then sharp left, and so on. He'd vary the pattern to keep himself from vanishing over the horizon and after a while we saw him come to a halt near a scrubby clump of mesquite. He was too far away for us to see the rods, but his arms were moving up and down and Jeff and I trudged off to join him.

"Got me a sizzle-sozzle fence-lifter this time," he said. Then rather dramatically he lifted his right foot off the ground and gave it a few hard shakes. The bunion was aching.

"Get us the depth," I suggested, believing that he ought to keep going while he was hot.

"I don't give depth," he said. "These people with their twigs jumping up and down, they give me the pure-dee whimwhams. How could a twig tell you the number of feet you have to dig to get at the water? Couldn't do it in a coon's age. Can a twig off of a willow tree think? Can a twig add and subtract and maltiply? Suppose you got a call from a rancher in Europe, say in Germany, where my people came from. You are a twig-man and so you take your twig and go over there and witch up some water, or pretend to witch it up, and this German rancher says, give him the depth, and so you put your twig to work jerking up and down and when it stops you say three hundred and thirty-three foot. God zooks! What a mess you got yourself in! They don't measure by the foot in Germany. They measure by the meter and the meter is about three foot. Can that twig *think* in German? I ask you!"

Cee Minus now sat down on the sand and began taking off his shoe so he could dose his bunion with water-miscible benzote.

"I cain't give you the depth," he rambled on, "but this I can tell you: you got a good one here. This bunion of mine is on fire. Lord-a-mercy! Niagara Falls must be down there!"

Jeff went searching for a rock to mark the spot and I asked Cee Minus if I could have a look at his rods.

"I'd rather you didn't handle them," he said. "There's an infinity between a man and his rods. Other people go to handling them and the chain gets disrupt. I had a grandfather in the Old Country was one of the last of the *Braunschweiger* dowsers. He hung a Brunswick sausage on the end of a silk thread and had the thread tied to his cane, which had been cut from a Swedish ash. Did you happen to know that water witchin' was invented by my people? I mean the Germans?"

"What happened with the *Braunschweiger* when it got over water?" I wanted to know.

"Teeter-tottered on the end of that thread. My grandfather was of the old school and what I started to tell you was that he died of despair and frustration at the age of eighty-seven. When he was in his early seventies a female cousin of his, an ignorant woman from Schleswig-Holstein, came to visit the family and he caught her with the *Braunschweiger,* ready to drop it in the skillet. He rasseled it away from her, but he was too late. He claimed that her handling of it, and her *intention* toward it, took all the Force out of it and took all The Power out of *him* at the same time. He was never able to witch another well after that and spent his declining years not speaking to people. Never spoke a single word after that *Braunschweiger* went dead on him."

There is more to water witchin' than meets the eye.

Following those two days of anthropomorphic witching and then the arrival of Smiley Kock with his drilling rig, I wore out a lot of rubber between Caliche and the Two Cross T.

On Jeff's instruction Smiley drilled first at the location where Flat Hat Irene had peach-pronged water at seven hundred feet. He cussed all through that operation as he did through the drilling of the well Cee Minus Hoffelinck found with his brass rods. Since he came from Uvalde I couldn't escape the suspicion that Smiley had absorbed his remarkable talent for cussing at the knee of Old Jack Garner—the same knee where Lyndon Johnson is said to have acquired his fluency.

Smiley Kock was unique in the cussing arts. He was a true musician. His barnyard strophes were always set to a beat. Sometimes when his machinery was running he'd stand off from the rig and cuss quietly, but in rhythm. In exigency he would lift his face toward the sky, spread his arms with the palms turned upward in an attitude of invocation, and cry:

Jee-   Christ   Him   Croo-   fied!
   zuss   and   the   see-

His poetic words could be heard above the clank and grumble of the rig. When he was getting ready to dig Cee Minus Hoffelinck's hole I observed him nailing a two-by-four rail onto his platform. He'd swing the hammer back and bring it down forcefully on the nailhead, following up with a second sharp blow, then the long backward swing, and again the two quick strokes, all done in perfect cadence. He set words to his nail driving just as he set words to the swish and thump of the rig. On this occasion he was bellowing his profane hymn . . .

Jee-   Christ   God   wood
   zuss   this   damn

  hard   poor   prick!
Is   as a   man's

There was no water at seven hundred feet in Flat Hat Irene's hole. We had him drill on to a thousand and the bit didn't even work up a sweat. He went down the same distance on the Hoffelinck-witched well and the grit at a thousand feet was dryer than the sand on the surface. Smiley called it "a suitcase hole," and defined the term: "Time to pack muh suitcase and get muh ass outa here."

After that he moved over to Emily's site, still marked by the palladium oxhide boulder. Smiley knew nothing at all about our experiment, beyond the certainty that he was dealing with lunatics, with a lady twitcher lurking somewhere in the background. Yet, as he started the final hole, he observed, "This here looks more like it."

He hit water at three hundred and eighty feet. Clean, cold, sparkling water—rivers of it, oceans of it.

He said, "If your lady witch witched this one, she did a good job."

"There wasn't any lady," I told him. "It was a pig. A pig named Emily witched up this one."

He looked at me a long moment, then said, "Same difference."

Jefferson Davis Cordee, grandson of a hero, was jubilant. Asia was happy. I was pleased. We summoned an immediate high-level conference beside the pool. Our hostess poured champagne in three glasses and then bubbled about a pint of the Pol Roger into a soup tureen and set the dish in front of our barometric pig.

Emily took one quick sniff and turned away. Jeff got out of his chair, seized her by the neck, and shoved her snout down into the wine. Emily made woofer-and-tweeter noises, spraying champagne around the tile flooring and, breaking free of Jeff's grasp, she stood and shook herself from stem to stern like a wet collie, apparently under the impression that her entire body had been drenched in the noxious juice. Then she looked up at Jeff with sadness and supplication in her eyes.

Jeff didn't seem to get the message, but I did. I said:

"Go get her a big dish of Big Dish Strawberry Swirl."

He picked up the bowl and started to leave the patio but Asia stopped him.

"Don't do it," she said. And both Jeff and I understood at once. The balance of nature must not be disturbed. Jeff went for a tureen of milk instead.

While he was indoors I softened down my voice, put some sadness and supplication into my own eyes, and spoke of how much I had missed being with Asia. I was trying for the old velvet phraseology, but fumbling as I always do, saying something about one more week of this deprivation and I'd break out with acne lesions the size of poker chips.

"Asia," I said, falling back on pure reason, "it is not the eagers that give a person acne, it's trying to avoid the acne that gives a person the acne. What I mean to say is . . ."

"I know what you mean," she said. "Let's keep it cool. Let's wait till Emily makes us all rich."

"You want me to self-destruct?"

She was laughing as Jeff came back into the patio with the bowl of milk. He put it down in front of Emily and when she made no move, he took her again by the neck and pushed her nose down into it. She drank the milk resentfully, in short pouty gulps, and when she paused to catch her breath, she'd cast a reproachful eye at her keeper, clearly saying, "You big ungainly two-legged farmer, you know I told you Strawberry Swirl!"

I now stated my opinion that Emily's success in the field could have been sheer chance and we needed more evidence of her genius before we could take her on the road. We would have trouble convincing the ranchers. A rancher will believe anything and everything of a supernatural nature except that one small pig can witch up one large water well. Moreover, he would expose himself to almost certain ridicule if he decided to give the pig a try.

Asia had a suggestion. "Why not let Smiley Kock spread the word around? I imagine he'd be able to convince some of the ranchers."

"Which means," I said grimly, "that I'll have to convince Smiley."

The Uvalde well digger was still pulling tool at the site of No. 1 Emily when we arrived with Emily herself in the back of the pickup. I stated our case as unctuously as I could and at first Smiley was indignant. He gave evidence that syncopated swear words were trying to burst right through the top of his head. But in the end sheer power won out—one tripartite cartel against one impious well digger, with the pig standing there in the truck staring at him with an air of knowing much more than a pig is entitled to know.

"We'll put a guarantee on our work," said Asia. "For the first three or four jobs I think we ought to offer her services without charge, because, after all, we'll still be proving out her talent. Then I think a fee ought to be set based on performance. No water, no fee. Does that sound fair to you, Mr. Kock?"

"Sure. I only know maybe two twitchers that never charge a penny for their work. Fist Phillips of Uvalde and C. J. McMoon of Bandera County. Them two both witch for free. They say their Power comes straight from the throne and oughten to be charged for. They'll always accept little presents, though, usely a horse or a calf or a crate of home-cured hams or a color TV. They won't socialize with any other twitchers, the ones that charge money, and won't speak to them on the street except sometimes to nod and say howdy."

Asia borrowed some paper and a pencil from me and with the help of Smiley, who is wise in all the angles and ramifications of well water, worked out a tentative system of fees for Emily. It came down finally to ten dollars per gallon of flow in tight country and five dollars in porous country. Smiley had to explain that most of the Southwest is tight country, where the ground is so compacted that the water can't seep in, and where a flow of forty gallons per minute would be average.

He said that people-type witches charge about twenty-five dollars a job whether they locate water or not, and so in his opinion our pig would be doing real good if she got four hundred dollars for a well that produced forty gallons a minute.

And Jeff polished off the proceedings with a personal observation.

"I'm sorta glad," he said, "that Emily's power don't come straight from the throne. I wouldn't want us to be takin' in horses and calves and TV sets."

"Not to mention country hams," added Asia.

Emily got her first assignment three days later.

Smiley Kock fell into conversation with a rancher named Gub-

bins in a Uvalde cafe and Gubbins, whose spread was in Duval
County, said he was in need of a heap more water than he had
been getting. He specified that he would want the proposition
witched. Somewhat timorously Smiley put the question:

"What would you say to havin' it witched by a pig?"

"I don't care if it's witched by the Lieutennit Gov'ner," said
Gubbins. "Wait a minute. Did you say *pig?*"

"That's right."

Rancher Gubbins arranged his face to represent mystification.
"You mean pig? Like a pig?"

"I'm talkin' about a little pig that belongs to some people over
in Blackleg County. This pig can find water where human people
fail."

"A pig," mused Gubbins, talking to himself. "A pig water witch.
Why not? Prob'ly *looks* a lot better than some we got around my
neck of the woods."

He gave himself a few moments of careful thought.

"Well," he said to Smiley, "people always say that Gubbins has
got guts. I think I'd like to try it with a pig."

Smiley was working over a slab of chicken-fried steak and apparently had lost the thread of the discussion.

"Try what with a pig?" he asked.

Mr. Gubbins was regarded by himself and by several of his
close friends as a salty dog.

"How does this pig go about witchin' a well?" he inquired. "Does
he run around holdin' a stick in his mouth? Don't tell me that when
he gets over some water, the pull of gravvidy jerks the curl outa
his tail."

Mr. Kock responded with a nervous laugh. Mr. Gubbins, for
his part, flapped his arms against his sides and guffawed.

"It's a girl pig," said Smiley. "All she does is walk around and
sniff and when she hits water she lets out a squeal, lets out three
grunts, and you got the Galveston flood on your hands."

Rancher Gubbins had a moment of skepticism.

"It don't seem reasonable," he ruminated, staring at the
scrofulous paint on the ceiling of the cafe. "Goes against the grain.
Still in all, there's that chicken of Jeb Wisdom's . . ."

He addressed himself once again to his companion.

"Mr. Kock, have you heard about Jeb Wisdom's hen down at
Cotulla? He's got this hen that can locate lost objects. Anything

from a missin' wristwatch to a six-year-old boy. The sheriff heard about this hen of Jeb's and came and borryed her because there was this six-year-old boy had disappeared, and they took the hen to the boy's house and turned her loose and she looked around a while and then let out a hen-holler and started walkin' and she led them out to an old sandpit that had water in it, and there, by George, was that boy right where he had fallen in and drownded himself."

"Can this hen witch a well?" Smiley inquired deprecatingly.

Ignoring the question and enraptured by his own narrative, the Duval rancher plowed right on.

"Jeb Wisdom says she's a Cochin-Chiney. After she found that boy people from half a dozen counties that had lost things like jewelry and valuable documents and even one man, a sheep rancher, that had lost a prozz ram worth upwards of six thousand dollars, had strayed off in the hills somewhere, and so Jeb Wisdom got smart and set up a Board of Equalization for his hen, and the Board of Equalization sessed the value of any article or like a ram that was lost, and Jeb charged one quarter of what the lost thing was worth, and he was cleanin' up but he took sour and grouchy about the whole thing because as he said the hen wouldn't live more'n a year and a half longer provided she didn't get took by the eagles and the coyotes, and he said this whole thing of givin' hens such a short life was an outrage against natural law, and . . . what I didn't mention, Mr. Kock, was that this Board of Equalization was nobody but Miz Wisdom his wife, and she's the one sessed the value of . . ."

"When you want the pig?" Smiley Kock asked rather sternly. He was getting good and sick of this hen story. Here he was, a legitimate civilian, you might say, come along with a pig that had miraculous powers and was capable of undermining the whole economy of the State of Texas, and this old windbag from Duval County had to start yammerin' his head off about a goddamn crazy hen.

"Any time you can bring 'er over," said Gubbins.

This transaction, between Kock and Gubbins, marked the Moment of Truth—the discovery that we had been grossly wrong to worry about Emily's acceptance as a geophysical prodigy. We had underestimated the intelligence of the average man. We had forgotten that in these times the American people, and especially the people of Texas, are starving for something solid and substantial that they can believe in, that they can put their whole faith in . . . such as the ability of a Cochin-Chiney hen to locate the bodies of lost and drownded boys.

Jeff drove Emily in his own car to the Gubbins ranch. He refused to haul her in the bed of a pickup, as if she were an ordinary pig, and during the journey she occupied the front seat beside him. At Fugglin's Hardware he had found a child's safety harness with a steel floor bracket—a rig that might have been designed with our baby pig in mind. It was talked around town later that when Gaylord Fugglin dug the item out of a crate in the back of his store, Jeff asked if he had it in pink.

In Duval County Emily squealed her squeal and grunted her grunts at the edge of a thicket of thorny shrubs. Jeff and Emily then returned home while Smiley Kock moved his machinery in and lowered the boom. A week of waiting followed.

I kept myself busy in town. For one thing, I was expecting a fresh explosion out of Fern. She had not contested my divorce action beyond telling anyone who would listen that I could no longer cut the mustard. When, in addition, she found out that she had been snookered out of the newspaper, I thought that she would come down and burn the joint to the ground. At the time of the foreclosure she had brought in a lawyer from El Paso, a public eyesore with a Snub Pollard mustache, but unknown parties friendly to me notified him that he had till sundown. He didn't even wait.

Then I got the phone call. Smiley Kock had hit at two hundred and forty feet. Water poured from the good earth at the rate of seventy-four gallons a minute, and Rancher Gubbins forgot all about Jeb Wisdom's hen and went around loudly proclaiming the divining genius of Emily.

I made scorch marks on El Camino del Zopilote getting down to the ranch. The phone had already started ringing and from now on Asia Battle's Spanish palace was to lose most of its calm.

Any news combining the elements of a cute animal with manifestations of the occult is certain to travel faster than sound. Within hours people all over Texas and beyond were talking about Emily. Newspapers were sending reporters and cameramen to put together handsome spreads concerning the Magnificent Mulefoot— a name invented by an Austin columnist. Magazine people were on their way, and television crews from the holy roller stations of West Texas were already racing down from Midland and Odessa.

Asia retained her beautiful serenity in the presence of all this razzle-dazzle; toward me she continued amiable but cool, friendly but frigid—tantalizing me with that Mona Lisa smirk which heartless women seem to enjoy bestowing on men who are dying in agony from the eagers.

During one fairly quiet interval Jeff asked me to go with him and Emily to the barn—get away from the house for a spell. It was the hour for the pig to take on a bait of cracked corn. At the pen Jeff poured the grain into a small wooden tub and while Emily went to work on it we sat down on a bench and chewed on a couple of straws.

"Grady," said my young friend, "nobody else knows about this, but I wanted to let you in on it. Things have been goin' so well for me that I've decided to propose to Holly Ann. I don't believe in luck, except that if a guy finds himself in a lucky streak, he ought to take advantage of it."

"You don't believe in luck, but you believe in luck," I said.

His mention of Holly Ann came almost as a shock. For days now I had all but forgotten about Mungo Oldbuck and Rancho Traseros and the Smiths. Yet I had known that this thing was coming, and that with it would come some pretty heady complications.

"You've told Holly Ann who you are?"

"Well . . . no."

"You've got to tell her."

He didn't respond for a while, thinking about it.

"I don't see why," he finally said, stubbornness showing in his voice. "That could cause trouble. Why can't it wait?"

"Things like that can't wait. You can't marry her and you can't ask her to marry you unless you tell her."

"Well," he grumbled, "okay, if you say so, Grady. I'd rather take a whippin'."

"And," I continued, putting stress on the word, "you've got to tell her father."

"Good Lord, Grady! You tryin' to break us up?"

"Certainly not. I'm sure Holly Ann will agree with me. Do you still meet with her out there in the woods?"

"Every couple of days . . . out at the crick."

"You go back to the house and get her on the phone and arrange to meet her out there right now, right this afternoon. Tell her. Get it over with. And make some arrangement about telling the old man. Chances are he'll kill you, but you've got to tell him. Go ahead. I'll take care of Emily till you get back."

And so he did it.

I played nursemaid to the pig for two or three hours and then he came riding back from Rinderpest Creek. He was as grim as glue. He and Holly Ann had quarreled bitterly. They had started off with an easy discussion. She was startled to learn that Jeff was The Virginian's grandson, but it didn't throw her. Not immediately. But somehow the tranquillity began to dwindle down and disappear, and Jeff said something of a goading nature, and Holly Ann uttered the rash charge that her grandfather had been murdered in cold blood.

From that point on it degenerated into a shouting match and the lovers parted, mounting their horses and charging away in opposite directions, each vowing never again to speak to the other.

That is the way it is with love.

They were estranged and deeply unhappy thereafter, until . . .

There are other matters that must be considered first.

I felt guilty about the bust-up, so I didn't say much. It was dark by the time I hit the road for town and my mind was all crowded up with portents and enigmas. About a mile north of Asia's cattle guard I saw a light flickering off to the right of the highway. I slowed down and came to a dirt road and turned in. A quarter of a mile from the pavement I found the source of the light.

A man was crouched beside a little campfire and a shabby-looking pickup stood nearby, showing its anemic purple paint in the light of the fire. The man didn't look up at me as I got out of my car. He was wearing jeans and a dirty shirt and he was fussing with something on the ground. It looked like a bow and arrow. I had never seen the man before.

"Cookin' yer supper?" I asked in acceptable Western prose.

Now he looked up. He glared stupidly into my face for a moment and grunted. He was ebbryated, and my eye picked up a quart bottle of whiskey nestled in the grass close beside him.

"Me Standcabbage," he said. It was, at best, an obscure statement. "Me Choctaw Indian. Me fix bow and arrow. Kill."

The words were spoken slowly, with an accent, but it was not the accent of a redskin—to my ear it was merely the thickening tongue of a man with too much booze inside of him. He was drunkenly trying to speak the language of the American Indian the way it was spoken at Republic Studios during the reign of Herbert Yates.

"White people steal my pig," he muttered. "Me kill." He picked up a small white jar of the kind used for cold cream. "Poison," he said. "Poison for put on arrowhead. Me make poison in Laredo. Take spleen of dead dog and stir up with powdered ants so Standcabbage can kill white people."

A glimmer was beginning to get through to me.

"Tell me how the white people stole your pig," I said.

"Me go out of Oklahoma to Mexico," he said, waving an unsteady hand toward his pickup. "Six fine pigs in truck. One little pig fall out. I do not know where this happen—somewhere on this road." A wave toward the highway. "I go on to Mexico with five pig. Mexico no want Choctaw Indian. Mexico got plenty Indian already. Mexico no want pig. Mexico got millions of pig run around in street, run around in store, run around in church."

"They wouldn't let you in?"

"Me stay in Laredo. Many Mexican. Many Indian. Many pig. Standcabbage shine white man's shoes in barbershop. One day see in . . ."

"Hold it, Crazy Horse," I interrupted him abruptly. "If your name is really Standcabbage, then listen to me, Standcabbage. Drop the dialect. I think I know what you're trying to say, but I can't take any more of that pidgin Swahili. Give it to me in straight American."

He raised his head and looked me in the eye and spoke in straight American:

"The sons a bitches stole my pig!"

My God, how pooned up can things get?

He calmed down after that outburst and I told him that I knew where his pig was, that the people who had his pig were honest people and hadn't stolen the animal. They were taking good care of it and even feeding it ice cream and I was certain he would get it back.

"You were talking about Laredo," I said. "What happened down there?"

He turned sheepish, and hung his head. "I'm sorry," he said, "but I'm a little drunk. I started to tell you in that phony dialect that I was shining shoes in this Laredo barbershop and yesterday morning I picked up the local paper and there it was. Just a couple of paragraphs, but it was about my pig, and it gave the name of the lady and the name of the ranch and . . ."

"*Your* pig?" I challenged him. "Why do you call it *your* pig?"

"The newspaper said it was a baby girl pig, and a Mulefoot. It had to be my pig. Along here somewhere is the spot where she fell out of my truck. The newspaper said that these people have discovered that my pig can witch water, and that they will get rich. I drove here without a stop, drinking whiskey all the way. I want my Pushy back."

"Your Pushy?"

"That's her name."

"Her name is Emily."

"So the newspaper said, but that is not true. Her name is Pushy, after my wife, Pushmataha. I will get her back."

He showed indications of getting into another lather, so I gentled him down, and he asked my permission to take a medicinal drink, and I not only gave him the okay, but tilted the bottle once myself. I was in such a sweat that I couldn't think what ought to be done next, so I looked around the landscape and made out the dark hulk of a sand dune a few yards to the east of us. I walked back and circled behind it and then returned to Standcabbage, who now struggled to his feet and introduced himself formally, advising me that his first name was Victor. He teetered a little from the drink but he seemed to be all right. I told him who I was and that I was a close friend of the people who had his pig, and that we'd get it all straightened out for him. For the time being I recommended that he put out his fire and move his pickup and his whiskey and his poisoned arrows to a new campsite back of the dune, where neither he nor his fire would be visible from the highway.

"Me white man speak with Mulefoot tongue," I said. "I've got to hurry back to town and you stay put till tomorrow. Get behind that sand dune and stay there till I come back. How you fixed for provisions?"

"I have enough food," he said, "but me Choctaw, me thirsty, white man better bring more firewater."

"Will do," I said. It is not fashionable nowadays to kick an Indian around. I started to leave, then thought of something.

"Don't go scouting around that ranch across the way. Just leave everything to me. And tell me straight: are you beset by an overwhelming fondness for the pig, or is it an overwhelming fondness for wampum?"

"Wampum."

"You'll make out. Go ahead now and move your camp, and you can work on your poisoned arrows while you're waiting."

"Only one," he said, bending and picking an arrow off the sand. "Got it in souvenir store at Lake Amistad." He reached again and came up with the white jar. "This is not poison—it's oxblood shoe polish and pipe tobacco."

"Poison or shoe polish, just don't go shooting at anybody."

"What if U. S. Cavalry come?"

"Scalp the bastards."

So off I went again and this time I made it to the metropolis. There was a light on in the office and I found Gene Shallow sitting at my desk.

"Phone's been ringin' night and day," he called out as I came through the door. "AP callin', and UPI, and the TV people and *Time* magazine and newspapers from all over the blamed country, even clean over to Baltimore and Albuh-kirk. Grady, I don't know a thing. Looks like you could of let me know, me settin' here at mission control. All these people jabberin' at me and . . ."

"I've been busy," I said, "and I've got worries."

Then almost as an afterthought Gene gave me the news of the Great Water Witch Rebellion. He spoke of it in the same monotone he generally employed when he said it might rain but then again it might not although it looked a little like it would if a body could depend on how a thing looked which it wouldn't be a smart idy. What he said was:

"They're gettin' up a rally for tomorrow night. Over at the Undercroft. Looks to me like they're fightin' mad about it all. Some talk of hangin' the pig right on the courthouse lawn. That'd be good for arr front page, Grady. I don't think we've ever had a pig hangin' here before."

It was supposed to be a secret convocation, kluxer in character, but of course everyone in town knew about it down to the last detail.

It was preceded in the afternoon by an emergency meeting of the Caliche Ministerial Alliance. There had been quarreling among the clergy over theological points touching on witchcraft, demonology, and hog culture. At the conclusion of this afternoon's meeting the preachers adopted a resolution declaring that the proceedings were classified top secret, sub rosa, and not to be whispered in Gath.

By 4:12 P.M. it was known to the farthest reaches of the town boundaries that the Reverend Freestone Ector had bloodied the nose of the Reverend Hardin Hudspeth, and that the Reverend Kyle Biggerstaff had been called a summbitchin' atheist for having offered the Presbyterian Undercroft to the enraged Anti-Pig citizens.

At six o'clock I presented myself at the side door of the church and sought to enter the Undercroft (means basement).

Mayor Ford Winkler barred the way. In ordinary circumstances the mayor was a timid little guy, as jumpy as the Hungarian partridge, but lately evil forces had been closing in on him—first Big Jim Deehardt threatening his life and now this hell-sent pig.

"You will not be admitted!" Mayor Winkler announced to me. Back of him stood County Judge Daphne Whipple, her arms folded across her juicy bosom, her stance that of General Jackson at Bull Run. Behind Daff was Fern Mobeetie, glaring her hatred, poised to spring like a jaguar. I already knew that these three were the instigators of the uprising against an inoffensive and innocent little pig. I knew, too, that my former wife was the actual ringleader, and that she had been urging that I swing from a limb alongside the pig.

"The hell I won't!" I responded.

"You act smart," said the mayor, "and you will be thrown into the street. Bodly."

"Not by you, I won't."

"By me you will," a voice sounded at my shoulder. It was Virge Decker, occasional bed companion to Fern, proprietor of the plumber's snake. He was looming over me in a most menacing manner.

I glanced past the mayor and the two Gorgon sisters and saw that the Undercroft was jammed with people. Up front I spotted Gene Shallow, who was looking in my direction. I gave him a hard wink, accompanied by a nod, which meant that he was to cover for me, and I almost dropped dead when he indicated he knew what I meant. I also spotted Billy Yewclid, the chickenshit well digger, and Game Warden Foster Cowan, and Old Man Springer with a wad of Days Work in his cheek, and then I saw Cee Minus Hoffelinck, the scientific witch whose grandfather had dangled sausages at hidden German waters. On the off chance that he might feel some small obligation toward me and because I had need of undercover agents, I gave him the same wink and the same nod. He stared right through me. As in every other high school subject, he got Cee Minus in sign language.

Rather than risk ignominious death at the hands of an imbecile, I went home and fixed some popcorn and beer and watched a detective show on television and then went to bed. I had forgotten all about Standcabbage the Choctaw Indian.

Here are the highlights of the Undercroft Meeting as reconstructed from accounts of eyewitnesses:

Invocation by the Reverend C. O. Jones, pastor of the Inner Circumvented Christian Church, South. The Reverend Jones quoted Exodus 3:1, wherein Moses took some kind of a rod and struck Mount Horeb and brought forth water, and the Reverend said there had always been an argument whether Mount Horeb was the same as Mount Sinai but it didn't make any difference because shorely the taking up of a rod and witchin' up water is just as important in God's Eye as the Ten Commandments or Dooderonnamy law giving or anything else.

Mayor Ford Winkler assumed the podium and said that he was acting as temporary chairman. Whereupon City Councilman Wilbur Tarrant, who is known as a weekend twitcher and who has long looked with disapprobation on the very guts of Ford Winkler, leaped to his feet.

"I move," he called out, "that we suspend the rules and appoint our beloved brother Woolly Butt Suggs to be our permanent chairman." Before anyone could interrupt him, Councilman Tarrant ripped out a rapid-fire volley of words like this: "All-in-favor-say-Aye-the-Ayes-have-it-Woolly-Butt-take-the-chair!"

The mayor set up an immediate whine of protest, waving his hands around and complaining about steamroller tactics. He was howled down.

Woolly Butt Suggs needs explanation. He is known as the Dean of Blackleg County Dowsers and uses a wand cut from a Melbourne woolly butt tree, which is the Australian eucalyptus. He is a retired railroad telegrapher with graying hair that hangs clear down to his hip pockets. I have talked to him on occasion and as is usually true of men who wear long hair, he has a firm grasp of reality, views the world with balanced judgment, is smarter than a treeful of owls, and washes himself quite regularly on Saturday nights. He wears a strip of black rag around his head to keep hair from obstructing his existentialist view of mankind, and in addition to being pre-eminent in the field of water witching, he is a healer. He can cure a fever by holding the patient's hand. Nothing more than that. Nothing acrobatic. No mumbo-jumbo. He simply grasps the patient's hand and keeps a firm hold on it. One hour cures a fever. Two hours will get rid of arthritis. It takes him five hours to knit up a fracture of the skull.

Woolly Butt lives alone in a decrepit little house where one day each year he sets his table for two and his dead wife comes in and dines with him and they talk things over in a general sort of way. She never touches the food but upon her departure each year she tells him what to serve next time. He told me once that he would cut off his hair except that his healing power would be diminished. He said that all his special powers reside in that long hair and that he has a built-in thermostat for controlling the flow.

"If I turned it all loose in one big surge," he advised me, "it'd might nigh kill the patient. They wouldn't be able to bear up under that amount of power."

As I have suggested, he is not too tidy, and wandering children as well as dogs and cats circle wide past his residence, but he is greatly respected in Caliche as Thales was respected in Miletus, Plato in Athens, and Nixon in Yorba Linda.

Woolly Butt Suggs took the chair and called for expressions of opinion concerning the matter at issue: the emergence of a pig as the most talked-about water witch in the State of Texas.

Pandemonium. Everybody wanted to talk at once. Flat Hat Irene clawed her way to the platform, rudely pushed Woolly Butt away, and tried to take over, crying out for the pig's blood.

Flat Hat achieved new heights of rage during the Undercroft gig. She shrilled out that she had been tricked into witching a well that had already been criminally witched by the aforesaid pig and that it was her desire to be granted the privilege of strangling the aforesaid pig with her own magical and consecrated hands, plus the privilege of expectorating in the eye of the California jezebel who had brought the pig of the first part into this God-fearing land to begin with. Then Irene's delicate exercise in forensics took a slight evangelistic turn.

"I confess!" she cried, flinging up her hands to heaven. "I bare my miserable sinnin' soul! I done wrong! I witched where that dirty little pig had already witched! I ast forgiveness!"

This unexpected show of weakness on the part of Flat Hat had a surprising effect on Alferd Keller, he who had witched the T-bone steaks at Bub Gardner's Meat Market. Alferd somehow got the impression that he was attending a testification-for-Christ rally. He struggled to his feet, his ancient bones snapping and popping, and hit the sawdust trail.

"I admit it!" he announced. "I went around town makin' false witness about them T-bones. I confess here and now that Bub Gardner he put me up to it and he will fry in Hell for his sins. As for me, I . . ."

At the podium Woolly Butt Suggs, lacking a gavel, fished a two-pound pocketknife out of his coat and used it to rap for order. When he got it he uttered a Suggsian witticism.

"It appears," he said, "that we have got offa the subject of pork and onto the subject of beef. I recommend that . . ."

A man named Forepaugh, lately moved to Caliche from some town in East Texas, stood up and said:

"I happen to bleeve in what the gent'mun said about witchin' T-bone steaks. I know a gent'mun in Tyler, Texas, name of Calvin Klein, that can witch inside a person's house two hunderd and twinny-five mile away. Seen him do it. He taken his willa stick and held it up toward the city of Austin, Texas, where his brother lives, name of Corky Klein, and he ast the stick to tell him if his brother Corky was home from that trip yet, his brother Corky Klein had been out to Disneyland in California, and if he was in the house, and the stick nodded its head yes. I was there. I seen it done."

"I bleeve you, sir," spoke up Alferd Keller, forgetting that he had just confessed himself a fraud.

"But," continued the East Texas orator, "I wish to state at the same time that I do not bleeve in the modern school uh thought that says you can pray to a flower or a vegetable plant when it is sickly and all fulla bugs and larvy, and it will straighten up and get well and even act like it is *smolling* at you. I do not hold with that because it has not been proved out yet, but there might be something to it. I would like to hear Brother Jones's feeling on this subject."

"What subject is that?" asked Reverend Jones.

Mr. Forepaugh's answer was lost in a babble that broke out, a babble of protest. The crowd was here for serious business. The crowd wanted action against that pig.

Chairman Suggs asked if somebody would kindly offer a resolution providing that the town dogcatcher be authorized to go out to Miz Battle's ranch, seize the offending pig, bring it back to town, and put it to sleep.

"Put it to sleep at the end of a rope!" cried my former wife.

There were loud seconds to that last motion from around the hall. Fern Mobeetie had become an accomplished rabble-rouser. Gene Shallow told me later that Fern and Daphne Whipple were openly taking swigs out of a black bottle all during the proceedings.

The Reverend Mr. Jones now made an effort to get the discussion onto level ground.

"I think," he announced, "that we should establish if this Miz Battle is a Cath'lic or not. We already know that Cath'lics don't have The Power. Did you ever hear of a Mescan water witch?"

"I did," sang out Billy Yewclid. "This Mescan Joe that collects old used lumber, I asked him once if he knew any Mescans could witch water, and he says he could do it himself, and I was supprized because he can't hardly speak a word of English, but he went in his shed and come out with a post-hole digger and he says that post-hole digger is his witchin' rod, and I'd bet money Joe is as Cath'lic as they come."

Enter Henry Mutcher, a Sunday twitcher.

"Hey, Billy!" he called out across the room to Yewclid. "You 'member the time that Cath'lic fella come through town lookin' for wells to witch, had that thing he called his asperjizzlum, had this here holy water in the end of it, and he claimed that asperjizzlum could locate . . ."

"I remember him," Billy Yewclid shouted back. "A pure-dee dumbcuff. And a Cath'lic to boot. It is my professional opinion that a party starts usin' Cath'lic holy water in our business, it's hittin' below the belt."

"No it's not," spoke up the Reverend Kyle Biggerstaff, donor of the Undercroft. "I do wish you folks would keep in mind something you don't seem able to keep in mind, to wit: it is not the instrument you use that finds the water, and it is not the body of the man that is holding the instrument that finds the water, but it is the Holy Spirit that does the job. Thus it comes to pass that if the Holy Spirit chooses to act through a Cath'lic and even through an asperjizzlum with holy water in it, then we should not question, we should not stand by and scoff."

The man Forepaugh from East Texas got to his feet again, imbued with this freshening display of tolerance.

"I bleeve," he announced, "that the Reverend is right. Over where I come from, the niggers is sposed to be extra good at witchin'. They got a lot of superstitions connected with it. They always cut their stick from a persimmon tree, but the persimmon tree has got to have a possum in it at the very moment the stick is cut. So like the Reverend says, it *couldn'* be the stick that has the Holy Spirit in it."

"That is *not* what I said!" protested the clergyman.

"The pig!" came a cry from somewhere in the crowd. "What about the pig?"

Mr. Forepaugh was turning out to be a man of great durability.

"I heard about a hippie fella up in Fort Worth," he went on, "that wore about forty strings of beads around his neck and had more hair than our steamed chairman and went around without ever wearin' any socks and . . ."

From somewhere came five slow words of critical exegesis:

"Jesus . . . never . . . wore . . . no . . . socks."

". . . and this hippie found out he had The Power and he begun to witch water with his electric guitar."

A derisive cry from the crowd: "Whad he plug it into, a prairie dog hole?"

The door at the rear of the Undercroft opened and a man came in. He was of medium height, stocky, muscular, dressed like a grandstand cowboy—everything light blue from his Stetson down to his boots. He wore a gun belt with two empty holsters, and a pair of silver Chihuahua spurs with rowels as big as silver dollars. He was brown enough to have been a Spaniard and he wore a black mascara-line mustache. He stood in the doorway, calmly surveying the room with his dark glittery eyes. Then he walked forward, the silver rowels ringing out their music against the concrete flooring. Confronting Woolly Butt Suggs, he bowed slightly from the waist, then turned and faced the gaping audience.

"I have heard," he said, spacing his words, "that you good people have a pig you want taken care of. I am in the business of taking care of pigs." He paused and executed a throat-slitting gesture across his neck, going *zzzzzzzzzz-ick!* "It is my custom to charge a fee for taking care of pigs but in this case there will be no charge. I will work free. I do not like the lady who has this pig."

"Excuse me," spoke up Chairman Suggs. "Would you mind telling us who you are?"

"My name is Tinea Cruris. People call me Tiny. Perhaps some of you may have seen me from time to time on the streets of your city, for I was once employed by Mr. Mungo Oldbuck. But, then, I didn't dress like this in the days when I was a lowly ranch hand."

"You happen to be a hard gun?" came from the audience. The questioner was my star reporter, Gene Shallow. Tinea Cruris shot a hard glance in his direction and chose to overlook him.

"I know the ranch where the pig lives," the man in blue went on. "I know the pig's habits. I know where the pig's pen is located. I know the pig's first name."

Mayor Winkler twittered to his feet.

"When do you propose to . . . uh . . . to take care of this pig? And how?"

"Right now is a good time, this very night, and I will do what you people want me to do in the matter of taking care of the pig. I will cut her throat if that is your pleasure, or I will stab her through the heart, or I will hit her on the skull with a hammer."

"We'd want her to suffer some before she died," sang out my beloved ex-wife.

"Mr. Tiny," said Mayor Winkler, "would you mind stepping outside for a moment while we have an executive session?"

"To be sure."

Though he looked as if he had seen too many Roy Rogers pictures, the man in blue had a way about him, an arrogant and swaggering manner that was mitigated and rendered almost charming by the soft melodious voice and the courtliness of his bearing. He left the room and the mayor pulled together half a dozen of the top brains in the room. After a whispered conference, lasting no more than five minutes, Señor Tinea Cruris was called back.

"We have just a couple of questions," said Mayor Winkler.

"Shoot," said the sleek Cruris.

"Are you . . . would you be . . . by any chance . . . are you a Mescan?"

"No."

"You look Mescan."

"Well, sir, *you* look Po-locky."

Hearty laughter rippled over the room and the mayor scowled fiercely.

"Just what *is* your nationality, Mr. Cruris?"

"I'm an Etruscan. From the north of Etrusk."

There was a stir, and a murmur, over the room. Someone said, "Sounds Russian." And someone else replied, "No. An Etruscan is a kind of Jew."

Mayor Winkler glanced at his leading confederates and they nodded approval. An Etruscan was okay.

"You plan on doing this job alone?" the mayor asked.

"If you want a couple of your own men to go with me, as witnesses, I'll agree to such an arrangement. I'd prefer that the men be experienced in hunting and tracking."

Another whispered conference. Then consultations with various men in the crowd. The Reverend C. O. Jones was chosen because he was thought to be honest and he was generally known as an outdoors type because he sometimes went fishing in Moco Pond.

They tried to get Foster Cowan, the game warden, to go with the blue-clad killer but he declined.

"I'm with you in spirit, fellas," he said, "but my job won't let me do it."

"Bull leather, Foster!" protested the mayor. "You're just the man for this assignment. The game laws don't mention anything in regards to strangling a pig, do they?"

"All I know," insisted Foster, "is that in my job I'm supposed to be on the side of the animals."

The choice then narrowed down to Cee Minus Hoffelinck.

"I'm like Flat Hat," he said. "I was inveggled into witching a territory that had already been witched, so to speak, by a dumb animal. It was an insult to my calling. I will go along if I will have the right to take the first slug at this pig."

Mayor Winkler directed a questioning look at the cowboy in blue.

"Okay," said Tinea Cruris, "provided he doesn't get over-wrought and start yelling and cussing and raising the neighborhood."

"I promise," said Cee Minus, and the die was cast. There was some grumbling from Fern Mobeetie, who still demanded a lynch party, but the three members of the murder squad left. They would pick up a shotgun at Cee Minus's house and another at Foster Cowan's.

The mayor jostled Woolly Butt Suggs away from the podium and issued a call for the Reverend Mr. Biggerstaff to step forward and speak the Benediction.

"He had to go to the bathroom," someone called out.

"Well, then," sighed the mayor, "I guess I'll have to do it. Seems like some people are never up to their responsibilities. Let us all go home to our houses and go to bed and sleep contented that we have done the Lord's work here tonight, proceeding against a brute creature that was sent amongst us by Satan Himself to cheat and defraud the loyal worthy citizens of Blackleg County and may ever'thing turn out okay, amen."

"Hey, Mayor!" Daphne Whipple sang out. "Come to think of it, you *do* look a little Po-locky!"

"*Meeting adjourned!*" yelled the mayor, and the historic affair of the Undercroft was over.

Gene Shallow was one of those people who early in life have mis-
pronounced a word and then, all during their remaining years on
earth, have continued mulishly and defiantly to mispronounce
that word. Gene's word was *quote.*

He shook me awake around midnight soon after the Undercroft
meeting broke up. He was more incoherent than usual but he did
manage to convey to me that "a subcommittee of three desprit
min" was preparing to descend on Asia Battle's ranch with the
intention of murdering a pig.

He described the conclusion of the meeting.

"At the end," he said, "the entarr congregation gethered outdoors on the grass and was singin' a hymn that said coat we will
hang that piggy from a sarr apple tree uncoat."

I got out of bed and began slamming on my clothes.

"You know what I think, Grady?" Gene continued, trailing me
around the premises. "I think they aim to hang that pig like he
was a human." He mumbled on about some stranger, a man in a
blue cowboy suit who was a professional pig-killer, and I went
rampaging through a closet looking for the only weapon I own, a
.22. I found it and then took another five minutes locating the
cartridges, and then I climbed into Old Blue and the goddamn
engine wouldn't take hold and people could have heard the
swearwords in Amarillo. I got out and opened the hood and gave
the carburetor a long baleful glare, which is my way of witching an
engine, and then tried it again and it started. Gene Shallow had
been standing by, still talking.

"That onnery wife of yours," he said, "she was there, and I
reckon she's changed her mind about hangin' you alongside of
the pig on the courthouse lawn. After they sung the hymn I heard
her say that when they got the G. D. pig dead they'd ought to take

you and Miz Battle out and hang you both upside down like Mussolini and his lady friend."

I greeted this intelligence with controlled enthusiasm.

I was about to pull away from the house when Big Jim Deehardt came whirling around the corner from Menmunt Avenue, driving a brand new Land Rover. His tires screeched as he slid to a stop beside my Pontiac.

"Hold!" he cried as he leaped from his superjeep. I held. "Wink the Fink is behind it all!" he announced. "I stand ready to kill the son of a bitch!"

"For Jesus sake, Big Jim," I said. "Get hold of yourself." I was staring at the Land Rover. He must have witched up two pots of gold with his little black box. It didn't occur to me that he was already throwing body blocks against the cancer cells.

"I got word that you were in trouble, Grady, and that Winkler was behind it all," Big Jim explained. "Had an operative in that meeting. I've organized Deehardt's Elite Corps. Seven good men, counting myself. They are standing at ease, out at the ball park, awaiting my orders. Every man a crack shot. What'll it be? Scorched Earth?"

"Who are the men?" I wanted to know.

"Four ranchers," he said, "and a couple of retired cowboys. Patriots down to the marrow. All six immunized against cancer cells by my miraculous silver box. They are ready to lay down their lives for Big Jim. Say the word, Grady! Where do we fight?"

I couldn't think of anything else, so I asked him if he knew where Mungo Oldbuck's place was. He said he'd seen the sign. I told him to take his Elite Corps to The Pueblo and tell Mungo I had sent him.

"Get your artillery greased up," I said, "and wait for me."

"Will do! And listen, Grady. Watch out for a greaser in a blue cowboy suit. He's their head gunsel." The Hermit of Leydigs Duct snapped off a salute and I made tracks for the Two Cross T.

Another full moon was riding across a sky streaked with cirrus. Too much light, I thought, for a proper kind of raid, but then maybe this mysterious Little Boy Blue knew what he was doing. I tried to speculate about him, but there was little to go on. My .22 would be enough to handle C. O. Jones and Cee Minus Hoffelinck—those two would run from a slingshot. But the swarthy stranger with the two empty holsters?

I clipped along at eighty. I had no idea how much of a start they had on me, but after I'd traveled eight or ten miles I spotted their car up ahead. They were taking their time, probably talking over tactical procedures. They would have seen my lights and I considered taking the bold course and rambling right past them; then I realized that in the moonlight either the preacher or Cee Minus would have recognized me or my car. I needed a ruse of some kind, and one lay waiting for me—the entrance to the Wigfall ranch on the left—and this, of course, brought back into my mind the presence of my drunk Indian.

I turned in at the Wigfall cattle guard as if I belonged there and drove back to the sand dune and found Victor Standcabbage sitting again beside his campfire, this time drunker than eight guilt-ridden goats. He hadn't needed that firewater he asked me to bring. There was a tall bottle at his elbow and he was mumbling something about having seen great herds of buffalo coming out of two holes in the ground up in the Staked Plains. When he saw me he reverted deeper into savagery. He howled:

"If Standcabbage no get Pushy, white people die!"

I gathered up his sleeping bag, his bow and arrow, and his bottle of whiskey and stowed them in the back seat. Then I rasseled him into the car, trying to talk soothingly, trying to tell him that we were on our way to see his pig Pushy. A vagrant memory crossed my mind, of a Chinese laundryman I once knew in Greenwich Village who referred to the sex act as "pushy-pushy," and spoke of it often, philosophically. His Confucius-say on the subject, coated widely in my circle of friends, went: "Pushy-pushy one time, goooood. Pushy-pushy two time, goooood. Pushy-pushy t'ree time, no goooood. Make sick."

The entire operation of getting Standcabbage on the road was conducted with great speed. I left the lavender pickup standing beside the dune and I didn't even put out the fire. I drove back to the highway with my lights doused and turned south again and of course there was no sign of the Blue Boy's car. I stepped down hard on the gas and then I almost blundered into the enemy.

They had pulled off the pavement and stopped, and all three men were out of the car and fooling around across the bar ditch, doing something with the fence. Apparently they hadn't noticed my car swing around the long curve and I could see Hoffelinck dragging on some strands of wire. They were cutting the link fence, and it was Asia's wire. The only possible reason they could have for this action would be to get their car onto Asia's land.

The sinister Blue Boy, assuming him to be the master planner, was going to do it the hard way. I calculated his position as about fifteen winding hypotenuse miles from the ranch headquarters— rough terrain all the way with rocky arroyos to cross, boulder-strewn hills to skirt. Why hadn't he chosen the simple course and stayed on the roads. There was only one answer I could think of: he was a romantic . . . he had looked at too many Westerns at the picture show. Still, I was quite happy about it. He was giving me time.

I waited until they had struggled the sedan through the cut in the fence, gave them ten minutes to disappear into the wilderness, and then I scampered on south.

I estimated that I would beat the invaders to the headquarters compound by at least half an hour, and I ruffled my tail and gunned 'er up to eighty again. It was past one o'clock when I pulled up at the Spanish castle. I sounded a few blasts on the horn and waited a couple of minutes and saw some lights come on. In another minute I was kissing her, and she was protesting and pushing at me.

"Henry!" she cried out. "You're drunk!"

"No," I told her. "*He* is." I gestured toward the car, where Standcabbage was half hanging out the window, staring stupidly at the scene.

The Choctaw apparition frightened her. She gasped and grabbed at her face.

"Who on earth . . . ?"

"Never mind," I commanded. "I'll explain him later. No time now."

I told her as fast as I could pour the words out that a crazy raiding party, with guns, was this very instant crossing her land bent upon killing and rape and arson, and I ordered her to get into some slacks and prepare to defend the old homestead.

"It'll take them a while yet to get to the barn," I told her, "but hurry. And see if you can dig up a gun."

She was momentarily addled, not comprehending a word I had said, and I thought she was going to disintegrate, so I yelled at her:

"Goddamn it, woman, they're coming in to kill the pig! Throw on some pants and get a gun and hurry down to the big barn. I'll wake up Jeff and Jaybird."

She looked again toward my car and her eyes grew wide and she repeated herself:

"Who *is* he?"

"A Choctaw Indian . . . named Standcabbage!" I almost yelled.

"Oh, my God!" she cried, and, turning, ran back into the house.

There was a light on in Jeff's cottage but he was nowhere in sight. His grandpappy's Colt was on the sofa in the living room and I found two boxes of shells in a table drawer. I drove over to Jaybird's 'dobe and got him out of bed. He rounded up a rifle and a shotgun and a Post Toasties box full of ammunition. I gave him a quick briefing as we drove on to the barn. Asia was already coming down the path, carrying a twelve-shot Browning automatic. She was holding it away from her body as if it were a poisonous snake.

"I'm afraid of this thing," she said. "It was Uncle Crawford's."

"You mean you don't know how to use it?" I asked.

Jaybird spoke up. "She knows how to point it and pull the trigger—I showed her that much. Somebody'll have to reload for her if she empties the magazine."

"Where the devil is Jefferson Davis Cordee?" I now asked. Nobody knew. So we went at the task of getting Standcabbage out of the car and into the barn. It was a struggle, and through it all he clung to his bow and arrow and his whiskey. The Plimsoll mark on his bottle indicated that he had been taking on additional fuel. There was a tack room of sorts in one corner of the barn and we got him in there with his sleeping bag and he conked out before we could get him stuffed into it. A good sensible Indian.

It was time for a battle plan. I suggested that first we should get Emily out of her doghouse and into the barn. Jaybird hurried outside to perform this chore. I took a quick survey of the interior of the building, noting doorways and windows, giving special attention to the north wall. I opened three windows facing the direction of the enemy's approach.

It seemed to me that if they ever made it across that rough country in the sedan, the time was growing near for them to arrive. They would probably travel the last half mile on foot.

I was enjoying the role of commander-in-chief.

"The best bet," I said, "would be to scare the bejezus out of them. That'll be easy with the preacher and the carpenter, but I don't know about Blue Britches."

"Who is this guy?" Jaybird wanted to know.

"The Lone Ranger, gone bad. I wish I knew. He turned up at the meeting in town and out of the goodness of his heart offered to come down here and kill Emily."

"Let me have first shot at him," Asia said, turning as hard as Calamity Jane. I smiled in admiration and she squeezed my arm and I took two romantic seconds to strike a dramatic pose and declaim, "When I'm gone, my dear, have them search my old foot-locker—they'll find a broken heart among my souvenirs." Then quickly back to resolute command.

"Here's how we'll work it," I said. "I'll take the west door and the northwest window. Asia, you stand over there at that middle window. Jaybird gets the east door and the window near it. Asia stands at her window and shoots at the moon. I run from door to window and back to door, shooting at flights of owls. Jaybird does the same at his end. They'll think we've got at least six guns going against them. Where in farfing hell is that Jeff?"

"Henry Grady," Asia purred, "you're a genius."

We settled down to wait. Emily was tethered to a post at the foot of the wooden stairway. She was yawning a good deal, and looking around with great curiosity, probably wondering about Jeff, thinking perhaps that all this ruckus might lead to a tub of Big Dish Strawberry Swirl. Now and then she emitted a soft grunt, expressing neither satisfaction nor chagrin. She just liked to shmooz around when she was with her people.

Jaybird spotted them first. They were coming in on foot, slowly and cautiously. They would probably circle around to the south side of the barn, where Emily's Castle stood with no Emily in it. They had no seeming suspicion that anyone was laying in ambush. As they cat-footed toward us they were, at first, no more than shadowy figures in the night, and then as they came closer, we were able to make them out individually. The cowboy in blue was in the middle, carrying what looked to be a rifle, and I took note of the fact that his holsters were no longer empty. Preacher Jones and Cee Minus Hoffelinck had shotguns and Preacher Jones was shouldering his as if he were on dress parade in a Laurel & Hardy film.

They were less than fifty yards away from the barn when I heard Asia's gasp.

"That's him! That's the man on the terrace!"

I took a closer look at the middle figure and now I recognized Blue Boy. He was the dog who worked for Mungo Oldbuck under the name Anadarko. I looked at his boots, and there they were—glinting in the moonlight—the silver spurs with the rowels that made the ringing noises on the tile outside Asia's bedroom.

I turned my eyes back to Asia, thinking that she might be taking dead aim. The butt of her Browning was resting on the floor and she was staring through the window. The three invaders halted; they peered intently at the big barn; they had heard noises.

I ran to the doorway, stepped into the open where they could see me, and fired a shot into the air. Anadarko responded with wild rifle fire, but I had already ducked back into the building.

I strode quickly to my window, laid the barrel of my .22 across the sill, took careful aim, and laid one into his right shoulder. He yelped like a hound dog and his rifle fell to the ground. Jaybird now fired one shot and Asia let go a bullet at the moon.

The preacher and the carpenter were already scattering sand as they loped toward the horizon. Anadarko lingered briefly, immobilized by the suddenness of it all and by the pain in his shoulder.

He couldn't see us, but he stood boldly glaring at the barn and, using his left hand, he made the throat-slitting gesture and went *zzzzzzzzzz-ick!* Then he turned and went trotting off, his right arm hanging dead at his side. He didn't even bother to pick up his gun.

Our valiant defending force (*generales, 1; soldados, 1; soldaderas, 1; cochinillos, 1*) now retired, swollen with victory, up the path to the big house for a coffee break and a conference. No one seemed to object to my having assumed the role of commander, although during the firing of the triumphant fusillade of three shots, Emily had interrupted her gentle grunting with an extended squeal; it could have been a pig-cry of protest. Neither the shots nor the squeal awakened the Choctaw. We left him in the tack room, alone with his gods.

Jaybird Huddleston carried the pig in his arms as we made our way to the Spanish castle. Asia and I were arm in arm and beginning to act kittenish until I realized that I should not even permit *thoughts* of such things to distract me from my military duties.

No futzing around, and so I announced loudly that I had some reconnoitering to do. For a moment I thought I'd better explain about Standcabbage, and then I decided to let it wait. There was a war on.

"They'll head back to town," I said. "The Etruscan has to get that wound fixed up and the other two are anxious to get into bed and drag the covers over their heads. I'll take my car and go out to the highway, to the spot where they cut the fence, and wait for them. We've got to be sure they've left the ranch."

"Let me go with you," Asia suggested.

"No. And don't *you* get the eagers. Not yet. Once I see those three gooks on their way back to Caliche, I'll turn around and head for Mungo's place and see if I can find Jeff. We're likely to need him, along with any other help I can get."

"For what?" The question came from Jaybird.

"Those morons in town," I answered him, "will be in a rage when they find out their task force has failed and their Blue Hero is shot. I've got a hunch they'll send out a whole army next time. And don't forget one important thing: *this is a religious war.*"

Somebody ought to hire me to teach at West Point.

I drove north and located a ragged clump of mesquite close to the
pavement where I could conceal Old Blue and keep an eye on the
break in the fencing. Then I settled back and waited. They were
a long while coming out. They probably took time to wrap up Anadarko's wound before undertaking the rough passage back to the
highway.

After maybe forty minutes the car came bumping across the
Texas veld, chugged up the slope to the pavement, and hightailed
it toward town.

When they were well on their way I wheeled around and drove
south.

Lights were on in The Pueblo and I could see more lights burning out back at the Smiths' house. Big Jim Deehardt's Land Rover
was parked at Mungo's entrance and across the way were his storm
troopers—six men lounging around two jeeps, six middle-aged
guerrillas, each with the appearance of being seven feet tall and
secure in his mind against encroachment of the dread carcinoma.
They nodded and howdyed as I went quickly past their bivouac,
headed straight for the Smith house.

Jeff and Holly Ann were sitting on the front porch and came
bounding down to greet me with news that this world was trying
to be the best of all possible worlds and pretty much succeeding
at it; Holly Ann's pappy had given his hearty approval and they
had set the date for the wedding. Jeff seized me by the arm.

"Come up on the porch, Grady," he urged. "I got to tell you
how Mr. Smith has changed my whole life. He told me . . ."

"Not now," I said sharply. "Tell me about it later. We've had
trouble at Asia's place and there's more of it on the way."

"What kind of trouble?"

"Shooting. Gunplay."

I gave them a quick résumé and asked Holly Ann to go get her

father. He had been asleep and he was yawning and scratching his
ribs when he came onto the porch. I said I'd like to have all three
of them go with me to Mungo's house.

As soon as we started on the walk, Jeff broke out in emotional
fever again.

"I was there in my house, ready to go to bed, and Holly Ann
knocked on . . ."

"Stow it, Jeff," I said. "We don't have time right now."

The proprietor of Rancho Transeros was in his office with the
Hermit of Leydigs Duct.

"Grady!" shouted Big Jim, leaping to his feet. "Great balls of
fire and frustration! Man, am I glad to see you! I've been trying
to tell your friend here about Winkler the Finkler and his mob,
and the danger you and your friends are in, but he just brushes
me off and keeps begging me to . . ."

Mungo was wearing a broad grin as he kept his gaze on Big Jim.
He was actually contemplating the con man from Illinois with an
air of admiration.

"This man," said Mungo, "has been telling me something of his
life story. It's great! A classic! Grady, help me talk him into putting it all in a book and by God I'll go back into publishing. How
about you ghosting it for him?"

"You made me promise I'd never write a book," I reminded
him.

"A whim, and you know it was a whim, and I know you've been
banging away at a book for months. So kindly can the crap, Grady.
Your friend Deehardt here is a natural. Greatest thing since
Trader Horn. He's a fraud and a swindler and he belongs in the
pen, yet his attitude toward the human race is almost exactly my
own. Namely: screw the entire stupid species! I insist that
we . . ."

"Mungo, listen to me. There's a good chance that a whole
battalion of mad water witches and their supporters will be arriv-
ing soon at Asia Battle's place, bent on killing us all. This is no
time for an editorial conference."

"You're hallucinating, son. Nobody's coming out here to kill
you. Certainly not those clods in Caliche."

"Sit still and listen," I insisted. And I quickly gave the assem-
bled company the story of Anadarko's raid on the barn. Mungo
was first bug-eyed, then furious.

"I fired that snake six or eight months ago," he said. "Right after they caught him tom-cattin' around over at Asia Battle's. Possibly the rottenest human being I've ever encountered wholly outside the literary establishment."

"You fired him, Mungo," I said, "and the snake hasn't forgotten *that,* either. He may have you on his list for a little bloodletting. He's wearing a gun on each hip and carrying a rifle."

I recommended that Mungo and Big Jim get all their people together and draw up some plans for a forced march to Asia's place. If the soldiers of superstition came they would come in numbers and they'd likely come soon after daybreak. Would Mungo be able to arm his yeomanry and get them over to Asia's by then?

"Hell yes," he said.

"I'll take Jeff back in my car," I said.

Jeff removed his arm from Holly Ann's waist and turned to Mungo.

"If you don't mind, I'll leave my horse here. He might come in handy."

"God's teeth, boy!" Mungo responded. "We've got enough horses to take on the Cossacks at Balaclava."

"Attention! *Achtung!*" This clarion cry came from Big Jim Deehardt. He had swung an arm upward and was pointing dramatically toward the ceiling. "I'll now take command of the brigade at this end," he announced. "That's why I came—I knew you people would need a born leader. Now, Mr. Oldbuck, how many gunhands can you dig up for me?"

"Simmer down and shut yer big mouth!" came a second voice, high-pitched and commanding. It was Rustler Smith, who now appeared to be coming full awake. "You'll take command of nothin', you oversize drugstore dude! I'll . . ."

Big Jim showed mountainous astonishment. He took a couple of steps toward The Rustler, then looked around the room, and inquired:

"Where did this fragment of shredded buffalo chip come from?"

"Listen, buster," shrilled Old Smith, "I've fought twenny pitched battles fer ever time your mama switched your ass . . ."

"Daddy!" from Holly Ann.

"Set down and obey orders!" The Rustler snapped at his daughter.

Mungo got to his feet behind his desk, throwing back his head and swelling out his chest.

"The bugs fight among themselves," he said in oratorical tones, "and the rag has been torn from the rosebush, and I'm telling you both to cool it. This happens to be my ranch and I'll command all divisions of the Army of the South. On a big black horse."

He carried it off so impressively, with such a grand display of military aplomb, that both Deehardt and Smith quickly relinquished all claim to leadership.

Jeff and I now hurried out to the car and started back for the Two Cross T. We hadn't traveled eight inches before The Virginian's grandson tried it again.

"The things he told me, Grady . . . well, it was somethin' like I had already been gettin' by mental telegraphy, and . . ."

"Jeff! Please hold it a while! I've got serious plans to work out."

"But, Grady, this has been the biggest night of my whole life."

"Soon as the fightin's over."

When we arrived at Asia's house we learned two things. Gene Shallow had called from town to report that an armed mob was forming up and that a lot of the people were so worked up that they were speaking the name of the Lord in vain. Gene said a cavalcade as big as the Memorial Day parade would soon be rolling south. Item Two: right after Gene's call Asia tried to get me on the phone at Mungo's and the line had gone dead. It had been cut, obviously.

How would they come? By the dirt road in from the highway? Or through that cut in the fence, over the route taken by the despicable Anadarko and his two cowardly subalterns?

"That Indian of yours is still at the barn," Jaybird Huddleston advised me.

"He's not *my* Indian. He's *our* Indian." I took a moment to sketch in a few details of Victor Standcabbage's story, and I advised all hands that the pig's real name was Pushy, and that she belonged to the Indian and that he wanted her back.

"This news," said Asia, "doesn't exactly break my heart. I don't think any pig in history has caused as much trouble as this one."

"Asia, darling, Emily is our *casus belli*. You can't just take a *casus belli* and throw it in the garbage can." I wasn't at all sure about what I was saying.

"I'm sorry I said it," she murmured contritely.

"I won't give 'er up," Jeff announced. "Emily is like a brother to me. I mean sister. And I won't call her Pushy."

"I wish we could all get a little sleep," I said, suggesting that everyone was tired and fretful. "But it wouldn't be wise. I'd say the kooks are already on the road. We need to get organized down at the barn, and we ought to put out sentries. Jeff, do you know how to fix a telephone wire if . . . ?"

A roar of motors came from outdoors. I grabbed up my rifle and ran to the front entrance. One car and one truck, and I could tell at a glance that they were Chicanos.

The first one I recognized was Horca Quemajosa, proprietor of La Chinche, a cantina in the Chihuahua section of town. He got out of his car and came forward, greeting me with an *abrazo* that loosened ligaments in my rib cage.

"We are to the rescue, Señor Grady!" he cried. "Look, *por favor!*" He swept an arm proudly toward the car and the truck, from which were emerging a motley assortment of dark-skinned gentlemen. "The Mexican Army she has arrive!" Don Horca was capable of doing a much better dialect than this one, but some smartass Gringo once told him that if he richened it up he would add a fine flavor to his cafe and attract mucho turistas.

There were eleven of them, counting their leader. I recognized a few whom I knew pretty well, and the others I had seen around. Among them were Sánchez Mondragon, who clerked in Irving Susann's store; Ignacio Acuña Landa y Escandon, maintenance engineer at the elementary school, and Joe Braniff, who claimed that his people were high rollers in Mexico City during the Carranza years and who also claimed that his *parientes* invented the airline that bears their name.

I told Horca Quemajosa that I was pleasantly surprised and what the hell had inspired him to organize such a formidable army?

"First place," he replied, "I am a little dronk. Second place, most of these hombres are a little dronk. Ever'body in my cafe was a little dronk last night, and we talked of the good Señorita Battle. We lawve the Señorita becoss . . ."

His explanation of that lawve had something to do with Asia's steadfast refusal to hire Mexican wets, and I said I was confused because I had always understood that the hiring of wets was a noble and philanthropic and brotherly act, of vast benefit to all concerned, and Don Horca responded with a brief expository oration which I think would have pleased John L. Lewis; as I understood his theorem, the hiring of wets might be a splendid thing for the wets, and for the ranchers, but a refusal to hire wets meant jobs for the Chicano citizens of Caliche, usually at wages commensurate with and equivalent to the wages paid to Anglo ranch hands.

In any case, here they were, hoisting rifles and shotguns out of the truck, and our strength was now swollen to approximately sixteen men (some a little dronk), one extremely able-bodied woman, one enfeebled Choctaw Indian, and one pig. I could only hope that Mungo's army was already marching.

I dispatched three of the Mexicans up the long road to search for the break in the telephone line. We might need to yell Mayday in the direction of the Texas Rangers, the FBI, Matt Dillon, the Swiss Guard, Robin Hood and His Merry Men, and all available doctors in Caliche.

Jaybird Huddleston was instructed to saddle a horse, take our one pair of field glasses, and ride cross-country to the place where Anadarko had cut the fence; there to conceal himself and his mount and watch for the arrival of the foe, determine his intentions, and then ride like hell for home. As Jaybird departed, the first whispers of dawn appeared in the sky.

With the telephone out, I still needed to get word of the impending assault to Mungo. Jeff volunteered to go, displaying all the mettle of Lancelot, plus valor beyond the call of duty, and a burning desire to look upon Holly Ann after forty-five long minutes of absence from her side. I said no. The taut warrior must not be devitalized before battle.

Out of the eleven Chicanos there was only one who could ride a horse, Prisciliano Aguilar, bartender to Don Horca Quemajosa. Off he galloped in the general direction of The Pueblo.

He was never seen again until the war was over.

The big barn would serve as our fortress once more and our entire battle plan was now orchestrated for that sector. All vehicles were moved to the barn and lined up against the back wall, pointed southward. A good general has to anticipate temporary setbacks and even retreat. Our mobile equipment consisted of two jeeps, a station wagon, Jaybird's pickup, Asia's Thunderbird, my Pontiac, Jeff's Plymouth, and the Mexican truck. While we were getting this glistening fleet lined against the barn wall, the missing car arrived—the one the three men had taken out the road to search for the break in the telephone line.

They came clattering up to the barn waving their arms in near ecstasy and shouting, "We find him! We find!" They had found, all right. The wire had been cut half a mile in from the highway and their counter-sapper operation had been a quick, memorable success. Except that the break hadn't been repaired.

"Need pair pliers!" they cried. They were making happy clipping motions with their hands—their way of impersonating a pair of pliers—and I felt a deep need to fall to the ground and beat my head against the turf. I told them to forget the wire—it was now too late to worry about it and, anyway, the valiant horseman Prisciliano Aguilar was already thundering toward Mungo's house.

While I was busy assigning people to their stations in and around the barn, Victor Standcabbage wandered out of the south doorway carrying his bow and arrow, a haggard Choctaw with a crazy notion that something important was going on. He was no longer speaking in tongues; he didn't quite know where he was or how he happened to become a member of this select company of lunatics. He sensed that he had met me somewhere before, and he approached me.

"I think I am supposed to kill somebody with this," he said, nodding toward the bow. "Please point out the party and I will do the job. For the sake of all humanity, I will kill."

I told him to go back into the barn and sit down and rest himself.

The sun was now up and we seemed to be ready. I stood beside Asia, who was at her window position with the Browning.

"Your uncle," I said, "how did it happen that he built such a big barn?"

"He had a premonition," she answered with that little smile, "that some day we'd be attacked by a horde of savage water witches."

His premonition was sure as hell right.

Chapter Thirty describing how Asia
Battle goes to war with a length of harness
leather

30

From time to time, since World War II, I have uttered the judgment that General Patton demonstrated his true worth when he said that all his life his ambition had been to lead a lot of men in a desperate battle.

Why was I now finding a strange inner pleasure in my role as Supreme Allied Commander in an actual shooting war? The question went flitting by me, and pointed an accusing finger, but I was too busy to start thumping my chest and murmuring *mea* likewise *culpa.*

I had to concentrate on the possibility that Jaybird Huddleston, who had gone to reconnoiter the movements of the foe, had been captured and hung from a coat sarr apple tree uncoat.

I was buzzing with the fidgets, so I left my post at the west doorway of the barn and went around to the south wall to check the positioning of the vehicles.

A tall ladder had been thrown up against the building and a young man with a Zapata mustache was halfway up it. A second young man with a Zapata mustache stood at the foot, ready to follow after the first. I yelled, halt, desist, *pare,* what the hell you *pendejos* think you're doing?

The one up the ladder called down:

"We want to be lookouts, and it is more better to shoot down from the top than shoot out from the bottom."

"Yes," said his friend on the ground. "It is the way Pancho Villa always did it."

"Up Pancho Villa's!" I shouted angrily, and then lest there be any mistake about my meaning, I flashed the universal sign of the middle finger, meaning *that* for Pancho Villa! "Get the hell down here!" I called out. "What happens to you guys if we have to retreat in a big hurry?"

"We will lay flat," said the boy up above, "and maybe the *hijos de puta* would not see us."

"If I know my *hijos de puta*," I informed him, "and I think I do, they will burn down the barn, with you two guys on it." The boy on the ladder descended quickly to earth. "And anyway," I added, "that's *not* the way Pancho Villa always did it. Pancho Villa always did it astride a dark señorita."

Great laughter from the two Chicanos. My quip made Pancho Villa even more of a hero in their eyes.

Thus it happened that I was off engaging in badinage with a couple of Chicano boys when Jaybird Huddleston was sighted, riding hell-for-leather out of the chaparral, headed straight for the barn.

He didn't leap from the saddle, but eased himself off in a gentle slide, favoring his arthritis and his dry bone-sockets.

His report was simple and concise. He figured between forty and fifty of them. A dozen cars and jeeps and pickups and two motorcycles. They held a powwow beside the highway and then eight of their vehicles crossed the ditch, went through the fence, and started bumping across Asia's uneven acres. Two other cars moved off south.

"Armament?"

"Everybody I could see had a gun," Jaybird responded, "including what looked like a couple of women that rode off in the second bunch. Looks to me like that second gang aims to come in by the road."

"Could you tell who's running the show?"

"The one making the most noise, running around like a turpentined dog, was that knothead mayor you got up there in Caliche. And right alongside of him that Anadarko cuss. I whipped his ass once and I suppose I'll have to do it again. I don't think you hurt him much, but his right arm is in a sling."

"Did anybody see you?"

"Don't think so."

"Good work, Jaybird. You are hereby promoted to lieutenant junior grade."

"From what?" he demanded.

"Scout."

He didn't see anything funny about it.

I turned to go back into the barn and a bug of curiosity suddenly bit me.

"Did you see anything of the preacher and that beanpole carpenter who were here yesterday with Little Boy Blue?"

"I looked especially. Not hide nor hair."

(I learned later that when the canaille started gathering in town for the raid, both the Reverend C. O. Jones and Cee Minus Hoffelinck excused themselves and said they would be right back. The Reverend Jones went home and got out his thirty-two-dollar Concordance and searched around a good long while and finally came up with: "They are altogether become filthy; There is none of them that doeth good, no, not one." He read it over a few times, wondering how he might apply it. Were those people at that ranch altogether filthy? Was the unruly mob downtown altogether filthy? Did the pig doeth no good? Adding it all up, he reached the conclusion that the reference was clearly to the Anti-Pig crowd. Then he sighed his relief, poured himself a root beer and drank it, and went to bed. Meanwhile Cee Minus had gone home and said to his wife, "Anybody asks for me, tell them I have been called to witch a well in Fleesianner Parish on the yon side of Louisiana." Then *he* went to bed.)

I was now able to reorganize and correct my defenses. Eight or ten janissaries, including armed women, were coming in from the east. The main body would arrive at a slower pace from the northeast. I'd need to make a slight alteration in the avenue of retreat.

Standing off to the southwest of the barn was a miniature mesa, or butte, its steep sides weathered into symmetrical stone pillars —the whole table set in the open, away from any other topographical irregularities. If the invaders came on with fire and ferocity, we would have to flee in this direction, racing around the nearest corner of the escarpment to escape their shelling and heading for a possible rendezvous with Mungo Oldbuck's advancing battalions.

We shifted some of the cars into better position for a quick getaway and resumed our sharpshooter positions. The barn would now be vulnerable on the north and on the east. The first danger signal came from the latter direction.

The two cars that had traveled the highway route came through the white gateposts and halted directly in front of Asia's lawn. The invaders were well out of our range as they piled out of the cars and gathered in a knot at the edge of the grass. A dumb move. Real dumb. They could have been shot to shreds if we had been waiting in the house instead of the barn. I quickly got the glasses from Jaybird's car and had a closer look. Nine warriors in all, three of them women—Fern Mobeetie, Daphne Whipple, and Flat Hat Irene. I made no attempt to identify the six men, beyond noting that they were all candidates for the wheelchair. It was clear that the finest flower of the Liberated Women's Movement were running this phase of the assault.

I set to wondering if Asia's rifle would carry that distance, so I might clunk one into my ex-wife, nicking a fragment of whale meat off of her ass. Then a concerted yell sounded inside the barn and I knew that the main enemy force had come in view.

There were about thirty men in the disorderly mob that was moving slowly toward us, all on foot. They had stashed their vehicles somewhere back in the chaparral. I surveyed the enemy through the glasses, noting Mayor Ford Winkler walking about four inches out front, bent forward in the sort of half-crouch a man employs when he's searching for nightcrawlers. I could almost make out the pallor in his face—every movement of his ridiculous little body proclaimed his cowardice. He was coping with the greatest crisis of his entire life, and facing up to that crisis with the heroic posture of a sniveling, designing, and detestable sneak.

Walking in the immediate wake of the mayor was Anadarko and he, at least, was holding himself erect. Winkler had a shotgun at the ready but the scoundrel in blue appeared to be unarmed . . . until I made out the butt of the revolver in his left holster.

I made a quick decision, dashing inside and telling everybody that we'd wait until they were a hundred yards off. "The same length as a football field," I added for the benefit of the majority. "And when I give the command," I went on, "we'll let go a single volley and then run like hell for the cars. Before we get into the vehicles, we'll give them one more fusillade from the corners of the barn, then hi-yo silver and away for the organ-pipe mesa. They'll have to turn and run back to get their own pursuit cars, and that will give us time to round the butte and swing toward the south."

A loud bang sounded. It came from the direction of the house, and I thought, Oh, Jesus, I've blundered and the goddamn evil women are gonna win this war hands down and put us all to the torture and cut off my *cojones* and roast them over an open fire the way it was in that Hemingway bull book.

I hurried out to the corner of the barn, expecting to find them already on top of us.

They were still up there at the front of the house, but now the six men and three women were lined up against the automobiles, arms spread against the car tops, their backs toward Asia's castle. A lone figure stood on the walkway holding a shotgun. It was Rosa Chupador, the beautiful Mexican girl. We had completely forgotten Rosa and now she had, with a single shot fired over their heads, captured the auxiliary force.

I yelled excitedly at her, but she couldn't hear me, and she didn't take her eyes off her prisoners.

Rosa's shotgun blast set the approaching force in the field to shooting wildly, and they were coming on now at a faster clip.

I yelled, "Fire!"

Thirteen guns roared (two of the Chicanos had neglected to load, or had put their shells in backwards, or couldn't locate their triggers).

The advance in the field halted and the invaders began milling around. At least two were on the ground, dead or wounded. Half a dozen more could be seen running away from the carnage, back in the direction of the highway.

I changed signals. We not only could stand them off, we could beat them handily. They were now a disorderly rabble, close to total panic, and their leader, Winkler the Finkler, was looking around the landscape with the air of a frightened animal, searching for a tree or a boulder to hide behind. Then he made up his mind. He turned tail and ran after the other defectors.

Hell, I said to myself, we can go right out there and take them!

I turned and looked at a barn almost emptied of people. Asia was standing near the back door, looking toward me, her rifle in her right hand.

"Come on, Henry!" she cried out. "Hurry!"

My troops had followed orders. My army was outside, ready to roar away by car and by jeep and by truck. There was nothing I could do now to stop them. They wouldn't come back for more fight. I ran to Asia's side and took her arm and led her out to her car. The instructions for a second volley had been forgotten. Well, it wasn't needed. The foe was still in disarray and Anadarko was now trying to regroup them and call back those who had fled.

I still had to rescue Rosa Chupador up at the house, and so I ran to my car, and then I thought of something else. The pig. Where the hell was Emily? The last I could remember, she had been at the house . . . Rosa had said something about feeding her outside the kitchen door.

And one more oversight!

My Choctaw Indian was still in the barn.

I yelled at Jaybird, who was sitting at the wheel of his pickup. "Go get Rosa! See if Emily's up there! We'll cover for you!"

Asia suddenly leaped away from my side, ran to the pickup, and climbed in beside Jaybird. He looked startled and then glanced at me and shrugged. Lord-a-mercy! She'd probably forgotten to bring her lipstick. Or wanted to see if she'd left any burners on in the kitchen. I waved Jaybird on and as he headed up toward the house I hastened back into the barn.

Victor Standcabbage was sitting on the floor in the shadows, his back against a wall. His bow and arrow were in his lap and he was staring down at them.

"Come on, Choctaw!" I shouted at him, bringing him out of his stupor. "We've got to run for it . . . or get killed!"

He got to his feet with surprising agility.

"I was asleep," he said, "and then I heard the shooting."

"Let's go!" I commanded, and with his tribal weapons in his hand he trotted alongside me, out to my car. Apparently the snooze had restored his equilibrium.

"Where are we?" he asked. "What is this place? Who is doing all the shooting? How did I ever get into such a wahoo mess as this?"

I was too busy to answer him. I grabbed the glasses and trained them on the scene in front of the house. Jaybird was out of the pickup and standing beside Rosa Chupador, talking to her. Then I saw Asia get out and begin scrabbling around in the bed of the truck. Finally her hand came out holding what looked to be a length of leather tug. I watched her, fascinated, as she turned and said something to Rosa. The Mexican girl raised the barrel of her gun slightly. Her nine prisoners still stood in surrender, their backs to the gun.

Asia walked briskly straight up to Fern Mobeetie and without preliminaries, flailed her across her insolent buttocks with the heavy strap. Five hard blows, and then she applied the leather to Flat Hat Irene's meat, and Irene showed fight. She whirled and was about to assault Asia with her claws when Rosa let go with another blast from the gun, firing into the air. Flat Hat Irene took the hint, turned back to the car, and Asia gave her a couple of extra licks that must have raised welts the size of Braunschweiger sausages. She then moved on to Daff Whipple and the county judge danced up and down with both pain and rage as the blows descended on her juridical prat.

I watched as Jaybird gathered in all the weaponry belonging to the auxiliary nine, throwing the guns into his truck, and then Rosa dashed inside to get the pig. In another thirty seconds the mission was accomplished and the pickup was speeding back toward the barn.

Jaybird came skidding in beside my car, waving frantically.

"Hit the road!" he yelled. "Whole new army's comin' across the fields!" He pointed out north.

I raised my hand and gave the cry: "Forward! *Adelante!*" We went roaring off for the crenellated mesa and as we cleared the corner of the barn I caught sight of the enemy reinforcements just zooming over a rise of ground, looking at first like a panzer division coming down on Poland. I lingered long enough to count the new vehicles—there were only five altogether. By this time my people were whirling around the western end of the mesa, and I still held back, watching the new arrivals as they came abreast of their compatriots. It was evident that they were going to have a conference in the field and this would give us time to get well out ahead of them.

So now I tromped on the gas and went charging after my command, exuberantly ignoring the rocks and the hummocks, passing one vehicle after another, waving cheerfully at the occupants of each, getting out in front so I could lead my army to the sector where help might lay.

From the moment he took command in front of The Pueblo, Mungo had insisted that his troopers should move north on horseback. He was able to convince Idaho Tunket that he, the former rodeo champion, should ride the grandnephew of Midnight, the same steed I had taken on the safari to Leydigs Duct. Rustler Smith argued that he had achieved an age where creature comforts were important in warfare, and he wanted the soft back seat of an automobile. Big Jim Deehardt contended that his new Land Rover would have served the Iron Duke well at Waterloo, and if he were compelled to ride an animal, he wanted a mule.

Idaho snorted at this last proposal. He surveyed Big Jim's six feet plus and observed: "You ride a mule into battle and you'll be a purty sight. You'll have to wrop your back laigs up over your shoulders, bringin' them in from behind, and then farr your weapon straight acrost your crotch."

The Hermit had, as always, a quick response.

"As I told the Kiwanis Club in Jeff City fifteen-sixteen years ago," he said, "whenever I'm using a rifle or a shotgun I like to have something solid and substantial to rest the barrel on."

At first Holly Ann said she didn't want to go, that she didn't believe in war. Then her thoughts turned to Jeff Cordee, and her principles were beginning to subside, and then her father spoke to her.

"Girl," he said, "you don't have to kill nobody. You could come along and make coffee and carry farrwood, somethin' on that awder."

There was an attempt to enlist two wet Mexicans who had been working several weeks at the ranch. Emiliano, the yard man, said he stood with Señorita Smeeth, detesting war with every bit of sinew and bone marrow in his slender frame, and that if nobody minded he'd like to be a conscientious objector. Nobody minded because his statement of principle was couched in Durango Spanish and nobody understood what he was saying. His friend Manuel, a stable scraper, proclaimed himself to be a hard-shell Quaker from Topolobampo, and would the Señores take note, *por favor,* that both of his eyes were slightly crossed and the chickens needed to be fed.

Then Mungo met further defeat. The six tall men who had come down with Big Jim—six Authentic Cattlemen of the True West—asserted flatly that they would withdraw if it was required that they get on horses. They told Mungo that the day of the horse is long gone in the West, and they advised him that he should grow a mustache, quit wearing socks, and get with it.

Voices were being raised, and Mungo was determined that his dynamic authority should prevail, and then he solved his problem by splitting his command into two divisions—the Traseros Cavalry Brigade up front, and the Deehardt Reprehensibles bringing up the rear. Thus the combined force rode out in the following classic Allenby formation:

1 General Oldbuck on Motilla, the black stallion whose ancestry dated back to the time of Hernan Cortez.
2 Idaho Tunket on Midnight.
3 Rustler Smith on Juicy Fruit, a first cousin of Black Jack, the Army's riderless horse that follows the caissons in presidential funerals with boots reversed in the stirrups.
4 Holly Ann Smith, astride a Copperbottom roan named Copperbottom, from the fact that he was a direct descendant of Copperbottom, one of the most celebrated sires in American horse history.
5 Big Jim Deehardt riding Emma, a polka-dotted Appaloosa, vaguely kin to Nelson, the horse George Washington sat on when he was looking at battles.
6 Two jeeps carrying the Reprehensibles.

Thus the total Oldbuck command, a savage and feral fighting machine, asking no quarter and offering none—a gristly and resourceful band that would have wrung terror from the hearts of both Marion the Swamp Fox and Light-Horse Harry Lee.

Mungo bestrode the great black stallion clad in white linen slacks and a vienna green sports shirt. He was about to order the advance when he noticed that something was missing.

"Where's Christchild-Muckeridge?" he called out.

"He drove to Alpine," Idaho Tunket responded, "to get some constipation medicine. It's my personal opinion, if you ask me, that he's . . ."

"Praise Allah for small favors," Mungo said. Then he led his army off toward Rinderpest Creek.

A half mile up the trail and Juicy Fruit began to crawfish and then to crowhop, these being preliminary gesturings which ordinarily would lead to his swallerin'-his-head and throwing Old Smith twenty miles north of Amarillo. The spectacle of the ancient Rustler aboard a bucking horse sent Idaho Tunket into spasms of laughter, for his own cayuse was the one with the bucking bloodlines. The Rustler resolutely cussed Juicy Fruit into quiescence, a virtuoso performance in vulgarity that impressed all hands, and then he cussed Idaho a right smart, and there was bad blood between the two men for the duration of the war.

The Army of the South came in sight of our mechanized division as both forces approached the banks of Rinderpest Creek, not far from the grove of live oak where Jeff Cordee had rejected the dragass prose of Faulkner and the rantipole enigmas of John Barth. I flung a snappy salute across the Rinderpest and Mungo returned it. Then Jeff Cordee broke ranks on our side and ran into the dry bed of the crick and Holly Ann dashed in aboard Copperbottom and everyone heard her cry out, as she pointed downstream toward the trees:

"Our place!"

We crossed to the south bank and when I had pulled Old Blue up alongside Mungo, he drew a pistol out of his pants, waved it aloft, and demanded, "Where's the enemy?"

"They're coming," I told him.

"How many regiments they got?"

"Two and a half."

"What's half a regiment, General Grady?"

"One with three half-witted women in it, General Oldbuck."

"Which direction do you think we ought to run in?"

"Let's sit down and rest awhile and then decide."

"Right," Mungo agreed, "but first, let's move our troops out of this goddamn heat and into those goddamn trees over there."

It was, indeed, a hot day. As Jaybird Huddleston had remarked thirty minutes earlier, the temperature stood at the oven setting that's considered just right for cornbread.

We straggled into the oaks and hid some of the vehicles on the south side of the copse. I slid the Pontiac into a spot up front where I'd be able to glimpse the enemy when he arrived, and Mungo tied Motilla to a tree and got into the front seat with me. He was grunting from the ache in his thighs.

"In case you want to know the truth," he said, "I've had just about enough war for one day. I propose that we strike south for The Pueblo and get drunk. I will furnish quality booze for the officers and cold beer for the enlisted personnel."

"No, Mungo. We've got to teach this rabble a lesson."

"You mean let them feel the temper of our steel?"

"Yes, and the steel of our temper."

"Grady, I believe you are already drunk."

I had to get a man out to scout the enemy's movements, so I sent a Chicano named Guillermo López Figueroa, who was serving as my batman, to go find Jeff. In a few minutes the big cowboy arrived with Holly Ann, and right behind them came Idaho. I told Jeff I wanted him to ride back up the trail and scout the enemy, find out if he was moving on us and, if so, how soon we might expect him.

Holly Ann pleaded with me to send someone else on the mission but I told her I had a corollary reason for getting Jeff out of camp. "This is a military installation," I told her, "and the way you two have been strolling under the trees, holding hands and grinning at each other . . . well, it's simply not good for morale. While Jeff is out on the trail you can go around and see that every soldier has his gun loaded and knows where the trigger is."

Jeff himself was a little unhappy about the whole arrangement but he asked Mungo if he could borrow the black stallion and then rode across the creek and up the north trail. Then through the trees came Asia. Idaho Tunket had been standing by with a sheet of paper in one hand and a pencil in the other, but now he stepped aside to give Miz Battle precedence.

She said, "Field Marshal, sir, we can't stay out here very long. We forgot to bring a scrap of food, and we have no water. People are beginning to complain already."

"Asia, dear," I said, "I don't think we'll be here long. We ought to know within the hour."

Idaho Tunket now spoke up. "At the Alamo," he said, "they had somethin' like sevendy-three kags of pork meat and they opened 'em up and the mackrobes and the maggots had got to all that meat and it was spoiled. They didn't complain a bit, John Wayne and Chill Willis and Booey and them."

"And you know where *they* ended up," said Mungo. There in the midst of all that tension Mungo's line made me think of a story about . . .

1st man: You happen to know who won the Hundred Years War?

2nd man: Sure.

1st man: Who?

2nd man: Nobody. They're all dead.

We weren't making much progress toward fighting a war, yet the little human touch, the sentimental incident, is always there, even in the midst of battle; it seems strange that all those full-blown military historians such as Bruce Catton and Trevor-Roper and Hanson Baldwin fail to note the little individual incidents that flesh out the full and complete portrait of your average holocaust.

Asia now addressed Mungo, who was still sitting at my side.

"General," she said, "do you know of any regulation that says a camp follower cannot kiss a commanding officer?"

"There is no such regulation in my army, mam," he replied.

She leaned in and kissed me, lusciously and lustily.

"I, too," said Mungo, "am a general, mam."

She hurried around the front of the car and kissed him, chastely on the cheek.

"Yum," said the Commander of the Army of the South. "That delightful gesture compels me to issue a frontline writ of covenant. I have never publicly apologized to you, mam, for my behavior in that hassle over the cow critters. I do so now. Let us be warm friends from this day forward, right down to the Big One at Armageddon."

She leaned in again and kissed him, less chastely, on the lips.

"Now," I said, "let us not be sickening about this thing. Asia, please go at once and spread good cheer among the hungry and the thirsty and the homesick."

The moment she had departed, Idaho stepped forward and stationed himself at Mungo's elbow.

"With us goin' into battle and all," he said rather sheepishly, "well, I found this piece of paper and pencil in a glove compartment back yonder and I been tryin' to write a letter to my mama. She lives back in Eagle Pass and I don't rightly know how old she is but it must be ninety er a hunderd. I'm never much of a hand to write letters so I woosh you gentlemen would see if I got ever'-thing spelt right and if I left anything out."

He presented the sheet of paper to his employer and in spite of myself, in spite of the desperate urgency of the moment, not-withstanding the fact that I could hear already, in my mind, the roar of the cannon and the thunder of hoofbeats . . . I leaned over to read a son's farewell missive to his old mother, written in crisis. This is the way it went:

Dear mama.

How are you. I am fine. How is your helth. Is everthing ok with you. I am ok. The weather has been so so. Rain all day last Tusday. Ranchers like it. I live in hopes I will live to see Eagle Pass at lease one more time as well as you. Dont worry about me. Prostrate trouble about the same. Trees beginning to bud. Hot sun today. Yr. loveing son francis x. tunket.

"It's newsy enough," said Mungo, "and the style is Joycean." He corrected several misspellings and then suggested that Idaho locate another piece of paper and make a clean copy ere time for the next dispatch rider to go thundering out of camp.

As Idaho vanished into the trees, Mungo's eyes followed him and I thought I detected an air of affection.

"Too bad they shot Lincoln," he murmured. "He'd have en-joyed that letter." Then he told me he had a confession to make.

"You want to know why I'm out here playing the fool and get-ting ready to have my earlobes shot off by some crackbrained Texas water witch? Well, I think I told you once that Crawford Battle was the only man who ever knocked me down. I lied. I want to correct that statement. That son of a bitch Tiny Cruris stretched me on the sod the day I fired him. I'd like to get just one shot at him before . . ."

I saw puffs of dust rising out north. It was Jeff Cordee riding back with a burr under his saddle. He crossed the creek bed and came straight to my command car.

"Here they come!" he cried out.

"Where?"

He waved at the horizon. "Just over the hill!"

I turned to Mungo.

"Damn it, General, why didn't you bring a bugler?"

I had to get out of the car and holler up the troops, let them know the enemy was approaching. I advised them that we would fight guerrilla-style, shooting from behind trees when trees were available, or from behind the clay banks of the creek. I turned back to ask Jeff the size of the enemy force and I saw that he was pointing north. The first vehicles had come in sight.

I'm sure they didn't even suspect that we were hidden in the trees.

They came bouncing over the rise without slackening speed, and a jeep traveled out front of all the other enemy vehicles. In it, riding alone, was the blue-clad scoundrel Tinea Cruris, better known now as Anadarko. He was driving with one hand, and he was within forty yards of the creek bank before he realized he had blundered straight into his enemy's lap. He stopped the jeep and leaned forward, peering into the woods. I let my eyes leave him for a moment and surveyed the long slope behind him. There were perhaps two dozen vehicles coming over the brow of the hill. They came rolling down the slope and pulled up in ragged formation some distance back of their leader. A deep stillness settled over the landscape. It must have been thus as Montgomery faced Rommel across the sand at El Alamein.

Anadarko, now certain that his enemy was hidden among the oaks, calmly pulled a white handkerchief from his pocket and climbing out of his jeep, he took a few steps forward and began waving it from side to side. I was astonished that he would call for a truce.

I grabbed Mungo's revolver and got out of my car and walked into the open. Nobody could see it but my knees were shaking.

The Blue Boy called out to me:

"Grady, you son of a whore, you did this to me!" He touched his left shoulder. "Now I'm going to drop this handkerchief and when it hits the ground I'm going to put a bullet right through your heart!"

I grew faint all over. Bitterness came up in my throat. The bastard was going to kill me. I glanced down at the gun in my hand but I knew that I was no match for this saloon fighter, that I wouldn't be able to bring it up and aim it before he'd drill me. I wondered where Rosa was keeping the pig. I could offer to let this black-hearted son of a bitch have Emily. Then I thought of Asia. She was back behind me in the trees, watching.

"*You and who else!*" I yelled defiantly.

Slowly the white handkerchief fluttered toward the ground.

"Make your move!" Anadarko called out. On that instant came the thud of hoofbeats and he whipped out his gun. A horseman had ridden in from the east, traveling along the bend of the creek. Anadarko squeezed off a shot at him and the newcomer swerved his mount, crossing the stream and charging headlong upon the man in blue.

Then I recognized the rider. It was Ian Christchild-Muckeridge. He rode straight at Anadarko with the clear intent of knocking the man down, but Anadarko got off another shot, the horse veered away, and the Englishman toppled from the saddle.

Anadarko turned slowly back to me, his gun straight out in front of him. Mine was still hanging limply at my side. I tried to haul it up and get off some kind of a shot, but the damn thing was made of lead and weighed twenty pounds. I was a gone coon. I knew it. I looked straight at Anadarko and his gun, and all my Dutch courage vanished. He sensed my belly-wrenching fright, he knew I was frozen where I stood, and he took his sweet time. Villains have more guts than heroes.

Then a deep voice came from behind me.

"Comanche!"

A whirring noise, a zzzzzzzwish!

Anadarko's body stiffened. An arrow was sticking in his chest, in his heart. The extended arm fell slowly and the gun dropped to the ground. A look of great astonishment flashed across the evil brown face, and then he collapsed.

Victor Standcabbage stepped forth from the trees.

"A Comanche dog," he said to me, quite calmly. He still had his bow in his hand. "I do not like Comanches."

"How could you tell he was a Comanche?"

"It is easy. A Comanche's eyes never hold still. Even among friends he knows he is among enemies, and his eyes are always shifting from side to side and darting about like little mice. Didn't you notice?"

"I was looking at the hole in the front end of his pistol."

Anadarko's warriors had not moved. They stood now beside their sedans and their jeeps and their trucks and stared across the river and into the trees. Two men lay on the ground out in front of them, and they were bewildered, not knowing what to do next. Mungo took a couple of steps in their direction, raised his right hand, and then whipped it downward in a gesture of contempt.

"*Go home!*" he yelled at them. "Go home and get your sugartit!" Some of them were ranchers, like himself, and a few were wealthy, like himself, but Mungo differed from them by having no hypocrisy in him, and no idiot superstition.

Big Jim Deehardt, who had been with his tall brigade on our right flank, now came up, demanding to know the whereabouts of Winkler the Finkler.

"I feel like slapping him around a little," said Big Jim. "My boys and I didn't get a bit of action. Who the hell was that scarecrow who came charging across in front of us?"

"That," Mungo announced loudly, "was my favorite author."

"And I forgot to tell you," I said to Big Jim, "that the mayor thumped his tail and took off like a jackrabbit the minute the first shot sounded in our opening skirmish."

"I'll get him at a later date," said The Hermit.

Idaho Tunket and a Chicano had crossed the creek and were bending over Ian Christchild-Muckeridge. The Englishman was showing signs of life—Anadarko's slug had creased his scalp and knocked him cold. He came out of it quickly, giving his head a couple of shakes and then demanding:

"Where is the bostard? I'll wrench off his foul codpiece and stuff it . . ." He glanced around, looking for his man, then touched the wound on his head. "Now I remembuh. He shawt me! A bit much, what? Narrow squeak, and all that. Where is the blighter, Idaho?"

"Right yonder on the ground, deader'n Sam Bass's grandmaw."

I stared up the slope at the people who were turning their vehicles and heading back toward town. Two men had picked up Anadarko and put him in the back of a truck. I turned and surveyed the edge of the copse and Asia came running, and we embraced in front of the entire victorious army.

"In the history books," I said to her, grinning, "this'll probably be known as the Battle of Rinderpest Creek." I looked toward the spot where the only real action had taken place—where Anadarko and Ian had fallen. "It sure wasn't Austerlitz—not exactly Gettysburg—but it'll do me for a while. I don't mind telling you, Asia my love, I was scairt plumb down to my heels."

She hugged me.

"Nonsense! You were superb. You were Lochinvar, D'Artagnan, Sergeant York . . ."

"Ichabod Crane," I appended.

"Scared? *You* scared? *I* was paralyzed!"

"So, don't stay that way, gal. Ah aim to marry you."

This will be something more than an Instantaneous Replay, concerned with certain melodramatic phenomena in which romance and flat-out love get some additional attention in our chronicle. We needs must deal with the rapprochement between Jefferson Davis Cordee and his future father-in-law. For the benefit of serious literary historians, we must describe the final cleaving together of the warring clans—for we have here a modern-day *Romeo and Juliet* without recourse to the vial of poison and the cruel dagger.

During the same hours the Sabbat of the Water Witches was unreeling in the Undercroft of the Presbyterian Church, Holly Ann Smith came riding a chestnut mare across Asia Battle's broad acres. She skirted the oak grove on Rinderpest Creek and wept a little, and went on through the night past occasional huddles of white-faced Herefords.

She tied her mare to a fence and walked the last couple of hundred yards to Jeff Cordee's little house. She was bone-tired; she'd had the deep vapors, the miasma of broken love, since the day of the quarrel and hadn't been able to sleep much at all for a week.

Jeff was in bed, awake and fighting the pillow, when he heard the hesitant tapping at the screen door.

No words were passed. They fell into each other's arms and the embraces were fierce and the kisses wild. When they could get back to near normal breathing, Holly Ann told Jeff that they must not delay one more minute, that there had to be an immediate confrontation between Jeff and her father.

The young lady returned to her horse while Jeff hurried across to the stables and lashed a saddle on one of Jaybird's brush horses. He soon joined Holly Ann and they rode in the starlight toward her home.

Part of the time when their horses were shoulder to shoulder they held hands. No way wise, but excusable under the circumstances. There is a saying in these regions that lovers should never clasp hands while on horseback, because a horse looks upon such conduct as unnatural and perhaps even degenerate, and might bolt and kill everybody in sight; and that if such lovers have an irresistible compulsion to hold hands, they should dismount, secure their horses, stand on solid ground, and hold anything they feel like holding.

When they reached the Smith house Holly Ann went inside and awakened The Rustler. He purpled up the atmosphere with strong language, as he usually did on being hauled out of bed, and when his daughter informed him that Jefferson Cordee had come to see him, he demanded to know who in the ceaseless goddamn hell was Jefferson Cordee?

"The young man from Wyoming, Daddy. The one you hit with the chair."

"What chair, for God sake?"

"The young man who wanted to know why you were eating your cherry pie backwards."

Old Smith's grizzled head began twisting from side to side and he took tentative steps in half a dozen directions.

"Come fer a showdown, has he!" he shouted. He dashed to a table on the far side of the room, then to a closet.

"Whirr'd I put that damn gun?" he screeched.

It took her a few minutes to convince him that Jeff had come on a mission of peace, that the young cowboy only wanted to meet and shake hands with the old man, that he had a couple of simple questions to ask about conditions in Wyoming. From shouting, Old Smith subsided into growls, and then mumbles, the gist of it all being that he had learned his stealth and distrust and wariness from the *good* Indinns in the Teton Mountains, and he knew who this young man was and that he came with treachery and murder in his heart.

Then the old man launched his moment of high drama, planting himself in front of his daughter, shoving his chin forward and snapping his eyes, leveling an index finger at her nose and giving it to her straight: "Girl, he's dye-rect kin to the man that killed your grampaw!"

"I already know that, Daddy. He's not wearing a gun. He thinks *you* want to shoot *him*. He started to strap one on but I talked him into leaving it home. I promise you he won't harm a hair on your head. And anyway, Daddy . . . I'm going to marry him."

Another outburst of roaring and ranting and cussing, with words and phrases scattered through it all, but none of them forming up to make intelligible sentences.

At length Holly Ann got him into the living room and into a big chair, and extracted a solemn promise from him that he would not move out of it.

"Only unless I'm attackted," he said, "er drawed on."

She settled for that, and went to the door and summoned Jeff, and as he came into the room she went out, closing the front door behind her.

She paced up and down in front of the house for a while. She could hear the rumble of Jeff's voice and the high-pitched tones of her father, but there was nothing in the sounds to suggest which direction the conference was taking. She quickly grew tired of the nervous pacing and went onto the porch and stretched out on a green-padded chaise. The rumble and clack of the voices went on, but she could not make out the words.

Then came the laughter. It broke through the walls loud and vigorous and convulsive. It continued without any sign of letup.

Holly Ann smiled and dropped her head back and in five seconds fell dead asleep.

When she had closed the front door on the two men, they stood and looked at each other warily, and both showed surprising signs of shyness. The old man finally settled his stare on the carpet and held his thin lips tightly shut, and then Jeff spoke up and said the most important question on his mind was, would Mr. Smith give him permission to marry Holly Ann?

No response.

"For a long time," Jeff told The Rustler, "I've had a strange sorta hunch that you knew something about my granddad that I'd ought to know."

Now Old Smith broke his silence.

"It's got to do with the hangin' of Steve, ain't it?"

"Maybe. Tell me anything. Just anything."

"Let's set down," said The Rustler. "I aim to be honest with you, boy. Your hunch was a good one. The way it happened, my old man told my old lady about Horse Thief Pass, and when I got a little older my old lady told it to me. I spose you know that a dude from the East name of Wister wrote a whole book about it. Had big long words in his book and two er three thousand lies. Holly Ann read it all the way through fer me, out loud. Took a whole week because it strung me out. If I wasn't feelin' sorrowful about my old man, I was laughin' myself sick at the way the facts was bollixed up."

"What facts?" Jeff asked, unable to hide his eagerness.

"Like at Horse Thief Pass. What you don't know, and what that Wister didn't know, was The Virginian he didn't take no part in the hangin' of Steve, and fer a good reason."

"What reason?"

"Now, don't get over-excited, son. After they all rode off to the cottonwoods fer the hangin' my old man come out of the woods and crep' up to that stable and found a crack he could see through and . . . I'm sure sorry I got to tell you this, boy, but your grand-pap was layin' in there, flopped down onconscious on a pile of hay and manure."

"You mean he'd been knocked out?"

"Knocked out hell! The thing this Wister bird didn't know was, *The Virginian drank!*"

"Of course he drank!" Jeff said. "Wister wrote about him goin' in saloons and havin' a drink with his friends."

"No, that ain't what I mean. I mean *he drank*. He was a *drunk*. Couldn't handle it. He had rode up there to put a stop to that hangin' and so they fed him a little red-eye and like it always was with him, he couldn't stop, and next thing you know he was layin' in the manure."

"Glory be!" cried Jeff. "That's the best news I ever heard!"

There was more to it—but that's enough to clear the record. I could understand Jeff's exultation—like me he was a Southerner with strong family sentiment, and now the only smirch standing against his father's good name had been wiped away . . . unless you consider a distaste for the poetry of Robert Browning to be a smirch.

It comes back to me now, the scene in front of the Smith house when Jeff and Holly Ann were first telling me their joyful news. I had shut them off, being preoccupied with the knowledge that armed men were marching against me and my friends. I had shut Jeff off later, and rudely, in the car. But I do remember how they were fair bursting with the news that The Rustler had given them his blessing, and that they had already set the date. There was one other matter.

"When you drove up," said Jeff, "we were sittin' up there on the porch tryin' to decide on the name we'll give our first boy."

"I know," I said. "Cyril Tharp Cordee."

"Nope," said Jeff. "We thought of Cyril, and then we thought of Henry, and Trampas, and even Grady. But we weren't able to . . ."

"Trampas Cordee . . ." I said. "Sounds good. Has a nice ring to it. But what if it's a girl?"

"That's easy," said Jeff. "I'll settle for nothin' less than Emily."

These concluding pages are being written a month after the great Battle of Rinderpest Creek, and this is the only chapter in my book not composed in that dingy office of the Weekly *Mud Dobber* between the hours of 3:30 and 6 A.M.

No more of that foolishness.

This is going to be the final chapter, and the shortest.

Asia Battle and I were married three days ago.

So what am I doing up?

Well, I need to put the finishing touch to this lyrical western romance so that six days hence, on our way to Bavaria for our honeymoon, I can drop the manuscript into the hands of Miss Bertha Wollenschlager of Thirty Rockefeller Plaza, New York, New York, One Oh Oh Twenty. Miss Wollenschlager, you may remember, was once upon a time my New York girl friend, in a day when I was around forty and she was in her mid-twenties.

Asia has recommended that I convert one of the guest bedrooms into a study, line the four walls with bookshelves, and settle down as author in residence. Maybe, but probably not. I have no thought of writing other books.

For the time being all I plan on doing is loving Asia Battle till she hollers calf rope.

Jeff Cordee and Holly Ann beat us to the altar by ten days and Jeff will become ramrod of the Two Cross T at the end of December, when Jaybird Huddleston retires to the little house he owns in Caliche.

Holly Ann's pap, Old Rustler Smith, stayed on to see his lovely daughter wed to the grandson of The Virginian, then he lit a shuck for his home country. They wanted him to live here at the ranch, but he stubborned up and said, no by God.

"I'm goin' back to God's Country," he said, "whirr a man can git himself hung in peace." In an aside, spoken behind his hand in tones so loud that everyone on the ranch could hear, he said to me: "Truth of the matter is, I got me a lady friend up there in Buffalo, got tiddies on her like a Jersey cow makin' fer home at sundown."

Things sometimes turn out surprisingly well. The Old Rustler had poetry in his soul.

And what of the mighty Standcabbage, who saved my life?

And Emily?

The Choctaw brave, slayer of Tinea Cruris, tried to give his pig to Asia, and she turned him down; he offered Emily to Jeff, but Jeff said all his affections were held in escrow for Holly Ann. Would I take her? Indeed not . . . I am bespoken.

"We all love Emily," I told Victor, "but she is really not Emily —she is every Mulefoot inch a Standcabbage, correctly named Pushy."

"I'm going back to Oklahoma," said the Choctaw, "back to my wife. Now I know what to do. I will flog her a little bit each day. I need to beat around on her, perhaps a half hour or so, just before breakfast. It will make her a good woman."

"Mr. Oldbuck will endorse that procedure," I told him.

Would he set his pig to witching for water in Oklahoma? He had given thought to it, but he didn't know how to go about it.

I had Jeff give him a few instructions.

Standcabbage rebelled at first when Jeff told him he would have to speak baby talk to the pig, that he'd have to say, "Go get wah-wah." A Choctaw's larynx, Victor protested, is not arranged to accommodate language of that character.

"Then she won't find water for you," Jeff told him.

"In that case, I'll speak the white man's words."

"And don't forget the Big Dish Strawberry Swirl."

"Maybe I won't be able to get Big Dish Strawberry Swirl in Mc-Alester, Oklahoma," Victor suggested.

"Then you'll have to buy you an ice cream freezer and learn to make it yourself."

"I'm beginning to think," said the Indian, "that I'd have been better off if I'd stayed at that barbershop in Laredo."

And so our beloved Mulefoot pig was taken into the lavender pickup and hauled away forever.

Let us not overlook Ian Christchild-Muckeridge. After it became known that the true author of *Descent into America* was

Mungo Oldbuck, the Englishman announced to the public that his real name was William Stumps. The Battle of Rinderpest Creek had changed his whole life. Shot out of the saddle by a full-blooded Comanche Indian! Crikey! What more could an Englishman ask for? He rented a house in Caliche, began writing cowboy novels under the name of Bill Stumps, and at last report was wearing wildly patterned slacks and messing around with Iolanthe Peeler, the Girl with the Iron Claw.

That left Mungo, Idaho Tunket, and Spiro Keats pretty much alone at Rancho Traseros. They are happy. Mungo is about ready to start on another book. I saw him a couple of days ago and he said:

"Grady, all other parts of my body are youthful and vigorous, but my stomach has suddenly begun to grow old. I have just instructed Idaho to cut down on the French cooking and to lay in a couple of tons of Gerber's baby food. There is little chance, under the circumstances, of my embracing a belief in a kindly and considerate Supreme Being."

And, finally, let me tip you off to something important. The woman I married is a paragon. She has no faults, not airy a flaw, and her sweet and forgiving nature is a wonder to behold on this earth. When we were discussing where we should go to get married, she floored me by suggesting that the ceremony be performed by County Judge Daphne Whipple.

"Great balls of fire, Asia!" I cried. "The woman conspired to have us slaughtered in our beds!"

"Oh, that was a long time back, Henry. I don't think she really meant us any harm. It would be a good thing if we forgave her and asked her to tie the knot."

I finally agreed, but I stipulated that the great event would have to be at the courthouse, not in Daphne's home. In the latter eventuality, I was too fearful that she'd invite us to stay for chicken-and-dumplings *à la* Beaumont.

"And what's wrong with chicken-and-dumplings?" Asia demanded.

"Not a thing," I said. "I love it."

P